The stranger walked up to Harriett and took her chin in a firm hand, tilting her head so that the hood of her cloak fell back. He studied her face for a moment and the flaming red hair that surrounded it in a riot of wispy curls. Harriett stood quietly beneath his gaze, though she knew she should have been outraged that he had taken such a liberty with her, a man to whom she had not even been formally introduced.

"My name is Harriett Haversham," she said, deciding to take matters into her own hands.

"Not the name of a wood sprite," he commented, releasing her chin, but continuing to gaze steadily down at her. "But then, who would be a wood sprite? Always flitting about and never settling in one spot."

Harriett swallowed, blinked, and returned the stranger's dark gaze. No one had ever talked to her like this before. Almost as if . . . "Are you flirting with me, sir?"

He chuckled. "Yes, Harriett Haversham, I believe I am."

If her heart had been pounding before, it quite thundered now. She was twenty-four, a spinster with no pretensions to beauty beyond a pair of lovely gray eyes and a quite engaging smile. Still, she had always thought herself content with her lot . . . until now.

An Easter Disguise

Emily Maxwell

ZEBRA BOOKS
KENSINGTON PUBLISHING CORP.

ZEBRA BOOKS are published by

Kensington Publishing Corp.
475 Park Avenue South
New York, NY 10016

Zebra and the Z logo Reg. U.S. Pat & TM Off.

First Printing: March, 1994

Printed in the United States of America

For my father, Willy Schwab,
for his love, support, and
Little Willy stories

One

"I tell you, if Camilla has ruined us, I shall never speak to her again. Never!" Augusta Haversham put down her coffee cup, her chin quivering at the thought of her brilliant future, now quite dashed by her sister's uncaring behavior. "And after I lent her my pink hair ribbons, too. How could she!"

"Augusta, if you will insist on creating a scene at the breakfast table, you may go to your room," Mrs. Haversham instructed her youngest daughter. "You know I cannot abide hysterics first thing in the morning."

At this unkind parental injunction, Augusta burst into tears, covering her face with her hands.

Harriett Haversham, the eldest of Parson Haversham's three daughters, buttered her toast and observed dispassionately that Gusta should cease to make such a ninny of herself, since it scarcely helped matters. "And besides upsetting Mama, it is making your eyes all red."

"It is?" Augusta stopped crying at once and ran to the mirror over the sideboard. "Oh, you are right, Harry. How dreadful I look. I must bathe them in rosewater at once. What if some-one should see me?"

Since it was hardly likely that anyone would call at such an early hour, no one replied. Not that such a thing mattered to Augusta, who had already quit the room so that she might lie down with cold compresses over her eyes.

"She is still very young," Harriett excused her sister. "At seventeen, I daresay such things seem most important. And if you should like me to go with Papa, I shall certainly be agree-able."

Mrs. Haversham sighed. If only her other two daughters could be as sensible as Harriett, life would be so much simpler. "I shall go with your papa, my dear. I know how very sick you become, riding in a closed carriage. And there is no telling how far they may have traveled. Camilla's note was found this morning, but there is no way of knowing when she and Tom—" Mrs. Haversham ceased to speak for a moment and with trembling hand reached for the cup of coffee that sat beside the plate of cold toast which she had found herself quite unable to eat.

"I'm sure you will catch up to them before nightfall," Harriett assured her mother. "For even though Tom Watkins knows horses, he cannot have much money to hire fresh ones."

"No." Mrs. Haversham put down her cup and pressed her lips together. "But I am terribly afraid. . . . Oh, Harriett, how could your sister have done such a thing? I know I begin to sound like Augusta, but I simply do not understand why Camilla has run off like this. And with Lord Weston's groom, who always seemed such a nice young man, and besides coming to church every Sunday, used to drive old Mrs. Northcourt to see her daughter whenever a carriage was free. And as if that were not enough . . ."

Pushing her plate away, Mrs. Haversham folded her hands together and looked up at her daughter with worried eyes. "I have discovered that the garnet eardrops Grandmama Haversham left you are missing. I'm afraid Camilla may have taken them while I was out visiting old Mrs. Carmichael."

Harriett swallowed and looked down at the piece of toast she had been nibbling, not sure what to say. "Does Papa know?" she asked in a subdued voice.

Mrs. Haversham shook her head. "I could not bear to tell him. It would kill your poor papa to learn of this on top of all else."

"I think you underrate Papa," Harriett answered, doing her best to cheer her mother. "For he has always preached forgiveness, and while he must be upset at first, I am sure in the end he would not hold it against Camilla.

9

Besides, you know that with my red hair I should not wear garnets, in any case." She gave her mother a little smile, and stood, brushing the toast crumbs from her fingers.

Unfortunately, neither the words nor the thought cheered her mother overmuch, serving as they did to remind Mrs. Haversham of yet another worry—namely, her eldest daughter's unhappy resemblance to her dear papa. Mrs. Haversham sighed and looked at Harriett's wildly curling red hair, thin cheeks, and rather long nose, all of which unmistakably proclaimed Harriett her father's daughter. What was well enough in a husband could be more than unfortunate in a daughter.

"If only we were rich," Mrs. Haversham said wistfully. For a fair fortune quite erased the misfortune of a less than fair face.

"I don't mind, Mama," Harriett said, with false cheer. "I am quite content."

"But you should not be," Mrs. Haversham protested. "You are the kindest, sweetest of my children and to think that you shall never marry—"

Harriett blushed, her fair skin turning so bright a pink that the freckles scattered across the bridge of her nose were for once quite invisible. She was twenty-four and had been on the shelf for the better part of six years. Surely she must be inured by now to her own inadequacies. But she was not, as she privately acknowledged. If only her sisters were not quite so attractive, the very opposite of Harriett, it

10

might not have been so bad. But while Harriett was tall and large boned, with red hair and strong features, her sisters were petite and daintily featured, with hair of an attractive chestnut hue.

"It really doesn't matter," she assured her mother once again, and walked to the long window of the room that served as both breakfast parlour and dining room. Her papa had gone to the local livery stable to hire a carriage, for while the parsonage boasted a curricle and pony cart, neither was deemed adequate for what might prove a long and arduous journey. At the sound of wheels on the drive, therefore, Harriett tweaked aside the drapery and looked outside. "Papa is here with the carriage," she announced, glad to change the subject.

"My portmanteau is all but packed," her mother replied, rising hastily from the table. "It will take me only a moment and I will be ready." Mrs. Haversham walked quickly to the doorway leading to the hall, her skirt of winter twill brushing against the mahogany sideboard. She hesitated for a moment. "Do see if you can persuade your papa to partake of some breakfast," she said, glancing at the covered dishes on the sideboard. "I am sure he has eaten nothing since—" she swallowed and closed her eyes for a moment, "—since Mary discovered Camilla's note when she went in to wake her. There is no telling when we shall have a chance to eat again."

Harriett nodded. "I shall do my best, but

you know how Papa is. He shall not want to stop for such a trifle. In any case . . ." Harriett's voice trailed off, for she was now speaking to her mother's back as that lady hurried into the hallway and up the stairs.

In the end, it made very little difference, for Cook was there with a large basket of food to be placed in the carriage and Mary with a hot brick for Mrs. Haversham's feet. "For it's still that cold, it bein' March an' all," she told her mistress.

"You are very good." Mrs. Haversham took the little maid's hand and thanked her with tears in her eyes. "Pray God that we are soon returned, Mary." She then turned to her eldest daughter, who stood next to the carriage, a shawl wrapped about her shoulders. "Look after your sister, Harriett. I leave things in your hands. It is my hope that we shall have returned before nightfall, or tomorrow at latest. If not—"

Mrs. Haversham turned, leaving her sentence unfinished, and allowed her husband to assist her into the carriage. The three who stood watching knew full well what it would mean were the vicar and his wife not returned by tomorrow. Camilla's reputation would be in ruins and all possibility of marriage to a respectable gentleman quite at an end.

"We will say that Camilla has gone to stay with my aunt, should anyone inquire," Harriett told the other two, as they turned to go back inside.

12

"Indeed, Miss Harriett, you've no cause to be worryin' about any of the servants saying anythin'," Cook replied, hands folded in her apron. "We're that loyal to your papa an' all."

"I know that," Harriett said with a sigh. "It's Augusta I'm worried about. Though it is in her own best interest to speak to no one about Camilla, you know what a runaway tongue she has at times."

Still, Augusta's runaway tongue would almost have been welcomed that morning, for the parsonage seemed unnaturally silent and the hours passed more slowly than Harriett would have believed possible. When she tried to read, she found her thoughts more on Camilla and her parents than on the characters in the book, and it seemed that the hall clock had never ticked so loudly nor so slowly before. With a sigh that seemed to echo in the silent parlour, Harriett put down her book and rose to her feet. She would take a basket of food to old Mrs. Micklewaithe. She had intended to do it later that afternoon anyway, and the walk in the crisp March air would do her good.

Though Augusta rarely accompanied Harriett or her mother on such calls, Harriett stopped to inquire if Augusta would like to join her. "The wind is gusting a bit today, but it will blow the cobwebs from our minds," she told her sister, trying to sound as cheerful as possible. "And I'm sure Mrs. Micklewaithe would be happy to see you."

Augusta, who had been quite thankful to

find that her eyes were not red after all, was sitting with an old issue of *The Lady's Magazine* propped open on the dressing table as she attempted to copy one of the fashionable hairstyles pictured therein. A bowl of sugar water, a row of hairpins, and a frown of concentration accompanied the effort. "As you see, I cannot possibly go anywhere at the moment," she said, twisting one stiffened lock into a curl and pinning it in place. "And surely someone from the family should be home, in case Camilla changes her mind and returns?"

"I only wish she would," Harriett said, watching as Augusta dipped her comb in the sugar water.

"In any case, the cold makes my nose turn a most unbecoming pink," Augusta continued, turning back to the mirror with an air of finality. "You may no longer care what you look like, but I, for one, should not care to be seen like that."

Harriett, biting back the retort that any woman not yet cold in her grave cared what she looked like, turned and walked quietly downstairs. Her sister was very young and admittedly a bit selfish, quite unable to enter into the feelings of anyone but herself at present. Augusta did not mean her remark to be unkind . . . I am sure she did not, Harriett repeated forcibly to herself, doing her best to keep at bay the mad desire to rush upstairs and dump the entire bowl of sugar water on Augusta's self-absorbed head.

With Cook's help, Harriett packed a basket of cold meat pasties, a bit of bread and cheese, and some of last summer's apples, a bit withered by now but still quite tasty and sure to be enjoyed by the invalid. When everything was ready, Harriett pulled on a pair of stout boots, donned her warmest wool cloak, and clutching the basket in both gloved hands, set out down the road to Mrs. Micklewaithe's small cottage.

The old lady had been confined to her home after slipping on a patch of ice and breaking her leg early in February. Though it was hoped that she would soon be on her feet again, she could not yet manage by herself, and was almost embarrassingly grateful to see Harriett, pink nose and all.

Harriett sat for a while, listening to the old lady's stories and petting George, the elderly, orange and white striped tom-cat, who made himself at home upon her lap. Her thoughts, however, were not on Mrs. Micklewaithe, most of whose tales she had heard before, nor on the silky orange coat of George, but on her parents as they traveled over roads rutted from winter's frosts in search of their runaway daughter.

Oh, Camilla, how could you? Harriett thought. Don't you care that you have broken Papa's heart, and that by your own selfish conduct, you may have caused the whole family to suffer? This, and Augusta's earlier lament, were in fact no more than the truth.

The Reverend Haversham held the living of

Upper Mourouby at the behest of the Earl of Weston, who had turned out the last vicar, a Reverend Smythe, for driving his curricle on a Sunday. Though Harriett and her sisters had never met Lord Weston, Reverend Smythe had informed them that the earl was notoriously high in the instep and was called Lord Stiff Rump by the locals. Whatever would such a gentleman say if he learned that one of Reverend Haversham's daughters had eloped with his groom? Harriett gave a little shiver.

"Ay, there's quite a draft," Mrs. Micklewaithe said. "Them windows have never fitted proper-like. I should keep the curtains drawn, I know. But it's that dark in here then, and a body needs a bit of sun, I say. Besides, George there likes to lie on the sill and watch the road, don't you, boy?"

George twitched his ears in the direction of his mistress's voice but declined to open his eyes. He had just had a small bowl of milk and a bit of the meat pasty Harriett had brought and was in no mood to do anything but sleep upon a warm lap.

"I do hate to disturb him," Harriett said. "But I really must be going."

"Ay." Mrs. Micklewaithe nodded. "It's just you and your sisters, then, is it?"

Harriett's gray eyes opened wide. Did everyone know about Camilla already? Surely the gabblemongers had not begun to chew upon her sister's reputation so soon? Harriett forced herself to continue stroking George as if nothing were wrong and waited for Mrs. Micklewaithe to continue.

"Saw the Reverend go past on the way to the stable." The old lady rewarded Harriett's patience. "And then your mama and him drove past in a hired carriage. Something amiss, I asked myself?" She waited to see if Harriett would bite on the bait, and when Harriett remained silent, continued with her own speculation.

"But then I thought, maybe your mama is just goin' on a visit to her sister. Though it's an odd time to be goin' visiting, what with Easter comin' on, and they do say as how Lord Weston might be comin' to stay. Leastways there's been all sorts of preparations and such up at Yarwood. More'n time, if you ask me. We haven't seen hide nor hair of him in many a day. Still, anyways you look at it, seems like it's not the best time for your papa to be away."

"Actually," Harriett looked down at her gloved hand as it stroked George's broad orange stripes and pondered the lie she was about to tell, "actually, it is my sister Camilla who has gone on a visit to my aunt."

"Ah." Mrs. Micklewaithe nodded. "Didn't see her in the carriage. Is she stayin' long?"

It is as Papa always says, one lie can but lead to another, Harriett thought, wondering what her reply should be. "I believe Camilla will be— oh dear, look how late it grows." She dumped George unceremoniously from her lap and stood up. "I'm afraid I must be going, Mrs.

Micklewaithe. Augusta will be wondering where I am."

Mrs. Micklewaithe gave her a sharp look, but only said that she should look in the kitchen cupboard for the bit of stale bread she'd been saving. "Can't get my teeth into the heel of a loaf to save my soul," she said. "Leastways not when its more'n a few days old. But I know as how you feed those birds of yours, so you might as well take it with you. No sense in it goin' to waste around here. 'Sides, I seen as how you was goin' to stop." She nodded to the small bag of bread crumbs Harriett had placed beside her reticule.

"Thank you, Mrs. Micklewaithe," Harriett said, feeling herself blush. It was the curse of her fair skin that the least embarrassment caused her to turn a shade of pink that Augusta had once told her in a fit of pique, clashed quite horribly with her hair. "I am quite aware that I should not be feeding the rooks or crows. The farmers consider them a nuisance, but there has been so little for them to eat this winter."

"Ay, and it's been a hard winter for man and beast," Mrs. Micklewaithe agreed. "Do take that bit of bread with you now, and never mind what others may say. To my way of thinkin' and your father's, too, I wouldn't be surprised helping God's creatures can't be anythin' but good."

Harriett was not sure everyone would have agreed that this applied to the crows and rooks

18

that had grown almost tame since she had begun to feed them in Lord Weston's home woods. Still, she could not bring herself to stop what with the weather still so cold and so little on the ground for the poor creatures to eat.

Walking down the footpath that led from Mrs. Micklewaithe's cottage, Harriett proceeded across the meadow where the cold wind blew strong, and into the small woods that marked the beginning of Yarwood, Lord Weston's estate. Once among the trees, the wind ceased to blow and everything grew calm and quiet. There were few birds to be seen, but Harriett knew they were there, waiting to see if she were friend or foe. She stopped at a small clearing where there was a fallen log upon which she might sit while she watched the birds enjoy their repast. It was not only the rooks and crows that came, but a few hardy thrushes and a chaffinch as well.

Harriett emptied her bag of bread on a small patch of winter-pale grass, then stepped back and raised her head to the skies.

"Cawwww. Cawwww, cawwww, cawwww. Tea is being served, gentlemen and ladies," she announced to the air, fancying herself a bit of a cross between a butler and a crow. "Most unladylike, Harriett," she chided herself with a small giggle, and then sat down to wait.

Rusty Brown was first. He was a large rook Harriett had named for the brown sheen to his otherwise brilliant black plumage. Being the bravest or perhaps greediest of the birds, he always arrived first, picking up the largest piece of bread in his beak and then trying to grab as many smaller pieces as possible without dropping the first.

"It will be warm again soon," Harriett told him. Rusty Brown cocked his head in her direction, fixed her with a beady black stare for a moment and then, knowing she would do him no harm, continued to peck at the bread. "Easter is early this year, less than two weeks away," she said, continuing her conversation. "Soon you will have to concern yourself with feeding your young. And you must not think I will be providing bread crumbs for you all summer."

"I am sorry to hear that," a voice replied.

Harriett jumped to her feet. At first she thought Rusty Brown had spoken to her. But then she turned, and saw a tall gentleman wearing a many-caped driving coat leaning casually against an oak tree. "Oh, I thought you were Rusty Brown," she exclaimed, realizing how inane the words must sound only after they were spoken.

"The rook?" he asked, nodding to the bird which had flown to the branch of a tree and was now watching them with beady-eyed concentration.

"Yes, I . . . um . . ." Harriett twisted her gloved hands together. She never knew what to say to gentlemen. Especially strange gentlemen. Especially large, strange gentlemen, she thought, as the stranger advanced and she had to tilt back her head to see his face. He was not wearing a hat, and his hair shone with the same brown-black brilliance of Rusty Brown's feathers.

"Do you live around here?" he inquired, his lips curving into a most charming smile.

"I . . . um . . ." Not only was she tongue-tied, but Harriett knew she was blushing as well. Oh, why must she always act the ninny-hammer!

"Or are you some wood sprite who inhabits the forest hereabouts?"

"Wood sprite? Me?" Harriett was startled out of her confused embarrassment. No one had ever thought of Harriett as any kind of sprite before. She looked down at herself in her old dark green wool cloak, all five feet seven of her, and then grinned back at the stranger. "I am hardly a sprite, sir," she said, her gray eyes sparkling with amusement. "A giantess, perhaps?"

The tall gentleman shook his head. "Not to me." Which was true enough. For beside the stranger's tall form, Harriett felt almost as if she might, indeed, be a sprite.

"You are very tall, sir."

"So I have been told," he agreed, causing Harriett to blush and become quite flustered again.

"I am sorry, it was rude of me to comment on your appearance," Harriett replied stiffly, looking down at the scuffed toes of her sturdy

21

boots. "My sister, Augusta, says I am quite hopelessly lacking in the social graces."

"Ah, I take it that Augusta must be a wood sprite, then?"

Harriett nodded. "Small and dainty and quite lovely."

"And possibly quite dull."

"Dull, sir?" Harriett left off the study of her boot tips and looked up at the stranger again. "I do not think most gentlemen would find Augusta dull."

The stranger walked up to Harriett and took her chin in a firm hand, tilting her head so that the hood of her cloak fell back. He studied her face for a moment and the flaming red hair that surrounded it in a riot of wispy curls. Harriett stood quietly beneath his gaze, though she knew she should have been outraged that he had taken such a liberty with her, a man to whom she had not even been formally introduced.

"My name is Harriett Haversham," she said, deciding to take matters into her own hands.

"Not the name of a wood sprite," he commented, releasing her chin but continuing to gaze steadily down at her. "But then, who would be a wood sprite? Always flitting about and never settling in one spot."

Harriett swallowed, blinked, and returned the stranger's dark gaze. No one had ever talked to her like this before. Almost as if . . . "Are you flirting with me, sir?"

He chuckled. "Yes, Harriett Haversham, I believe I am."

If her heart had been pounding before, it quite thundered now. She was twenty-four, a spinster with no pretensions to beauty beyond a pair of lovely gray eyes and a quite engaging smile. Still, she had always thought herself content with her lot . . . until now.

The voice of someone hallooing sounded in the distant. The stranger turned his head, a look of annoyance on his face. "I'm afraid I must go, Harriett Haversham," he said.

Harriett's heart stopped thundering and dropped to her stomach. "But I do not know your name," she blurted out, quite before she could stop herself, and then bit her lip in consternation. How forward she was. She had given the gentleman a disgust of her, she knew she had.

The stranger hesitated for a moment. Harriett frowned and found herself for some unknown reason quite close to tears. "I should not have asked," she said. "It is no business of mine, I am sure." She gave him a small curtsy. "I will bid you good day, sir."

"Phillip Sinclair," he said as she turned away. "My name is Phillip Sinclair. I am staying with a party of friends at Yarwood."

"With Lord Stiff Rump?" Harriett asked, and then covered her mouth with a hand. Would she never learn to control her tongue? She either said nothing or the first thing that came to mind. And she had accused Augusta of having a runaway tongue.

Phillip Sinclair's dark eyes narrowed. "I beg your pardon?" he asked, his voice as chilly as the air.

"Lord Weston, I meant to say," Harriett replied in a small voice.

"Indeed?" When he looked down his arrogant nose like that and raised his eyebrows, Phillip Sinclair did not look at all attractive, Harriett decided. He looked, in fact, as stiff as Lord Stiff Rump was reported to be.

Harriett raised her own eyebrows, and though it was quite impossible for her to look down her nose at someone so much taller, she did the best she could. She should not have said what she had, especially if Lord Weston were a particular friend of the gentleman's. But still, there was no reason for Phillip Sinclair to poker up so over what was no more than a simple slip of the tongue. Why, one would almost think—

Harriett gave a little gasp. "You aren't . . . ?"

He nodded. "I am."

"Oh, dear." She had certainly landed herself in the suds this time. And he even knew her name because she had been so foolish as to gift him with it. Harriett lowered her eyes, desperately trying to think of some way she could rectify the matter. "You are standing in my bread crumbs," was the first thing that came to mind.

"You are standing in my home woods," was the reply.

"And you said your name was Phillip Sinclair," Harriett accused.

"Phillip Sinclair, Earl of Weston, as you should know if you are in the habit of trespassing on my grounds. And," he continued, getting to the heart of the matter, "I fail to see why I have been given the epithet 'Stiff Rump.' "

"Probably for the same reason I named the rook 'Rusty Brown.' Because it describes you so well."

Lord Weston's dark eyes flared for a moment, causing Harriett to take a hasty step backward. "I am sorry. That was uncalled for," she apologized in a small voice.

"It was." His voice was harsh, not at all the pleasant, teasing baritone it had been earlier.

Harriett stole a quick glance upward. Lord Weston was frowning down at her, not a whit mollified by her apology.

"I, um . . . had best be going," she decided.

"Yes, as must I . . . if I am going to organize a rook-hunting expedition in the home woods for tomorrow."

"What? But—"

"It is my woods, is it not? And rooks are considered by most people hereabouts as no more than a nuisance, taking the grain that would be better left for the game birds."

Harriett looked to the branch where Rusty Brown had been sitting. He was no longer there, but he would be back. And so would Lord Weston, with his party of friends. Harriett bit her lip and looked away. There was nothing she could do, of course. These were, as Lord Weston had said, his woods.

Pulling the hood over her fiery curls with hands that trembled, Harriett turned away. She did not trust herself to speak. Lord Weston would come tomorrow with his guns and his friends and they would shoot the poor birds that had come to think of this small clearing as a sanctuary, a safe place where food could be found. She had taught the birds trust and it would be their death.

"Miss Haversham."

Harriett hesitated at the edge of the clearing, but did not turn. And I do not care a whit if it is rude, she thought.

Lord Weston stepped in front of her. Harriett compared her scuffed but sturdy boots with his shining Hessians and refused to look up.

"Miss Haversham, it is my turn to apologize. But surely you knew I was only teasing you."

Harriett sniffed and blinked and opened the reticule that dangled from her wrist in search of a handkerchief.

"Miss Haversham, if you are going to be a watering pot, I shall truly organize a rook-hunting party."

Harriett sniffed again, but this time she did look up, her great gray eyes shining with tears. "You were only funning?" she asked, her voice muffled by the handkerchief she was holding to her nose.

Lord Weston nodded. "I doubt that my

guests would consider rook-hunting any sort of sport, and in any case, I could hardly shoot Rusty Brown. He was the one that introduced us."

Harriett blew her nose with a bit too much vigor, and stuffed her handkerchief back in her reticule. "Actually, I am not sure Mama would consider Rusty Brown the proper sort to perform that office," she said.

"Miss Haversham?"

"Yes?"

"Are you flirting with me?" Lord Weston asked.

Harriett looked genuinely shocked for a moment. "Am I? I don't think so. I mean, I have never been accused of flirting before. But if I am, I must say it is a rather agreeable thing to do," she ended with a small smile.

"Indeed it is," Lord Weston agreed. "May I escort you home, Miss Haversham? I should like to meet your parents."

"My parents?" Oh, dear, Harriett thought. What am I doing? Standing here talking to Lord Stiff Rump, when he must on no account find out about Camilla eloping with his groom and Mama and Papa being gone. "I'm . . . I'm afraid that would be quite impossible," she said.

"May I ask why?" He was frowning down at her, not looking at all pleased by her evasion.

"Phillip?" A voice called at the edge of the clearing. "Hallooo?"

Harriett sighed with relief. "I believe someone is looking for you, Lord Stiff Rump," she said. "I mean . . . oh, dear!" Harriett gave him a quick curtsy and fled, her face flaming to match her hair.

Two

Lord Weston adjusted his cravat in the glass over his dressing table and frowned.

"Too much starch, milord?" inquired James, his valet.

"Not you, too, James." Lord Weston scowled more fiercely.

James raised his eyebrows. "I beg your pardon, milord?"

Lord Weston twisted around on his dressing stool, hands upon the knees of his trousers. "Do you think I am, in fact, too full of starch, James? Too rigid, an unyielding stickler, too stiff-rumped, in fact?"

James pursed his lips. "Perhaps the yellow waistcoat, milord?"

"Then it's true?" Lord Weston sighed.

"I merely suggested that the yellow waistcoat might be better with the blue frock coat, milord."

"You think me as stiff-rumped as all the rest," Lord Weston stated unequivocally. "Whenever you evade a question, I know it's because you think I don't want to hear the answer."

James held out the yellow waistcoat and Lord Weston rose to slip it on with the complete trust a gentleman has for a truly admirable valet. The yellow waistcoat must be preferred. James had said so. Lord Weston then shrugged into his frock coat of blue superfine and accepted the watchfob and snuffbox that James held out.

"Do we know any Havershams in the district?" Lord Weston asked, putting the watchfob in his waistcoat pocket.

James paused in the act of straightening an infinitesimal wrinkle in Lord Weston's coat. "We are so seldom in the district, milord, I am not sure . . . but is there not a Reverend Haversham who has the living of Upper Mourouby?"

"Is there?"

"I believe so, milord When the last curate was removed from the position due to an unfortunate incident with his curricle, I believe your secretary, Mr. Adams, suggested a Reverend Haversham for the living."

"Ah, yes, I vaguely remember meeting the man. Has a shocking head of red hair and several daughters, as I recall, though I never met the family."

"I believe that to be correct, milord."

"Hmmmmm." Lord Weston gazed absently at his image in the cheval glass, while James waited for his nod of approval. Instead, Lord Weston frowned.

"Is something amiss, milord? Would you have preferred the puce waistcoat?"

"What? Oh, no, James, no, the yellow is fine. It is just that I seem to grow out of touch with things here. We should visit Yarwood more often."

"I believe your mother prefers your property in Somerset, milord."

"Yes, she does, but that is no excuse. I have always thought absentee landlords deplorable, and I don't think I was at Yarwood more than a few days last year. Well, I shall consult with the estate manager tomorrow. Meanwhile, I should like to know more of this Haversham family. See what you can find out, will you?"

"Very good, milord. And now I believe the dinner bell will be sounding in a few minutes and your guests are no doubt awaiting you in the library."

Lord Weston accepted his valet's prodding without demur, his thoughts on a thin, freckled face with no pretensions to beauty, beyond a pair of lovely gray eyes, an engaging smile, and a way of looking up at a man—

"Milord?"

"Coming, James, coming."

Lord Weston joined his guests who were, as James had said, already gathered in the library. His mother, the dowager Lady Weston, smiled at him as he entered the room, but her eyes were glacial. He was late. The lower classes might be late, having an inferior sense of time, but a Weston never was.

"My apologies." Lord Weston smiled, but offered neither explanation nor excuse. His mother pressed her lips together in a tight line of disapproval. Lord Weston, affecting not to notice, turned to greet his guests. There were only six, including the dowager, and only one had been invited by Lord Weston. This was his old friend George Reading, a chum since school, who was thought by Lady Weston to have a bad influence on her son. The fact that Lord Weston was thirty-six and had been on the town for some sixteen years, notwithstanding.

The other guests, all chosen by Lady Weston, were Miss Dade and her mother, and Miss Smalbathe and her sister. All had been given the singular honor of being asked to spend the two weeks before Easter at Yarwood. All had accepted with alacrity, for it was well known that Lady Weston was seeking a wife for her son. Lord Weston's opinion on the subject was not known. Nor did it seem to matter greatly.

"Miss Dade, you look quite charming, as always." Lord Weston smiled down at Laurenda Dade, who dimpled up at him and fluttered long lashes over her justly famous blue eyes. Though a diamond of the first water, Miss Dade had failed to take during her first Season. Some said it was due to the vacant mind behind the beautiful face. Others said that her mother, in hanging out for a duke or an earl, had miscalculated how much her daughter's beautiful face would bring in the marriage mart.

Miss Smalbathe cleared her throat. It would not do to have Lord Weston gaze at the dazzling Miss Dade too long. Gentlemen's minds were known to be weak when it came to such things. Not that Abigail Smalbathe was an antidote, far from it. Oh, she might not be quite as beautiful as Miss Dade, but she was quite able to hold her own, thank you.

With a sharp mind hidden behind a simpering manner, Miss Smalbathe intended to have Lord Weston in the parson's trap before the final blessing on Easter morning. And if Lord Weston seemed not to favor her (there was no telling with men, who could be capricious creatures, when all was said and done), there was always her sister, Prudence. Though Abigail considered her sister a total imbecile, on a par with Miss Dade, the marriage settlement would be considerable no matter which sister he married. That was the important thing.

"Mrs. Dade, it is easy to see from whom your daughter has her beauty." Lord Weston continued to greet his guests in his leisurely fashion, while conspiracies of which he was well aware roiled about him.

"And Miss Smalbathe," he paused over Prudence Smalbathe's hand. She giggled up at him. Her eyes were gray, but otherwise the vacant stare in them was identical to Miss Dade's. Lord Weston gave a small sigh before turning to Abigail Smalbathe.

"We were looking everywhere for you earlier, Lord Weston," Abigail Smalbathe chided, smiling so that he would know she was only funning. "Mr. Reading thought you might have gone for a walk around the grounds. I must say, it was quite naughty of you to abandon your guests in that way."

"Indeed?" Lord Weston raised one eyebrow and stared down at Miss Smalbathe. What a boring, presumptuous woman she was.

Lord Weston was attracted to her, Miss Smalbathe could tell by the way he was staring. Well, that was all for the good, she supposed, since he was rumored to be worth at least thirty thousand pounds a year. Still, it was a pity he was so very tall and dark. Miss Smalbathe did not admire such men, and would have preferred someone of slighter form and paler complexion. But then, one could not have everything in a husband.

And how admirable it would be to return to London and announce to the ton that she was engaged to Lord Weston. It would be the talk of the Season, and make up for last year, when she had received only one offer, and that quite unsuitable. Yes, she would accept when Lord Weston made his offer, for despite his unfortunate looks, the earl was considered quite a catch. Abigail Smalbathe smiled and looked about the library, mentally redecorating it to suit her tastes.

The evening was, as Lord Weston had expected, quite interminable. The dinner, a ragout of veal, had been excellent. But Lord Weston had been seated, by some mad act of fate or his mother's planning, between Miss Prudence Smalbathe and Miss Dade. Conversation had been exceedingly tedious, to say the least, and he had all but thrown up his hands in rejoicing when the ladies had finally left the men to their port.

Thank God he had insisted that George be invited, Lord Weston thought. To spend two weeks alone with his mother and her candidates for the office of the new Lady Weston would be enough to make any man wave the white flag of surrender.

"They'll have you in a parson's noose before the Season ends," George predicted, leaning back in his chair and sipping his wine.

"You were invited to cheer me, George, not to send me into a fit of the dismals." Lord Weston poured some wine into his own glass from the decanter at his elbow. "Though sometimes I think I should just agree to my mother's choice of wife and be done with it."

"It would be the simplest thing to do," George agreed. "Though if it's to be that sharp-faced Smalbathe creature, I feel I must tell you, I'd sooner be drawn and quartered myself."

"Ah, then you prefer her sister Prudence? Or is it Miss Dade who strikes your fancy?"

George grinned and leaned forward, putting his glass on the table and reaching for a walnut from the dish which had been left on the table.

"At least you don't have to worry about them prattling on for hours. Not a brain between them, of course. But then, there are those who would say it didn't matter, at least, not when it comes to the Dade chit. Diamond of the first water there, Phillip, old boy. Only thing is, you'd have to worry about your children being brainless nodcocks. Awful risk, if you ask me."

"Hmmmmm." Lord Weston cracked a nut between his fingers, chewed meditatively upon the contents for a moment, and then asked, "George, do you think me too high in the instep?" He looked up at his friend, a frown between his dark brows.

"The man who was sent down twice? Once for adding vinegar to the proctor's wine, and the second time for that pig in the church pew? Hardly."

"The pig was your idea, as I recall, George. And the thing is, I seem to have acquired the name of Stiff Rump among some of the local gentry."

George poured himself another glass of wine. "Can't know you very well, Phillip." He shook his head. "Not that you don't poker up a bit stiff now and then. Or give someone a set down when you think he deserves it."

"Me?" Lord Weston paused in the act of reaching for the nutcracker.

George nodded. "Cut old Briartree direct the other day. Not that he didn't deserve it."

"Briartree refused to dance with Miss Taylor after they had been introduced at Almack's.

Worst of bad manners, besides embarrassing the poor girl almost to death. He wasn't being asked to marry the chit, just to stand up with her for the quadrille."

"Those teeth aren't her fault, in any case," George agreed. "Inherits them from her mother, poor thing."

Lord Weston pushed a small scattering of walnut shells into a pile and stood up, draining his glass. "If that's being stiff-rumped, I shall continue to be so," he said. "Now, I'm afraid we will have to join the ladies, George." He smiled apologetically down at his friend and flexed his broad shoulders as if getting ready to do battle. "I'd say I'm sorry I got you into this, but I'm not. The thought of facing all those marriage-minded females by myself makes me quake in my boots."

George Reading got to his feet and shrugged. "I don't mind, Phillip. Thing is, I'm not really rich enough to deflect their fire, old boy. They treat me rather like an occasional table: useful, but not deserving of much attention."

"Poor George. Well, you will be happy to know that not only will there be your favorite plum cake for tea, but I instructed the butler to hide the harp music immediately once Miss Dade's mother informed me that her daughter was an accomplished performer."

George laid a hand upon his friend's arm. "Bless you, Lord Stiff Rump," he said with mock sincerity, and was surprised to see Lord

Weston frown. "Surely that doesn't bother you, Phillip?"

"Of course not," Lord Weston replied. "And in any case, I intend to prove to certain young females that the epithet is far from fitting."

Harriett's evening was also proving interminable. She was on tenterhooks waiting for word about Camilla and as if that were not enough, she must deal with Augusta's continuous complaints.

"I must say I, for one, never expected Cammie to do such a selfish thing," Augusta announced as they sat at supper. "I mean, she might have thought of me. It is her duty to marry well so that I may have a Season. I am quite wasted at Upper Mourouby, and you know Papa will never come up with the necessary to send me to London. He must forever be giving money away without thought to the needs of his own offspring."

"Augusta, you know Papa only gives to those in the parish who are really in need," Harriett chided, putting down her soup spoon. "And we are hardly in want."

"That is easy for you to say, Harry, for you have never wanted anything. Why, you would be satisfied to spend your entire life in Upper Mourouby calling on such as Mrs. Micklewaithe. I want more than that, Harry."

Harriett nodded for Mary to remove her soup plate. "What is it exactly that you do want,

Gusta?" she asked. Sometimes Augusta could make her feel so sensible and staid, so . . . old.

"I want a Season in London, and I want to marry a very rich man, and I want that blue velvet dress that I saw in the window of Madame St. Germaine's when last we went to town."

Harriett frowned, giving her sister's want list serious consideration. It seemed there was really only one thing on it that Augusta had any remote possibility of getting at the moment. But, "What would you do with the dress?" she asked. "You do mean the blue velvet with the deep décolletage and the knots of ribbon and lace along the edge?"

Augusta nodded. "I should wear it, of course. Oh, you are thinking that I would not have the occasion. But I have heard that Lord Weston might visit Yarwood over Easter. Would that not be beyond anything? For he is sure to give a dinner party and must invite us. And then I should be able to wear the dress."

"Would not the blue velvet be a bit grand for a simple dinner party?" Harriett asked, helping herself from a dish of boiled parsnips.

"That is all you know," was Augusta's answer. "Ladies wear much more elaborate gowns to dinner parties in London, and I know I should look truly *au fait* in the blue velvet. If only Papa weren't so parsimonious and Mama so . . . so starchy."

"Starchy?" Harriett was surprised at her younger sister's choice of words, for she had never thought of their mother that way before. Mrs. Haversham was certainly strict. And it was true there were times when one found her dictates a bit confining, but . . . Harriett pushed the food around her plate with her fork and thought about the matter. Lord Weston's face seemed to stare up at her from the boiled parsnips. She had called him stiff-rumped, though she had no real reason to do so beyond what she had heard. And he had not seemed a bit starchy or stiff when he had been talking to her. In fact, he seemed to be one of the few men besides Papa who did not make her tongue-tied. Quite the opposite, for he had actually accused her of flirting with him.

"Why are you blushing so?" Augusta demanded. "I have told you it is most unbecoming. Members of the ton never blush, I have heard. It is not at all the thing."

"I was simply thinking . . . I, ah, met Lord Weston this afternoon."

"What!" Augusta's brown eyes widened. "But why didn't you tell me? It is above all things! What does he look like? What did he say? Does he—he doesn't know about Camilla, does he?" Augusta put one hand dramatically to her breast. "Say that he does not, Harry! I shall—I shall die if he does. We shall be ruined. My every chance of happiness gone! My London Season! My blue velvet dress!"

Harriett put down her fork. "Augusta, if you please!" she snapped. Harriett had seen her mother quell Augusta's hysterics enough to know how it was done.

Augusta blinked and sniffed, her eyes filling with tears. "You don't understand, Harry," she said. "How can you? You don't care for gowns and dancing and . . . and fripperies. But I do. If my life is ruined, if Lord Weston finds out about Camilla, I shall die. I know I shall."

"Really, Gusta." Harriett sighed. "I am sure Lord Weston does not know about Camilla. But that does not mean he is going to invite us to a dinner party. In any case, even if he did, he would invite Mama and Papa. You are not even out yet. Mama would never permit you to attend anything more than a family gathering."

Augusta looked stubborn, then thoughtful. "You know, Harry, I have been wondering about something."

"Yes?" Harriett asked cautiously.

"It seems quite out of character for Camilla to elope with Tom Watkins, don't you think? For though I will admit he is prodigious handsome, he has not a feather to fly with. And you know that Camilla loves clothes and fancies as much as I do. So maybe Cammie really is in love with Tom?"

Harriett shrugged. "I know little of the emotion."

Augusta gave her a sympathetic look. "I have been in love any number of times," she said, with some authority. "And I must say, I would not marry for such a reason. For it is my opin-

41

ion it never lasts beyond the first meeting or two."

Harriett signaled Mary that the covers might be removed and the dessert, a simple jelly and some fruit, might be brought in. Augusta remained thoughtfully silent while the dishes were being cleared by the maid and Joseph, the man who performed the tasks of both butler and footman in Reverend Haversham's small household.

"You don't suppose Tom Watkins is really a duke or something?" she said at last, spooning up a bit of the jelly. "You know, he might have been acting as a groom to win a bet. I'm sure I've heard of members of the ton doing that sort of thing. And it would explain why they eloped, for Tom cannot believe that Camilla has any money, even though Papa does give a great deal of it away."

"Only to those who are truly in need," Harriett replied.

"I am truly in need of that blue velvet dress," Augusta said. "And I know Papa would not give me the money for that."

"I doubt that Mama would permit you to wear the dress in any case."

"No." Augusta smiled. "But Mama is not here at the moment, is she?"

The jelly Harriett had been enjoying suddenly lost its flavor. "Augusta, you are not planning anything, are you?" she asked, putting down her spoon.

"Whatever do you mean, Harry?" Augusta opened wide, innocent eyes at her sister.

"You know quite well what I mean, Gusta. And you are no longer a child to be playing pranks as you did when Mama went to visit Aunt Sophie two years ago and you put salt in the sugar bowl."

"Of course not."

"It was not funny, Augusta. Old Mrs. Pierson put some in her tea and almost died from choking. She had to lie down on the sofa and afterward Papa had to drive her home. What may seem at first harmless may have consequences you do not expect. Promise me that you will do nothing of which Mama would not approve."

"Really, Harry, I—"

"Promise me, Gusta. And do not cross your fingers."

Augusta gave her older sister a rebellious look from under long eyelashes. "You spoil everything," she complained. "I swear, you are as stuffy as Mama. I think Cammie eloped so she could get away from here and have some fun. And I do not blame her."

"Even if Lord Weston finds out, and we are ruined, and all your hopes of a brilliant marriage are dashed, and to top it all, you do not get your blue velvet dress?" Harriett asked dryly.

"You do not understand," Augusta cried. "How could you? You've never had any hopes or dreams. You have always been quite content as you are. Well, I am not." With tears in her eyes, Augusta shoved back her chair and fled the room.

Harriett bit her lip and swallowed the lump in her throat. Never had any hopes or dreams? Ah, Gusta, if you only knew. Even plain girls have dreams. Dreams of the handsome man who will someday see beyond their plainness to the heart beneath. I do not know when we give up such dreams. Certainly I still cherish a few. Harriett picked up her spoon and gazed at the half-eaten jelly in her dish. She could not help but think of Lord Weston, though she knew she should not.

Phillip Sinclair. She smiled as she remembered the way he had told her his name, and then gave a little sigh. No matter what his name, he was still Lord Weston: rich, titled and very attractive. A tempting combination for any woman, surely. True, he may have flirted with Harriett for a few moments to amuse himself, but he would never be serious about her. Harriett knew that. It was a lesson she had learned when she was very young. But she had learned it well.

Harriett held up her spoon and gazed at her upside-down image in its silvery surface. No, Lord Weston would never look at Harriett Haversham, who fed rooks and was tongue-tied in the presence of strangers. Not that she had been tongue-tied in his presence after the first few moments. No, with Lord Weston, she had felt strangely comfortable, strangely at home.

But men did not marry women with whom they were comfortable. Men married women who were beautiful and exciting and had a bit of mystery about them. And I have none of those, Harriett thought, as she turned her spoon around and forced herself to finish eating the jelly.

Augusta returned in time to join Harriett for tea in the parlour. "For I do not want you to feel lonely," she told her sister, reaching for a piece of her favorite raisin cake. "Has there been any word from Mama or Papa?"

Harriett shook her head. "They have probably decided to spend the night at an inn. Unless they caught up with Camilla at once, it would be too late to return."

"I just hope they do not catch up with Camilla too late," Augusta said. "Imagine having a groom for a brother-in-law."

"I doubt it will come to that. In any case, I thought Tom Watkins was really a duke in disguise," Harriett said.

"I was only funning," Augusta excused herself, brushing crumbs from her fingers and sitting back on the upholstered settee. "Now, tell me more about Lord Weston and how you came to meet him. Is he prodigious handsome? How old is he, do you suppose? And is it true that he is not wed?"

Harriett choked on her tea. "Wed?" she asked, when she was able. It had not occurred to her that Lord Weston might be wed. But of course, he must be. A man of his attractions.

"Are you all right?" Augusta put down her tea cup and half rose from the settee, looking worriedly at her sister.

"Fine." Harriett cleared her throat. "I am fine. I just . . . the tea was too hot, is all."

Augusta continued to frown at her sister. "You had the most peculiar look upon your face, Harry. Are you sure you are not ill?"

"Quite positive," Harriett affirmed, unless you counted a sudden attack of the dismals.

"Well, then, you must tell me all about Lord Weston and how you came to meet," Augusta instructed, plumping back down on the settee and reaching for her tea cup again. "Go on, Harry. I want to hear everything."

Harriett looked down at the scalloped-top tea table. She wanted to talk about Lord Weston, yet at the same time, she did not want to speak of him at all. It was silly to feel that way, like some schoolroom chit who has had all her hopes of a ribbon quite dashed. Whether Lord Weston was married made little difference, really. It was not as if she, Harriett, would have had any chance with him anyway.

Across the tea table Augusta eyed her impatiently. "Well," Harriett began, "ever since Old John told me that the rooks were coming to the stable looking for bits of grain because food was so scarce this winter, I have been putting out scraps and pieces of stale bread for them."

"For the rooks?" Augusta asked, as if this were the most amazing thing she had ever heard. "But they are such great, ugly black things."

"Not really, Augusta. Not if you take the time to look at them. Their feathers are really a lovely purplish-blue, except for the one I call Rusty Brown. And they are truly very intelligent creatures. I have taken to feeding them in a small clearing in Lord Weston's home woods where they gather for the night."

"His game manager must be pleased."

"Well, of course, he is not." Harriett smiled. "But I think because I am the vicar's daughter he has decided to humor me. Besides, the clearing is almost at the edge of the woods, so the rooks don't drive away the game birds or do any real harm. And they were gathering there long before I started putting down scraps of food. You know, Gusta, I think if I took the time, I could quite tame Rusty Brown."

Augusta helped herself to some more tea, viewing her sister with the benign tolerance of the young for their elders, who will run on about things of no interest whatsoever. "Lord Weston?" she prompted.

"He came upon me while I was feeding Rusty Brown."

"The rook?"

Harriett nodded.

"Oh, dear. Did he . . . did he think you terribly odd?"

Harriett tilted her head to one side, considering the matter. "I do not think so, at least, he did say something about a wood sprite."

Augusta groaned.

"But I don't think he meant anything by it, Gusta. And he did mention wanting to meet Mama and Papa."

"Wanting to meet Mama and Papa? But why—oh, Harry, do you suppose he is going to make me an offer?" Augusta's eyes shone with hopeful anticipation

"Gusta! Do not be such a ninnyhammer. Lord Weston has not even met you. That is the most farfetched faradiddle you have yet come up with. And besides . . . he may be married."

Augusta shook her head. "I don't think so, Harry. Because Mary's sister is in service at Lord Weston's estate in Somerset. And when Mary went home for Mothering Sunday, she said her sister spoke only of the dowager. Which doesn't sound as if he is wed. And it is not so farfetched because even though we have never met, Lord Weston has doubtless heard of me. For you know how popular I am at the local assemblies."

This was true enough, and cause for some concern to their mother, who was not sure it was quite the thing to allow her young daughter to attend the local gatherings.

"Well, we had best hope Lord Weston does not call," Harriett concluded. "At least, not until Mama and Papa have returned with Camilla. I should hate to try and explain their absence."

"Heavens, yes," Augusta agreed. "Deceit is not your forte, Harry. Still, I am sure they will be home by tomorrow, and he would not call before then. Now do go on and tell me what Lord Weston is like in appearance. Mary says his estate in Somerset is so vast, her sister has yet to lay eyes on the master. Not that I would throw my hat over the windmill just for a handsome face, of course. I am not like Camilla."

"No, I—" At a sound from outside, Harriett rose from her chair and went quickly to the window. Parting the heavy drapery, she peered down the drive. "Nothing," she said, turning back to the parlour with a sigh. "I thought I heard the carriage, but it must have been the wind in the trees."

"You said yourself they must be putting up at an inn," Augusta pointed out.

Harriett resumed her seat in the brocade chair in front of the tea table. "Yes, I know, but I had hoped . . . well, no matter. I was going to describe Lord Weston, was I not? He is quite tall, and I should guess somewhere in his late thirties."

"Old." Augusta said the word as if it were Lord Weston's death knell.

"Not so very, "Harriett replied. "And he is quite attractive, I thought."

"Hmmmmmm." Augusta looked thoughtful. "Do you know how long he is to stay?"

Harriett shook her head. "Lord Weston did not say."

"It is a pity he is so very old, or I should make a push to engage his affections," Augusta said.

"I think you would only make a cake of your-

49

self if you tried," Harriett replied. "I am sure such as Lord Weston may have the pick of any London beauty. You are a very pretty girl, Augusta, but young and inexperienced in these things."

"And I suppose you are, Harry?"

The words stung as they were meant to. Harriett rose and rang for Mary to clear away the tea things. "I think it is time that we retired," she said in a tight voice.

"I did not mean—"

"I know you did not, Augusta." Harriett nodded but did not look at her sister. "We are both tired and worried about Mama and Papa and Camilla. When you say your prayers tonight, you must ask God for their safe return, as I know I shall."

"Yes," Augusta agreed. "And that Lord Weston has a dinner party and invites me," she added under her breath. "It would be above everything!"

Three

It was not as if Harriett sought Mary out the next morning. No. It was quite by accident that she met the little maid as she was hanging linens in the airing room. Mary dropped a quick curtsy and asked if there had been any news from the master and mistress.

"No." Harriett shook her head and sighed. "I must confess that I find all this waiting about quite trying. Still, as Papa would say, we must put our faith in Him who watches over all of us and will deliver us from every evil."

"Yes, Miss Harriett."

Harriett smiled at the grim expression on the maid's face. "Sorry, Mary, I did not mean to preach. It is from acting as first reader of Papa's sermons, you know. The words seem to stick in my mind and come tumbling out when I least expect them."

"That's all right, Miss. 'Tis to be expected, you bein' Reverend Haversham's eldest, an' all.

"Yes. Well, I had best be going, there is so

much to be done with Mama away," Harriett said, though she made no move to go, but remained standing staring down at the blue flounce on her otherwise plain muslin gown. "Um . . . I was just wondering how you enjoyed your visit home for Mothering Sunday."

"Oh, it was ever so nice seein' everyone again, Miss. And my mum was that pleased over the simnel cakes you and your mother made. She says as how they're even better than the ones Lucy brought. An' hers was made by that fancy French cook of Lord Weston's."

Harriett smiled. On Mothering Sunday, the fourth Sunday in Lent, the servants were always given a holiday to visit their families. Reverend Haversham gave everyone a few extra pence to buy flowers or presents for their mothers, and Mrs. Haversham and Harriett always baked the traditional simnel cakes to be taken home as well.

"Your mother doesn't prefer the other kind of cake, then?" Harriett asked, looking pleased.

"The one with the almond paste and candy flowers?" Mary shook her head. "They're good an' all, but we like the spiced ones with the currants and nuts. My mum, she comes from where they make that kind, the Bury simnel. So she's always liked it best."

"So do I," Harriett confessed. "I just wish we made them more than once a year." She hesitated, wanting to ask more about Lord Weston, but not sure how to do so without sounding like the worst sort of gabblemonger. "Um . . . did you know that the word 'simnel' comes from the Latin? Papa says a simnellus is a loaf of wheat bread baked for special occasions."

"Is it indeed?" Mary asked, stooping to take a sheet from her basket.

"Yes." Harriett nodded. "But Mama says she heard that the word 'simnel' comes from the first people who made the cake, who were named Simon and Nell."

Mary shrugged. "I don't know about any of that, Miss. I just know I like eatin' 'em well enough." She looked down at the sheet in her arms and then back at Harriett. "Was there somethin' you was wantin', then, Miss Harriett?"

"No, I just . . . um, I met Lord Weston yesterday.

"Did you, Miss?"

Harriett nodded. "Yes. I understand he will be staying at Yarwood until Easter with a party of friends. And I was just wondering if you'd heard . . . that is, Augusta and I had been talking, not gossiping, you understand," she looked up from her flounce at the maid, "but just talking the way people do about neighbors, and we were wondering, I mean we've heard about the dowager but not about, that is—"

"I don't believe Lord Weston is wed," Mary said, rightly guessing where Harriett was heading. "In fact, Meg, the upper maid at Yarwood, who's a friend of mine, was sayin', not gossipin', mind, that the dowager Lady Weston is lookin' about to find her son a wife. That's why the other ladies are visitin' Yarwood, most like. Hopin' they'll be the one he takes a shine to."

"How, ah, interesting," Harriett said, looking down at her flounce again to hide her avid curiosity. "Did Meg say anything more about these ladies with expectations?"

Mary finished hanging a sheet, then leaned a bit closer to her mistress and confided, "No, but I did see the one of them, and she's a real beauty, Miss. A true Incomparable, as they say. Wouldn't be surprised if she weren't the one he chooses, men bein' what they are an' all."

"Yes." Harriett had very little knowledge of what men were, but that they were susceptible to a pretty face she knew full well. And she had no reason to think Lord Weston would be any different. "Well, I mustn't keep you, Mary. Mama will probably be arriving soon, and I want to make sure Cook has a small nuncheon ready for her."

Mary gave a small curtsy. "Yes, Miss. And if I hear any more about the goin's-on at Yarwood, I'll be sure an' tell you."

Harriett blushed. Her avid curiosity must be quite obvious. But surely no one would think it was because she was interested in Lord Weston himself. No. Of course not. It was perfectly natural to be interested in one's neighbors. Especially when they were so rarely at Yarwood.

"In fact, I am not sure that they came at all last year," Harriett mused to herself, as she walked down the stairs to the parlour. Yarwood was only one of Lord Weston's estates, and apparently not a favorite. Though if it were mine, I should stay all year and forgo the London Season, Harriett thought. She had adored the estate ever since first setting eyes on it when she was fifteen and Papa had been gifted with the living through the recommendation of an old school friend. Before that the family had lived in East Hampton, in a comfortable but rather cramped cottage near the Reverend Haversham's church.

It had been their lucky day when Reverend Smythe, the vicar of Upper Mourouby, had taken that fateful Sabbath carriage drive. Though such a thing seemed a minor infraction when all was said and done, and certainly no cause to remove someone from the living, at least in Harriett's opinion. Still, that was what Lord Weston had done.

"He's a stiff-rumped, unforgiving soul," the Reverend Smythe had complained, when the Havershams had driven up one day to view the parsonage. "A real stickler, too high in the instep by far. Folks around here call him Lord Stiff Rump, and rightly so."

Reverend Haversham had not replied. But one could tell by the way he raised his eyebrows and pressed his lips together that he did not approve of the Reverend Smythe, being something of a stickler himself. Besides, the vicar of Upper Mourouby had hardly been thrown out into the cold. Far from it. The Reverend Smythe held absentee livings in several other parishes. Still, there was no gainsaying the fact that the living at Upper Mourouby, with its fine house and garden, was considered a real plum. The Reverend Smythe had been sorry to lose it. And the Reverend Haversham and his family quite happy to gain it.

Harriett stopped in the parlour to pick up the books she had left on the sofa table yesterday. It was one of her mornings to teach the younger children of the parish the rudiments of reading, writing, and doing simple sums. This was possible only during the winter months, when the children could be spared from other chores. Soon, most of them would be needed to help with the spring planting. Taking her old green wool cloak down from its peg, Harriett fastened it securely about her throat, and pulled on her gloves and stout boots, before setting out for church where the children were taught.

When she returned, it would be to the sight of her parents and Camilla sitting down to tea. Harriett sighed as she stepped carefully over puddles on the footpath. Waiting was so difficult; it would be easier having something to occupy her mind. Besides, she knew the children looked forward to their makeshift school, possibly because Harriett brought sweetmeats whenever possible. But also, she thought, because their young minds were so eager to take in everything possible, like the dry earth soaking up a spring rain.

Harriett herself was no scholar, but her papa had taught her Latin and a smattering of French, and she had read widely in his library. She had also had access to the library at Yarwood when Lord Weston was not in residence. Though somewhat neglected due to the absence of its master, the library still contained a fine collection of books, and the estate manager, Mr. Beauchamp, had been happy to give Harriett and her father the use of it.

That would not be the case now, however, Harriett thought. Not with Lord Stiff Rump there. Her foot slipped on a bit of clotted dirt and she twisted her ankle painfully. And no more than serves me right, she thought, limping a bit. For it is quite unfair of me to think such things of Lord Weston. After all, I hardly know the man, and he did not seem unkind when we met in the woods. No, it was just that she was feeling disgruntled and out of sorts because of what Mary had told her.

So Lord Weston was looking about for a wife and at least one of the candidates for the position was an Incomparable? Well, that had nothing to do with her. Though the knowledge would put Augusta's nose quite out of joint. Her sister was used to being the prettiest girl in the district, and though not yet out, quite the most sought after at the local assemblies. To have a diamond of the first water in the parish would certainly not be to her liking. Nor to Camilla's. For though not as pretty as Augusta, she was quite an attractive girl and there had been talk at one time of the squire's son . . .

But I am forgetting, Harriett told herself . . . Camilla has run off with Tom Watkins. And may have ruined herself in the process. Pray God it is not so. Harriett stopped and closed her eyes, saying a quick, silent prayer for her sister's safe return.

Her path wound around the outside of Lord Weston's estate and the surrounding hedge was full of the sound of birds. A jay flew screaming across her path, seeming to resent her intrusion. Harriett smiled. So beautiful, and yet such a nasty temper. Harriett had brought along the small bag of scraps Cook had saved for her to feed the rooks, and for a moment she was tempted to spread the largesse beside the path so that she might curry favor with the beautiful jay. "But I will not," she told the bird, "for you would not appreciate it and only think me a toad eater. I shall save it for my black-feathered friends instead."

The jay screamed its defiance from the branch of a nearby larch tree, and Harriett smilingly walked on. It was warmer today, and perhaps the periwinkles and violets would have begun to open in the meadow. When she stopped to feed the rooks she would look for them, she decided. The square tower of the church was visible now, and Harriett hurried her steps. It would not do to be late. Though it was not yet planting time, there were chores enough for the children, and only an hour or so to spare for schooling.

The church in Upper Mourouby with its long vertical windows was said to be of the Perpendicular style. Built toward the end of the sixteenth century, it was neither large nor small, neither plain nor elaborate, but comfortably in-between. Harriett entered through the tower doorway and stopped to pick up the bag of slates stored behind the tower stairs. Her small school was conducted in the south aisle, where a series of five plain benches served to accommodate the children.

On the other side of the church was the north porch, built by the Weston family as their own private entrance to the family pew. Elaborate carvings of foliage adorned this seating, to the despair of the poor woman hired to dust and clean the church. Harriett purposely avoided looking in this direction but busied herself in placing the slates along the benches. It was rare to see anyone sitting in the elaborately carved pew, but even as Harriett's hands were busy, she could not help but wonder if Lord Weston would be there for the Palm Sunday service.

Harriett felt herself blush a little at the thought, and knew she would never be able to concentrate on the sermon her Papa preached if that were the case. But then, she had usually read and often helped with the writing of the sermon beforehand, anyway. And Harriett doubted that there were many in the congregation so pure of mind and thought that they would not spend at least some part of the church service speculating on the Weston family. Especially if the candidates for the office of Lady Weston were there as well.

Harriett felt her spirits lower a bit at the thought, though there was no reason for such a fit of the dismals, no reason at all, she chided herself sternly. Some of the children began to arrive, either shyly taking their places along the bench or bouncing in with such vigor that Harriett was glad she would have them in her keeping for no more than an hour.

"Saw a thrush nest in the hedge, Miss," Johnny Rounsend reported, sliding into his place. "But I didn't steal any of the eggs, not a one. Can't say I didn't want to, though."

"Miss?" Susan Thromorten waved her hand at Harriett. "Will we be havin' Easter eggs this year? Mrs. Haversham made 'em last year and they was ever so nice."

Oh, dear, Harriett thought. She had forgotten about the Easter eggs, and she knew some of the children thought them a special treat. "Of course," she said. "We shall have the eggs on Easter Sunday as usual, and there will be the egg-rolling down Meyer's Hill as well. Now let us work on our alphabet today."

After the children had gone, Harriett stored the slates and chalk behind the tower stairs again, gathered her books together and set off for home, a slight frown between her brows.

With all the confusion over Camilla, she had forgotten about the Easter eggs, but they must have them. It was not only the children who looked forward to receiving decorated eggs, but the elderly and ailing among the villagers as well. Last year and for several years previous, her mother had gotten most of the eggs from Yarwood. Though the parsonage boasted six good laying hens, they could hardly be expected to provide the number necessary.

Harriett veered off the road that led between the hedgerows where Johnny Rounsend had found his thrush nest, and onto the little side path that led into Lord Weston's home woods. Primroses were just beginning to open in the little clearing, as Harriett had hoped, and the sweet violets and periwinkles had already painted a colorful carpet of blue and white upon which she could spread her bits of bread for the rooks. Rusty Brown watched and scolded her from a branch.

"I am not late," Harriett excused herself. "You forget, I teach the children their letters today." She stepped back, watching as Rusty Brown flew down to pick up as many scraps as he possibly could before flying away and allowing the other birds a chance. A small greenish-gray wren landed next, followed by some starlings and a chaffinch. On a branch of the larch tree nearby a bright yellow bunting sat. "A little bit of bread and cheese," it sang, getting up its courage to join the other birds. Harriett stood absolutely still, until the yellow bunting finally flew down, grabbed a few crumbs of leftover toast and flew back to its branch.

Smiling, Harriett waited until almost all the largesse was gone before turning away. She had thought, hoped, that she might meet Lord Weston again. There was no reason why she should, of course. He was doubtless busy entertaining his guests. Harriett's heart sank at the thought. She brushed the last crumbs from her little bag, folded it neatly, and was about to put it in her reticule when she heard voices approaching.

"La, Lord Weston, but I am not sure I should be walking the woods like this with you," a woman's voice teased.

"Then let us turn back," Harriett heard Lord Weston's deep baritone reply.

"No, no, we must—oh!"

The woman and Lord Weston emerged into Harriett's small clearing. Eyebrows raised, the sharp-featured woman regarded Harriett from narrowed, assessing eyes.

Why, she is not beautiful at all, Harriett thought, her mood lightening considerably. Pretty, perhaps, but hardly an Incomparable.

"Ah, Miss Haversham." Lord Weston smiled and strolled across the clearing. The woman hurried to catch up with him, taking his arm possessively. "Allow me to present Miss Smalbathe."

Abigail Smalbathe acknowledged Harriett with a nod.

"Feeding Rusty Brown again, Miss Haversham?" Lord Weston asked.

Harriett nodded, hoping she did not have crumbs trailing down her cloak as she sometimes did. "Rusty Brown and . . . and some other birds," she said, feeling herself grow tongue-tied under Miss Smalbathe's intimidating stare.

"What is this Rusty Brown?" Abigail Smalbathe asked, her tone one of amused condescension. "Some sort of bird, I assume." She smiled at Harriett. "I believe our cook in Etherington throws out crumbs for the birds as well."

Harriett blushed. The insult was clearly there, and she raised her chin a trifle. For all Harriett was a bit shy and not completely at ease conversing with strangers, she was not a carpet to be trod upon. "I have heard that the Prince Regent is fond of feeding the birds as well," she replied in a soft voice.

Miss Smalbathe's smile disappeared.

"Rusty Brown is a rook," Lord Weston intervened, before things could grow nasty. "He has become somewhat tame since Miss Haversham began to feed him."

"Indeed?" Miss Smalbathe put both hands in the fur muff she carried. "I must admit I cannot imagine why anyone would want to feed such a bird. Rooks are such ugly, nasty creatures, without even a song to recommend them. In Etherington, I have directed the gamekeeper to shoot them." She turned to

Lord Weston. "I think we should return, I am beginning to feel a bit chilled."

"Of course," Lord Weston nodded absently in her direction. "Would you care to join us at Yarwood for something hot to drink?" he asked Harriett.

The sun was shining down strongly into the little clearing, warming Harriett with its friendly rays. The last thing she wanted was to join Lord Weston and Miss Smalbathe for a tête-à-tête. And yet . . .

"Yes, I should like to join you," Harriett found herself replying. "In fact, I was on my way to Yarwood when I stopped in the clearing, for there is something I need to discuss with you, Lord Weston."

If Lord Weston was surprised by this, he did not show it, and a few minutes later Harriett found herself ensconced before the drawing room fire at Yarwood. Miss Smalbathe excused herself and went to change her dress, thus inadvertently leaving the field to Harriett.

"Would you prefer coffee or tea?" Lord Weston asked, ringing for the butler.

"Whichever . . ." Harriett stopped and pressed her lips together. She had been about to say, whichever you prefer, my lord. At the parsonage, principles of economy dictated that one brew either coffee or tea, not both. But I am not at the parsonage now, Harriett told herself. "I shall have coffee, if you please," she said firmly.

Lord Weston smiled at the blush which softly

tinted Harriett's delicate complexion. "We will be having coffee, Marston," he instructed the butler, taking a seat opposite Harriett.

Harriett kept her eyes focused on the ornate chimneypiece to one side of her. Swirls of leaves, a woman with a basket on her head, and a myriad of woodland creatures all crowded the plaster scene.

"I prefer a simpler design myself," Lord Weston remarked. "Though I understand it is greatly admired."

"Oh." Harriett's eyes flew from the chimneypiece to Lord Weston, then back to the chimneypiece. She cleared her throat nervously. "There . . . there is a thrush, however." She pointed to the plaster bird, which seemed to be twice the size of the tree upon which it was perched.

"But no rook."

"No," Harriett agreed. "No rook."

The butler returned with the refreshments then, mercifully cutting short the labored conversation. Harriett gave a sigh of relief, as one reprieved from a sentence of death. Her mother was right. It would have been totally useless for her to have had a Season. She'd have been miserable. Just thinking of spending every day trying to converse with strangers, she gave a small shudder.

"Cold, Miss Haversham?" Lord Weston asked, with polite interest. "May I move your chair closer to the fire?"

"No, no. I—" She accepted the coffee that

the butler handed her. "That is, I am not used to coffee quite this strong."

"You have not tasted it yet, Miss Haversham."

"Oh. I—" What an idiot she was! She sounded like a complete goose. And she had been so hoping . . . Harriett's fingers tightened around her coffee cup. She had spent a large part of yesterday rehearsing exactly what she would say to Lord Weston should they ever meet again, and now here she was, acting as tongue-tied as ever.

Lord Weston leaned back in his brocade chair, sipping his coffee and observing Harriett's confusion. "A great deal of polite conversation is quite empty," he observed kindly. "The trick is to say something without actually saying anything."

Harriett blinked across at him and then broke into a smile.

It was Lord Weston's turn to blink. Harriett Haversham had the most ravishing smile he had ever seen. It was wide and genuine, and revealed the most charming dimple at the side of her mouth.

"I find it quite difficult to say something about nothing," Harriett confessed, relaxing into the cushioned sofa on which she was sitting. "My sisters are quite adept at the art, I think, but I have never been able to master it."

"It is simply a matter of practice." Abigail Smalbathe sailed into the room, resplendent in a morning dress of sea-green gros de Naples ornamented with ribbons and worked muslin ruffles. "You speak of the pianoforte, do you not?" Miss Smalbathe continued, seating herself beside Harriett on the sofa. Lord Weston would now be able to view the two of them side by side and see exactly how superior she, Abigail Smalbathe was, compared to the little country nobody. Noting the blank way in which the other two were staring at her, she asked, "Do you speak of drawing, then? It, too, is merely a matter of practice, Miss Shaverham. I am quite the watercolorist, you know." She smiled at Lord Weston.

"Haversham," Harriett said quietly.

"I beg your pardon?"

"My name is Haversham," Harriett repeated.

"Are you sure?" Miss Smalbathe narrowed her eyes at Harriett. "I am rarely mistaken about these things."

"Haversham," Harriett stated with finality.

"If you insist." Miss Smalbathe gave Harriett a tight smile, though it was quite obvious she considered Harriett's insistence a bit rag-mannered.

Harriett sipped her coffee, trying to quell the growing dislike she felt for Miss Smalbathe. It was unchristian to feel so when she was barely acquainted with the woman. She knew her Papa would disapprove and say it was Harriett's duty to love her neighbor. But then, Papa had not met Miss Smalbathe.

Having accepted a cup of coffee, though as she said, she really preferred tea, Miss Smalbathe continued to extol her virtues. "I am quite proficient in the arts, you know, and have also an excellent voice. Though it is not *au fait* to boast of such things, I do not exaggerate when I tell you that His Grace the Duke of Nevernham was heard to remark that I have such a voice as would make angels weep. In fact, when I was last prevailed upon to perform, he must needs leave the room, for he declared that it quite unmanned him."

"The Nevernhams were never known for their fortitude," Lord Weston murmured, just as the doors to the drawing room opened and George Reading walked in.

"Here you are, Phillip. I have been looking all over for you, I thought we were to go riding." George Reading advanced further into the room, spied the refreshment tray, and quickly snabbled a lady finger.

"I don't believe you have met Miss Haversham, George," Lord Weston said.

"Oh, I say, I am sorry." George Reading swallowed his lady finger, dusted off his fingers, and bowed over Harriett's hand. "Didn't see you sitting there, I'm afraid."

Abigail Smalbathe smiled. It was quite obvious that the poor girl faded into insignificance beside her. No doubt it was due to the red hair and those quite horrid spots. Miss Smalbathe would suggest that she bathe her face in vinegar water, which was her mama's cure for freckles. Not that anyone in the Smalbathe family had ever had any, of course.

"I am very pleased to meet you, Mr. Reading," Harriett said. "Even though I am very fond of lady fingers myself."

"Then how lucky for us both that there are two left," George Reading replied, after a moment of startled surprise. His smile made the corners of his eyes turn up in a rather engaging manner, Harriett thought. He took the plate with the lady fingers and offered it to Harriett with the admonition, "Now only one, mind."

What a nice man, Harriett found herself thinking. Not disturbing and a little bit frightening like Lord Weston, but . . . nice.

"Miss Shaversham trains rooks," Abigail Smalbathe informed him. She was not interested in George Reading. He was a fourth son with few expectations, but she felt it her duty to warn him about the queer kick in Miss Shaversham's gallop.

"Indeed?" George Reading pulled a small gilt chair closer to the sofa. "How fascinating, Miss Haversham. How ever did you accomplish that?"

Harriett felt herself blushing. "I . . . I have hardly trained the rooks, Mr. Reading," she said, almost apologetically. "It is just that I have been feeding them because it has been such a hard winter, and the birds have learned to come when they see me or hear my call."

"Your call?" Miss Smalbathe gave Harriett an indulgent smile. "How do you call your rooks, Miss Shaversham?"

"I just . . . you know. I just imitate their way

of . . . of calling." Harriett took a large bite of the lady finger on her plate, praying that Miss Smalbathe would not ask for a demonstration. She could not, she would not, "caw" in Lord Weston's drawing room.

Mercifully, Lord Weston changed the subject by asking what it was that Harriett had wanted to discuss with him. "Unless it is of a confidential nature?" he added. "In which case, we can withdraw to the library."

"Oh, no, my lord." Harriett put her coffee cup on the occasional table and shook her head. "I merely wished to speak to you about some eggs. You see, at Easter, we color eggs for the children in the parish school, as well as for some of the elderly villagers. And on Easter Day there is an egg roll down Meyer's Hill. The thing is, we like to give each child several eggs so they may be shared with the rest of the family." Harriett leaned forward, all shyness quite forgotten. "Most of the children are from the poorest families in the district and the extra eggs are a great luxury to them."

"And you wish Yarwood to supply them?" Lord Weston asked.

"The parsonage hens cannot provide all that we need," Harriett answered. "It would be a great kindness."

Lord Weston smiled and stood, walking to the fireplace. "And would you color one for me as well?" he asked, turning to face her. "It has been a good many years since I have had a decorated egg at Easter, or rolled one down a hill."

"Of course." Harriett looked up at him. He was so very tall, and while not conventionally handsome, perhaps, so very attractive.

"What a good idea!" Abigail Smalbathe clapped her hands together. "We must all color eggs. It would be wonderfully charitable of us, and I'm sure I should enjoy it immensely." She smiled coyly up at Lord Weston. "And of course, I shall color a special one for you."

"What about me?" George Reading asked, around a mouthful of sponge cake. "Aren't you going to color an egg for me as well?"

Miss Smalbathe gave him a tight smile. "Miss Shaversham shall do that. Won't you, my dear? I'm sure you are much more experienced at this sort of thing." She leaned over and gave Harriett a pat on the hand. "At Etherington, I believe the cook or one of the undermaids colors eggs for the village children."

Harriett pressed her lips together. She would not say something uncharitable, she would not. "I should be more than happy to decorate an egg for you, Mr. Reading," she said at last. "Assuming there are enough, of course. The parish children must come first, and then there are the invalids I visit, who I thought might—"

"La, she is full of good works!" Miss Smalbathe exclaimed, giving a little titter of laughter. "You must remember that charity begins at home, Miss Shaversham."

"Upper Mourouby is my home," Harriett replied. "And my papa, Reverend Haversham, has always said that to give unto the least of his children is to give unto the Lord himself."

Miss Smalbathe's lips snapped together. "Well, really . . ."

Lord Weston straightened from his lounging stance beside the fireplace. "It hardly matters. I am sure there will be plenty of eggs to provide for everyone." He smiled down at Harriett. "Would you care for some more coffee, Miss Haversham?"

"No, I . . . I really think I should be going." Harriett stood up and began buttoning her pelisse.

"I shall escort you home."

"It is but a step, my lord, and you have your guests to see to." Harriett stooped to retrieve her reticule and the schoolbooks she had used that morning.

"George can take care of Miss Smalbathe," Lord Weston replied, walking into the hallway with Harriett. "Besides, I have not yet paid my respects to your parents."

Harriett paled. "They are not at home," she said at once. "At least, they are at home, but they are not *presently* at home."

"I see." Lord Weston gave her a quizzical look. "And when do you expect them?"

"Oh, at any moment. They must surely be home at any moment," Harriett reassured herself. "And I am sure Papa will call upon you as soon as he is able."

"Good." Lord Weston nodded, his dark eyes

intent upon her. "At any rate, we shall certainly meet tomorrow evening. I look forward—"

"Westie! Oh, Westie, there you are!" A young woman came into the hallway, her carriage so graceful she seemed to float rather than walk.

"You have been looking for me, Miss Dade?" Lord Weston asked.

"Yes, for Mama and I cannot decide which color ribbon is most becoming, the pink or the rose. She said I was to come and ask you." Miss Dade held out the two ribbons and smiled ingenuously up at him. The light filtering in through the high window over the door shone down upon the perfect oval of her face. Golden hair was twisted into a high knot from which a few curling tendrils had been allowed to escape and fall becomingly upon her forehead, where they shone like spun gold.

Harriett looked at the perfect complexion, the large, luminous blue eyes, and sighed. This, then, must be the Incomparable.

Four

Augusta was waiting for Harriett in the parlour. She had, in fact, been waiting for Harriett for some twenty minutes and was now in a highly agitated state. She smiled nervously at her sister, who seemed from the rather dour expression she wore to be a bit out of sorts. Augusta nibbled on her bottom lip and considered the matter.

"Would you like some tea, Harriett?" she offered. Tea was known to be as good a cure as any for a fit of the dismals.

"No, thank you." Harriett put her schoolbooks down on the sideboard and removed her pelisse and bonnet. For reasons of economy, the parlour was one of the few rooms in which a fire was lit, except on the coldest days of winter. Harriett now sank down in one of the matching stuffed chairs and leaned forward, warming her hands at its flames.

"Has it turned cold, then?" Augusta asked. "It seemed rather mild this morning."

Harriett attempted a smile. "The wind has sprung up again. One might almost suppose that March has turned its back on spring." She had walked home alone. Not that she had wanted Lord Weston to accompany her . . . far from it. But she had thought he might at least have noticed when she left. Instead, he had been so preoccupied with the beautiful Miss Dade, Harriett had been allowed to slip out the door without so much as a polite farewell.

"We have had a message from Mama," Augusta said, trying to gauge Harriett's mood by the way this information was received.

"Indeed?" Harriett sat up. "Is everything all right? Are they returning soon? Is Cammie with them?"

"Well, um, actually . . . no," Augusta admitted.

"No, what?" Harriett asked. "No, Cammie is not with them, or no—"

"No to everything," Augusta said. "Here— the message came this morning, just after you left." She handed Harriett the folded paper and then proceeded to elaborate on the contents before Harriett had a chance to read it. "A wheel came off the carriage five miles out of Nerburton, and it could not be repaired until today; and it seems that in alighting from the carriage, Mama slipped in the mud and broke her ankle."

"Oh, no!" Harriett stared down at the note and began to quickly scan its crossed lines.

"But it is not so bad," Augusta continued,

"because Mama says she is not in much pain and the innkeeper's wife has been very kind, and Papa will surely start off after Camilla as soon as the wheel is repaired."

Harriett looked up from the note. "I do not know how you can say it is not so bad, Gusta. What could be worse? Mama is in bed with a broken ankle, and Camilla has spent the night with Tom Watkins. Now they must be married at once, which is the very thing Mama and Papa hoped to prevent. And only yesterday you were in hysterics at the very thought!"

"Yes." Augusta nodded. "And I still think it very selfish of Camilla to have done this to me, but meanwhile we have received an invitation."

Harriett appeared not to be listening. She was staring into the fire with a frown worrying her brow. "I should go to Mama," she said, looking up at Augusta at last. "It is not right that she should be left alone at an inn while Papa is out searching for Camilla."

"But you promised Mama you would look after me," Augusta protested. Her big brown eyes filled with tears. "You cannot leave now, Harriett. It would ruin everything."

Touched by this show of sisterly love and trust, Harriett leaned over and patted Augusta's hand. "You would come with me, of course."

"But—but we can't. Not now. Harriett, you have not been listening," Augusta complained.

"Whatever do you mean, Gusta?" Harriett

76

sat back in surprise. "Of course I have been listening. Mama is at an inn outside of—"

"No, no, that is not what I meant. I mean, I am sure I am very sorry Mama is hurt and all, but oh, Harriett, it is such an opportunity!" Augusta looked across at her sister, eyes shining.

Harriett sucked in her cheeks and closed her eyes for a moment. The last time Augusta had had such a look was when she had cut the hem from the silk curtains in the parlour to decorate her hat. "Augusta, you haven't done anything foolish, have you? Not at such a time, surely."

"Of course not!" Augusta looked offended. "I am not a child, Harriett. There are any number of girls my age who are already married. And if Papa would only stop squandering his money on others and consider the sufferings of his own children for a change, I might have a Season and meet someone eligible as well."

Harriett sighed. Not that again. "You think that Papa should give money to you so you may waste it on fripperies, rather than use it to provide as such for Mrs. Allen and her children, who have been left destitute? Really, Augusta!"

Jumping out of her chair, Augusta put her hands on her hips and faced her sister. "You are just like Papa," she accused. "Never seeing any further than the nose on your face. Spending the money on fripperies for me so that I might have a Season would be an investment.

For I know I should marry very well, and then I should persuade my very, very rich husband to give money to such as Mrs. Allen."

Harriett gave her sister a skeptical look.

"I would. I am not quite the birdbrain you think me, Harriett. And if Cammie were not such a gudgeon as to have run off with Lord Weston's groom, for heaven's sake, but had married someone rich, as I'm sure I should have done in her place, she might have provided for Papa's charity cases."

"And a Season in London for you as well."

Augusta nodded. "It would be the least she could do, after I lent her my Limerick gloves and lace ruff, not to mention the hair ribbons which I had only worn once myself."

Harriett rose from her chair by the fire and picked up the pelisse she had abandoned earlier. "I know you think me a prosy bore, Gusta," she said with a sigh. "And much too old and . . . and stuffy to understand, but it is not true. I do realize that you want to have a bit of fun and do some of the things you are always reading about in Papa's *Gazette*. But it is beside the point now. We must go to Mama and see to her comfort."

"I think she would wish us to remain here," Augusta insisted stubbornly. "She said nothing in her note about joining her."

"Well, of course, she would not, but—"

"I think she wishes us to remain here so that the gabblemongers do not find out about Cammie and Tom. Which they will be sure of doing if we leave as well. And then Lord Weston will hear of it and soon everyone will know and my—our every chance of happiness will be at an end. Besides, I am sure Papa will find Camilla and bring her and Mama home tomorrow. It would be silly for us to journey all that distance only to turn around the next day and return."

Harriett, who had blushed at the very mention of Lord Weston's name, gave the matter some thought. After meeting the earl, she could not really believe he would repeat the sort of gossip that could ruin a young woman's life. But there were his guests to consider, especially a certain sharp-faced Miss Smalbathe. Harriett was quite sure Miss Smalbathe was the sort who would relish just such a bit of juicy gossip and consider it her duty to spread it as far as possible.

"You may be right, Gusta," she admitted.

"Of course I am." Augusta smiled and picked up the bonnet Harriett had left on the chair. "Besides, I have already accepted the invitation for both of us."

"Invitation?" Harriett blinked.

Augusta could not prevent herself from breaking into a grin. "It is above everything, Harriett. Only wait until you hear." She gripped the edge of Harriett's velvet bonnet tightly. "We have received an invitation to dinner at Yarwood!"

"Lord Weston has invited us to dinner?" Harriett put one hand to her breast and sat down, clutching her pelisse. "Where is the invitation? How was it addressed? Did he mention our names specifically?" She felt her heart hammering excitedly against her hand. Perhaps he was not indifferent to her after all. He might not be attracted to her as she was to him, but perhaps, just perhaps, he was not totally indifferent. She looked up at Augusta, who still stood mangling Harriett's bonnet between her fingers.

"Well, he did not mention us specifically," she hedged. "I mean he did, of course, but not by name. I mean, I'm sure he would have if he knew our names, but—"

"He knows mine," Harriett interrupted, feeling the sudden excitement begin to melt away like sugar crystals on a bun in the summer heat. "May I see the invitation, please?"

Augusta turned and walked over to the small walnut desk on which her mother wrote the household accounts. The invitation, with its fine black penstrokes marching precisely across the white paper, seemed to shine up at her like a magical promise. Augusta took a deep breath, crossed her fingers, and then handed it to Harriett.

"It is addressed to Mama and Papa," Harriett said.

"And family," Augusta quickly pointed out. "Which is you and me and . . . and Camilla. You couldn't very well expect them to invite each of us individually. Besides, remember how Papa said that the last time Lord Weston was at Yarwood he got Mama mixed up with the squire's wife? I think he visits so infrequently he cannot remember who everyone is."

Harriett frowned. She had a feeling Augusta was right. And when Lord Weston left Yarwood, he would probably forget all about Harriett Haversham and their two brief encounters. She unfolded the thick white paper, read the invitation twice over, and sighed. They must refuse, of course. There was no way they could go without Mama and Papa.

"I know what you are going to say," Augusta broke into her thoughts. "But there is a way we could go, and it would not be at all improper, if you would but agree. Oh, please, Harriett, say you will—just this once."

It would be torture to go and watch Lord Weston hanging on every word that dripped from the Incomparable's mouth. Yet would it not also be torture to stay at home and imagine Lord Weston and the Incomparable together? Harriett rubbed one finger along the edge of the invitation. She was tempted to agree, to accept the invitation. At least then she would see Lord Weston once more. "Are you sure it is not improper?" she asked.

"Not very," Augusta assured her.

"How not very?" Harriett knew her sister of old and was not reassured by the look of innocence and the bland smile.

"Well . . ." Augusta sat down in the chair opposite. "I take it you are worried because we must go without Papa and Mama."

Harriett nodded.

"And by the fact that we must not do anything that would cause gossip."

Harriett nodded again.

"Well," Augusta took a deep breath, "I have given the matter some thought while you have been gone, and it seems to me that we can hardly refuse on Papa's behalf without explaining where he has gone. Which we do not want to do." She waited for Harriett's agreement, and then continued. "I suppose we could say he is ill, but we would not want Lord Weston to think Papa sickly."

"And I have already told Lord Weston that Papa is not presently at home," Harriett added. "It would seem uncommon strange for him to be driving about when he is ill."

"Besides it being a terrible bouncer, which Papa is always preaching against," Augusta added shrewdly. "In fact, the only way to be sure of not incurring Lord Weston's wrath, with him being so high in the instep and all, or causing any gossip, is for Mama and Papa to attend the dinner. Or failing that, for Papa and one of his daughters to go."

"Yes," Harriett agreed absently. She was imagining herself stepping out of the carriage at Yarwood dressed to the nines and somehow transformed into a real beauty. She imagined Lord Weston's dark eyes lighting with admiration, while the Incomparable and Miss Smalbathe stood to one side, grinding their teeth. She was awakened from these pleasant thoughts by Augusta, who suddenly hurled herself across the room and wrapped her arms around Harriett's shoulders, hugging her with such ferocity Harriett could barely breathe.

"What?" Harriett gasped.

"Oh, thank you, thank you, best of sisters! I knew you were not such a fusty prose as you sometimes seem. And I'm sure Camilla will not mind if I borrow her blue satin with the net frock, for I have nothing truly suitable of my own, and I have already checked, and she did not take it with her. Now we must just find something of Papa's to fit you, which should not be too difficult, for you are much of a height."

Augusta bounced up and over to the parlour doorway. "Yarwood! Do you know I have never been there? At least, I have been on the grounds, but never in the house. I am so excited! Who would think that something good could come of Cammie's running away?"

Though Harriett also rose and walked to the door, she hardly bounced, but walked slowly, approaching her sister as one would a wild animal one was about to shoot. "Something of Papa's?" she asked, the words sounding as if someone had her by the throat and was determined to squeeze the life from her body. "What do you mean, something of Papa's?"

"If Papa and one of his daughters are to attend the dinner, and Papa is not here, then one of us must pretend to be Papa. You agreed that this was so." Augusta spoke slowly and made it all sound so reasonable, Harriett actually stopped to consider the matter.

"I am much too short to fit into Papa's clothes," Augusta continued, crossing her fingers behind her back for luck, "besides being too young and not resembling Papa in the slightest, while you—"

"Yes, yes, I know. People have been telling me I look exactly like Papa for years." Harriett glared at Augusta. "It is hardly a compliment."

Augusta pursed her lips and looked down at the polished floorboards for a moment. Harriett was obviously vexed about something, for she was usually quite sunny-tempered. "Well, I should be perfectly happy to go as Papa, were I tall enough," she told her sister, "for I think it would be quite amusing to pretend to be a man and find out what they really say when we are gone. But I hardly think Mama would approve."

"And you think Mama—or Papa, for that matter—would approve of me attending a dinner in disguise?" Harriett began to wonder if her younger sister had suffered some sort of brainstorm.

"Um . . . in the Bible, didn't, ah, Jacob disguise himself at a dinner or . . . um, something?" Augusta asked. "I'm sure Papa would approve if it's in the Bible."

"Jacob disguised himself as his brother Esau and brought his father something to eat so that he might win his brother's birthright," Harriett said, in some exasperation.

Augusta smiled. "There, you see? I knew I was right. And we shall do the same thing, only in this case, instead of one of those birthright things, which I recall Papa saying Esau didn't value properly anyway, we shall win an evening at Yarwood. Please, Harriett, do not deny me this." She bit her lip, widened her big brown eyes, and looked sorrowfully up at her older sister.

Tossing her pelisse down on a chair, Harriett turned to face Augusta, hardening her heart to the pitiful expression which she knew was only playacting anyway. "Even did I agree," she said, trying to sound reasonable and not simply exasperated, "you cannot have thought the matter through. What will happen when Papa returns and pays a call on Lord Weston? Or when Lord Weston attends church services and sees that the Reverend Haversham in the pulpit bears only a superficial resemblance to the man who sat at his dinner table?"

Her woebegone expression disappearing at once, Augusta explained. She had had several hours in which to work matters through, and believed she had an answer to any cavil Harriett, might raise. "The Weston family pew is at the back of the church," she ticked off her answers on her fingers. "With Mama's broken ankle and all, Papa cannot now return in time for Palm Sunday services anyway, and Mr. Marsh, the curate from Tilbering, must come instead, and . . ." she grinned up at her sister, "you know I can talk Mr. Marsh into doing whatever I ask."

That was true enough, Harriett thought ruefully. The poor curate had been besotted by her sister since they had met last year. "But Papa is sure to call upon Lord Weston as soon as he returns, and . . ."

"Mary told me that one of the footmen at Yarwood who is sweet on her, and gave her some ribbons which I must say are as fine as any I possess, was lamenting the fact that the family will be leaving Yarwood early next week. Even if Papa does return before then, I am sure we can contrive to keep him from calling on Lord Weston until it is too late and they have already left. No one will ever know, Harry. Please, it will all work out. And it means so much to me. If Cammie has disgraced us, as I fear she has and as I would never do no matter how handsome Tom Watkins is, we may never receive such an invitation again."

Harriett frowned. Somehow what Augusta said made sense. Or was it just that she wanted it to make sense? If Lord Weston was indeed leaving early next week, this might be her only chance to see him again. And Harriett was quite willing to cheat any number of Esaus out of their birthrights to do so. Besides, Augusta was right. It would be amusing to hear what men had to say to each other when women were not present. Why, Harriett might even be able to winkle out some notion of what Lord Weston thought of her.

"When the invitation arrived, of course, I knew we could not accept it," Augusta broke into her thoughts. "And I wracked my brain trying to think of some excuse to give for Papa so he would not be thought to shirk his duty and invite the wrath of Lord Weston. But then Old John brought in the note from Mama and I realized things could work out quite well. I could get my evening out in society, and Lord Stiff Rump need never know Papa is not here or that Camilla has run off with his groom. It is quite perfect. Truly, it is, Harriett." She looked at her sister anxiously, worrying her bottom lip once again. "Please don't be stuffy about it, Harry."

A mischievous twinkle appeared in Harriett's eyes as she continued to consider the matter, and then that elusive dimple peeked out beside her mouth. She did not look at all like the sensible, prosy eldest daughter of Reverend Haversham.

"There is only one problem," she told Augusta. "I mean, I do hate to put a caveat in your way, but Lord Weston is sure to recognize me. We have met twice now. He will know that I am not Papa, no matter how I dress."

"You underestimate me, Harriett," Augusta replied, and then broke into a grin. "Does that mean you will do it, best of sisters?"

"Yes." Harriett nodded, and then, more decisively, "Yes, Gusta," she said. "If you can find some way of disguising me so that Lord Weston does not know who I am, I will do it." She refused to be thought of as a . . . a stuffy ape leader. She might not be beautiful, like the Incomparable Miss Dade, but Harriett Haversham had a bit of spunk in her.

A sense of rising excitement filled Harriett until she felt like that hot air balloon that had landed in the meadow last summer and caused Mrs. Littleby to suffer a fit of the vapors. I shall look quite beautiful and . . . and daring in Papa's clothes, she decided. And I shall converse with Lord Weston as an equal, impressing him with my knowledge of literature and the arts. He, in turn, will speak to me of the virtues of one Miss Harriett Haversham, and when I reveal that I am, in fact, the lady in question, he will be amazed. In fact, he just might fall to his knees and propose to me on the instant, she thought, with a little shiver of excitement. Her gray eyes sparkled as she picked up her pelisse once again.

"I quite look forward to tomorrow evening," she told Augusta.

"So what did you think, George?" Lord Weston asked his friend the next day, as they walked back to the house from the stables. They had ridden through the woods and over the meadow that made up the western edge of Yarwood. It was a glorious day, cool but sunny, and they both arrived at the breakfast table feeling famished.

"What did I think of what?" George Reading

inquired, concentrating on the plate he was heaping with food from the sideboard.

"Miss Haversham," Lord Weston prompted. "What did you think of Miss Haversham?"

"Didn't think of her at all," George replied. "Why, was I supposed to?"

"No, of course not. I just—did you not think her an unusually attractive, sensible young woman?"

George Reading chewed his bacon, looking a bit like a contented cow, though there was a great deal more than bovine intelligence in his brown eyes, and they were not, at the moment, very placid. He swallowed, cleared his throat, and said, "Ah, yes. Sensible. Have you tried the buttered muffins? Your cook is quite without equal when it comes to buttered muffins."

Lord Weston poured his coffee and gave his guest an affronted look. "You did not like Miss Haversham," he said flatly.

"Of course I liked her," George protested. "I thought her very nice, rather companionable, in fact, but she is a bit long in the tooth to be called young, Phillip. Why, she must be twenty-four if she is a day. And to call her unusually attractive when Miss Dade is around is . . . is, well, I'm sorry old man, but I fear for your sanity."

"You have not seen Miss Haversham smile," Lord Weston stated unequivocally. "If you had seen her smile as I have, you would understand what I mean. She has the most attractive dimple at the side of her mouth, and her eyes light up. Most society beauties, including your Miss Dade, have smiles that look as if someone had painted them on."

George licked a bit of butter off his fingers and nodded. "Some of them are painted on," he said. "Had it from Bernie Bentwood. Some of the Diamonds refuse to smile, afraid they'll get lines if they do. So they paint the smile on and remain poker-faced. It's a fact. No need to look at me like I'm dicked in the nob. Ask Bernie."

Since Bernie Bentwood was known to be *au fait* on everything going on in the fashionable world, Lord Weston did not feel the need. What he did feel was the urge to continue talking about Miss Haversham. "Lovely hair, didn't you think? Unusual color."

"Red?" George chewed contemplatively on a bit of rare beefsteak. "Not fashionable, I'm afraid. Girl would never take."

"Is it necessary that everyone look exactly the same?" Lord Weston demanded, spearing the yolk of his egg with unusual ferocity. "I found Miss Haversham charming. Not in the common mode, perhaps, but that made her all the more striking."

"Trains those rooks, though," George reminded him. "Odd kick in her gallop. Lady Weston wouldn't approve."

"I do not need my mother's approval, George."

George Reading shrugged. "Didn't say you did. Just stating a fact, Phillip. Sounds to me as if you've been knocked a bit cock-a-hoop by this Haversham girl. Can't say I quite see why. I mean, nice little thing, but I can think of any number of females that surpass her in beauty and wit."

"If you will recall, George, it was beauty and wit that landed me in the briars last time."

"Cornelia Cumminham." George nodded, frowned, and reached for a piece of the boiled ham. "Thing is, you should never have proposed to the Cumminham chit. It's not as though you were in love with her. Didn't have any money to recommend her, either. Nothing but a pretty face."

"She was the most sought-after female of the Season."

"And you snabbled her and then decided you didn't want her."

"Good heavens, George, I didn't expect her to accept me. Everyone was proposing. I was sure she'd hold out for the Duke of Middleford."

"Used you," George said succinctly. "Meant to make old Middleford jealous, only it didn't work. He went and married that heiress from Norfolk, and there you were, left holding the bag—or more accurately, Miss Cumminham."

Lord Weston nodded. "Fortunately, Lord Braitherton came along. Once Cornelia found out how much he was worth, I was left in the dust."

"Fortunate for you."

Pushing away his plate, Lord Weston sat back

in his chair. "Thing is, George, they're all alike, these society chits. Money and a title are all that concern 'em. They wouldn't care if I had two heads and a tail, as long as I had enough of the ready. Miss Haversham isn't like that."

George raised a skeptical eyebrow over the coffee cup he was draining.

"It's true. Long as they think you're swimming in lard, most females will do anything, say anything to get you in the parson's noose. Once they've got you strung up, of course, it's a different story. Look at my father."

George took out a silver toothpick and assumed a lugubrious expression. The late Lord Weston had been a notoriously henpecked husband.

"But I tell you, Miss Haversham is not like that. Why, she was fairly tongue-tied when we met, blushing like a green girl straight from the schoolroom. Nothing dishonest about her, wouldn't know how to dissemble, I swear."

"All females know how to dissemble," George corrected his host. "They're born knowing. Truth isn't an absolute to a female, it's whatever the occasion demands."

Lord Weston rose from his chair. "You've grown hard, George," he said, slapping his friend on the shoulder. "Unrequited love, perhaps?"

"You know I'm not in the petticoat line, old boy. Never will be from watching my friend's amours. You don't have to be bitten to be shy of the biter, you know. And this leg-shackling business has never made sense to me. Get yourself a good cook, I say, and forget marriage. Mind you, being the younger son, I don't have to worry about an heir, the way you do. No, that's my brother Horace's business, and a good thing." George Reading smiled in satisfaction and followed his friend into the library where they sat down to the chess game they had abandoned the evening before.

"Know anything about the family?" George asked, surveying the board.

Lord Weston's hand hovered above one of his knights. "Family?" he asked.

"Miss Haversham's family," George said. "Best to investigate before becoming involved."

"James is taking care of that." Lord Weston moved his piece and sat back. "But her father has the living of Upper Mourouby, so there can hardly be any scandal. Unlike his predecessor."

"Oh?" George Reading raised his eyebrows but kept his eyes on the playing board. "Do I scent a good story there?"

"Bad one, really," Lord Weston answered. "The man was a bit of a tippler, according to the villagers, and more often than not, the neighboring curate conducted the Sabbath worship while Reverend Smythe was at home nursing a hangover. My family quite naturally did not view this with approval. So five years ago, Smythe, who was quite foxed at the time, was driving hell for leather to get to the service on time, knowing we were in attendance, and there was an accident in which a young boy was killed. It was a terrible business. Smythe was dismissed on the spot, of course, though he claimed it was the boy's fault for darting out into the road."

"And the living was given to Miss Haversham's father?" George Reading asked.

Lord Weston nodded. "I've invited the family to supper, so you'll get to meet him tonight. But I must say, Reverend Haversham came highly recommended. Was in school with a friend of my father's, and then married a Miss Tyler, daughter of a vicar from Norfolk. The Havershams are distant cousins of Sir Reginal Freemantle, in fact. Not rich by any means, and little in the way of expectations. But from all reports, they're well liked. James will sniff out any down-and-dirty if it exists, of course. But I don't think it does. The villagers think highly of the family, and you heard Miss Haversham speak of the parish school she conducts."

"Mmmmm." George frowned, and moved his rook. "Should think your mother is looking for a bit more pedigree, however."

"Being the daughter of an earl, Mama tends to look down upon lesser mortals. Are you sure you meant to make that move?"

"What? Why?" George scanned the playing board, saw the danger he was in, and gave a mild curse. "You've been distracting me apurpose," he complained. "You know that's the only way you can win a game. It will serve you right to be trapped 'neath the cat's foot."

Five

Daydreams and nightmares often have much in common. Or so Harriett was beginning to think as she stood with Augusta, surveying the contents of their father's wardrobe. What had sounded like a daring lark the night before, had, in the light of day, begun to seem merely foolish. "For if anyone finds out what we have done, it will cause exactly the scandal we have been at pains to avoid. I do not know what made me agree to this."

"I think, perhaps, Papa's second best suit," Augusta said, ignoring her sister's cowardice and frowning at the single-breasted coat with gilt buttons that she was holding. "That way, you need not worry about spilling something on it. Now, what about a waistcoat?"

"You may call me a prosy shelf-liner, if you wish," Harriett said, as her sister laid the dress coat over a chair, "but what we are proposing to do is the height of idiocy." She frowned at a pink waistcoat, said, "Not with my hair," and selected a white one embroidered in blue instead.

"A much better choice." Augusta nodded. "You will look quite the dandy, Harriett."

"Do you think so?"

"Of course." Augusta shrugged and held out Reverend Haversham's shirt for Harriett to try on.

Harriett eyed the garment with misgivings. Her conscience screamed that she was wrong even to consider this ridiculous masquerade. Unfortunately, Harriett was the only one of the Haversham daughters to possess such a vocal conscience. Augusta and Camilla never worried about their misdeeds, unless they were caught, of course. Harriett fretted even when no one knew of her guilt.

"Hurry it up a bit, Harry," Augusta urged. "There are other things to be done, and it is nearly noon already."

Unbuttoning the front of her morning gown, Harriett sighed, but did as her sister bid. She was the older, she had been left in charge by their mother, she was the one who should call a stop to this lunacy. But she knew that Augusta would cry and carry on and make her feel such a terrible monster that one guilt would simply be replaced by another. Soft hearts can be a veritable bane to one's existence, Harriett thought, slipping her arms inside her father's shirt, which hung about her like a shroud.

"We shall have to pin it," Augusta said, looking Harriett over with a frown, "there is not time to tack it in place. And I imagine the shirt will look much better when you are wearing Papa's coat."

It did not. In fact, the Reverend Haversham's coat looked much too large as well, but since there was no time to do anything about it, Augusta pronounced that it would do.

"Shall I try on the trousers?" Harriett asked, eyeing them doubtfully.

"Oh, I am sure they will fit," Augusta said airily. "And truly, there is barely enough time for us to grab a bit of nuncheon before I must start on your hair."

Harriett looked in the cheval glass mirror in her parents' bedroom. Certainly something must be done about her hair, that was true enough. Glorious red with golden highlights, it curled in riotous abandon about her head and over her shoulders without regard to fashion. Still, Harriett had always been rather fond of it. "Shall I tie it back?" she asked doubtfully. "I know that will seem a bit old-fashioned, but some men in the village still wear it so."

"We shall contrive something so that Lord Weston does not recognize you," Augusta replied, avoiding Harriett's eyes. "But now, I declare I am quite famished. We do not dine at Yarwood until five, you know, and since I had nothing but a cup of chocolate this morning, I must eat at once."

"Hmmmm." Harriett removed her father's coat and shirt and slipped into her own simple morning dress. She did not like the way

Augusta had avoided looking at her. Still, she did not see how her sister could be into any more mischief than she already was. Following Augusta into the dining room, Harriett did her best to swallow her foreboding along with the cold meat pasty Cook had laid out for them.

Surprisingly, Augusta went about her own endeavors after their light meal, and Harriett was left alone to fret over the possibilities of the evening ahead. It would be scandalous if Lord Weston should recognize her. Yet she would be disappointed if he did not. For surely, wearing her Papa's clothes would not make such a difference. And, Harriett blushed, if Lord Weston had observed her as closely as she had him, he would be an addlepate not to know her at once.

Of course, he might be too polite to say anything, Harriett thought. Perhaps he would speak to her privately about it. Ask what she meant by wearing such a disguise. And what would she say? Harriett sat down at the pianoforte in the parlour and picked out a tune. She was a good player, but only when she was alone. When she was asked to perform in public, her hands invariably froze upon the keyboard and all the carefully practiced pieces fled from her mind.

For a moment Harriett concentrated on a sonata by Joseph Haydn, becoming quite lost in the music and forgetting her worries over Camilla and the mounting doubts she had about that night's masquerade.

"Ah, here you are, Harry." Augusta swept

into the room, abruptly ending both Haydn's music and Harriett's peace of mind. "I have the scissors, some sugar water, and some of Old John's boot black, so we are ready."

"Ready?" Harriett asked, not liking the way her sister was looking at her.

"To begin your transformation. You said it would create a scandal were Lord Weston to recognize you. So we will just have to make sure that doesn't happen, won't we?" Augusta smiled expectantly at Harriett.

"I begin to feel a bit like a lamb being led to the slaughter," Harriett said warily.

"Oh, I hadn't planned anything quite that drastic," Augusta assured her. "And brunettes are fashionable this year, you know."

"Augusta . . ."

"It will look quite charming, Harry. Truly it will," Augusta said. "Now, just you sit here, and do not interrupt."

A towel was placed on the floor and around Harriett's shoulders, since it would not do to ruin either the carpet or the gown, even though both were old and in need of refurbishing. At first, Harriett was not unduly alarmed. Augusta meant merely to trim her unruly red curls a bit so they might be tied back in more orderly fashion. The boot black . . . well, Harriett refused to think about that.

A long red curl fell into her lap, and Harriett idly twirled it about her finger for a moment before suddenly realizing that it was a good six inches in length and should have been attached to her head.

"Augusta!" Harriett shrieked, jumping to her feet. "What have you done?" Running to peer in the mirror over the sideboard, Harriett took one look at her hair, shorn quite short on one side while still hanging in glorious profusion on the other, and became ominously silent.

"Augusta," she said again after a moment, her voice deceptively mild. "I believe that this time, I shall kill you."

Augusta, standing amidst the scattered red locks, held up her scissors in defence. "Thou shalt not kill, Harriett," she said. "It's one of the commandments."

"Let us consider the golden rule," Harriett said sweetly, turning back to Augusta. "Do unto others as you would have them do unto you." She advanced slowly but steadily across the carpet toward her sister.

"Harry, you . . . you wouldn't." Augusta backed behind the sofa, one hand going to her own luxuriant dark locks.

"Even I have my breaking point, dear sister."

"Well, I . . . I can understand that," Augusta admitted, her eyes darting about the room as she searched for something, anything, to distract her sister. "And of course, I am terribly sorry if you do not like your new hairstyle. But it is all the rage."

"Oh?" Harriett stopped for a moment, but did not appear convinced.

Augusta nodded vigorously. "I can show you pictures in *Ackermann's Repository* which I borrowed from Madame St. Germaine. Short curls are quite fashionable."

"Then you will want your hair to be fashionable as well, will you not?" As if Harriett did not know that the *Ackermann's Repository* her sister had borrowed from the local dressmaker was more than three years old.

Augusta, squeezed between the sofa and the mahogany side table, said quickly, "The thing is, Harriett, that whether you like it or not, you cannot leave your hair half-cut like that. It looks quite ridiculous."

Harriett hesitated and turned back to the mirror, surveying her lopsided hair with a frown. Unfortunately, she was cursed with a logical mind as well as a vocal conscience, and while her fingers might itch to get at Augusta's long hair, Harriett had to admit that her sister was right. Her hair did look ridiculous. It could not be left half-cut.

"Very well," Harriett said, turning back to the chair and readjusting the towel about her shoulders. "You may continue."

Augusta's sigh of relief was audible as she crept from behind the sofa.

"But," Harriett turned and speared her sister with a steely glance, "I shall not forget this, Gusta." She turned back to face the room, then swung around once more. "And don't you dare tell me that to forgive is divine!"

Augusta nibbled on her bottom lip and remained silent. When Harriett was angry, which was not often, but memorable when it happened, it was wise not to provoke her further. Fingers shaking slightly, Augusta finished clipping her sister's hair. Then she took a deep breath and walked to stand in front of Harriett.

"I . . . I will need to put some of my sugar water on your hair to tame the curls," she said, holding out a small bowl. "Else you will look much too feminine, Harry."

Harriett nodded her assent, her face stern and unsmiling. Augusta must learn that she could not do outrageous things and depend upon her charm to win forgiveness. She was no longer a child. She must learn that things had consequences. Such as vengeful sisters, Harriett thought, pressing her lips together to keep from smiling.

Augusta caught the gleam of humor in her sister's eyes and relaxed. Harry could never stay angry with someone for long. "You know, I rather like your hair like this," she said, tilting her head to one side to study Harriett. "It makes your face look fuller and shows up your eyes more. Really, Harriett, you will thank me for this."

"I doubt it. But get on with it and be done, Gusta. I must still get into Papa's clothes, and you will want to fuss with yourself, as usual. We have not that much time."

"No." Augusta was counting on that. If time were short, Harriett would not be able to change things but must go as Augusta had devised. Dipping her tortoiseshell comb into the sugar water, Augusta proceeded to subdue Harriett's curls. It was not easy. And Harriett still looked undeniably feminine, but Augusta was counting on her *pièce de résistance*.

"As soon as your hair is dry, we will put the boot black on," she told Harriett. "And you know, it seems to me—"

"Boot black!" Harriett's gray eyes opened wide for a moment, then shut in resignation. She might have known. In fact, she had, but ninnyhammer that she was, Harriett had been hoping she was wrong.

"Your red hair is much too noticeable," Augusta said, her logic as irrefutable as always. "Lord Weston would know you on the instant. But with dark hair and . . ." Augusta took a deep breath before continuing, ". . . and a moustache, I am sure he will not know it is you."

Harriett's eyes snapped open. "You may not have noticed, Augusta, but though I resemble our Papa in many ways, I do not have a moustache."

"Not yet," Augusta agreed.

"Not ever," Harriett averred.

Augusta smiled. "But Harry, you said yourself that if Lord Weston recognizes you, we shall be creating the very scandal we hoped to avoid. So it seems to me—"

"—that we should not attend the dinner. Send our excuses. Plead illness."

"Harry! We must go. I shall die if we do not."

"Wait until Papa is home, then, so he may give you the last rites."

Augusta's reply was a loud sniff. Tears sparkled in her big brown eyes, spilled over, and coursed down her cheeks to land with a plop in the tin of boot black. "You . . . you know how much this means to me, Harriett," Augusta said, her voice a ragged whisper. "I know it is asking a lot of you, and you are quite right to refuse, but I have never been to a dinner like this before, and now that Cammie has run off, I may never have the chance again."

Harriett sighed. She knew that Augusta had the unique ability to produce tears whenever things did not go her way, but she also knew that what her sister said was true. Mrs. Haversham kept a tight hold on her younger daughter's reins, and it was only in the last year that Augusta had been allowed to attend the local assemblies. To be invited to a dinner with people who moved in the first circles of society was beyond anything to Augusta's way of thinking, and might be as close as she would ever come to the delights of a Season.

"A small one," Harriett said, capitulating.

She was rewarded with a hug, a bit of spilled boot black on the towel, and the epithet "best of sisters." All smiles now, Augusta took one of Harriett's shorn curls, stiffened it with the sugar water, and then turned it from red to black with a swift application of the black polish. Harriett watched the process with distinct misgiving. But in for a penny, in for a pound, she decided, and tilted her head so Augusta could apply the boot black to all her stiffened hair.

I must be mad, Harriett thought an hour later, as she surveyed herself once again in the cheval glass. Totally, completely mad. And so I shall claim, when asked why I agreed to this masquerade. A brainstorm, I shall say; it came on me all of a sudden.

The figure that looked back at her could only nod in agreement. It was a figure she barely recognized. Sleek, black hair, a small, dark moustache, and a suit of blue superfine moved when she did, but seemed to have no other connection with her former self. Only her gray eyes seemed the same. And the blush that stole quickly over her cheeks when she looked at her trouser-clad legs. Most improper. Harriett shifted from one foot to the other in embarrassment. I cannot go out like this, she thought. Truly I cannot. Augusta shall simply have to forgo the pleasure of dinner. We will send Old John with a note saying there has been an unexpected illness.

Harriett scrunched up her nose—the moustache itched—and then tugged at the bottom of her father's frock coat, wincing as one of the pins at the back pricked her skin. Most uncomfortable. Quite impossible. Surely Augusta would understand.

"I'm ready, Harry." Augusta waltzed into the room, turning about once so Harriett could see how lovely Camilla's blue satin looked. "I am so glad you agreed to go, best of sisters. I vow, I shall never call you a prosy sapskull again." She twirled to a stop in front of Harriett, who had turned slowly to face her.

"Augusta, I am sorry, but I—"

"Why, you look positively dashing, Harry!"

Harriett looked down at herself. "I do?" She had never been called anything but passable before.

"Indeed, yes." Augusta nodded. "You shall have all the ladies quite agog." She stifled a giggle. "How funny, Harriett. And you shall get to sit with the gentlemen after dinner. I have always wondered what they talk about among themselves when we are not there, and now you shall have a chance to find out. No one will ever suspect it is you."

"No." Harriett turned back to the mirror. "I would not know it myself," she agreed. Perhaps everything would be all right, after all. Perhaps it really would be fun.

"May I help you on with your pelisse, my dear?" she asked Augusta with a bow.

Augusta curtsied in reply. "La, sir, I would be much obliged."

The lanterns beside the entrance to Yarwood glowed brightly in the cool spring air. Old John stopped the Haversham carriage smartly on the graveled drive and a footman came running out of the house to let down the steps. Harriett took a deep breath, touched the moustache to make sure it was still in place, and then stepped carefully down. Wearing trousers was quite different from wearing a skirt and petticoats. She felt quite naked and yet quite free at the same time.

Turning, Harriett held out her arm to Augusta, and together they climbed the seven steps to the entrance, where two large stone lions looked ready to pounce on the unwary.

"Now remember to speak in a low voice," Augusta warned. "If you forget and your voice gets too high, we shall truly be in the suds."

"I shan't forget," Harriett said. She ran one finger inside her cravat and swallowed. The neckcloth was a bit too tight, but there was nothing to be done about it now. Augusta had insisted on tying it in the mathematical, using instructions she had found in a book. The result was a bit of mangled linen that made Harriett feel as if she would choke at any moment.

Patting one of the stone lions absently in passing, Harriett stepped inside the imposing oak door, looking around curiously. Yesterday they had entered Yarwood from a side door. The main entrance was much more imposing, with what seemed like miles of marble stretching upward to a painted ceiling of clouds and cavorting cherubs. Beside her, Augusta gave a little gasp and tilted her head back to get a better look.

"Your coat, sir." The butler materialized

suddenly in the hallway to assist Harriett from her greatcoat.

"Thank you." Harriett lowered her voice to what she hoped Augusta would consider a proper masculine pitch.

"And your hat?"

"Oh." Harriett blushed and swept it quickly from her head, smiling sheepishly. She had forgotten that she was wearing her father's top hat.

As the butler turned to hand the garments to a waiting footman, Augusta sidled over. "You mustn't do that again, Harriett," she whispered.

"I am not used to wearing top hats," Harriett defended herself. "And I can hardly do it again, since I no longer have it."

"Not the hat!" Augusta hissed and then smiled as the butler turned to them again.

"If you will follow me?" he said, leading the way down a long hallway filled with columns and bits of statuary.

"What do you mean, not the hat?" Harriett asked, as they trotted after the butler, obedient as a pair of sheep.

"The smile. You must not smile like that," Augusta said. "It makes you look like a female."

Harriett frowned. "Deuce take it, Gusta, I am a female, and I know only one way to smile."

Augusta blinked. She had never heard Harriett speak that way before. "Well, you must . . .

you must think of yourself as playacting," she instructed, as they sidestepped a marble column with a bust of a Grecian gentleman on top. "You know. Ophelia."

"Who?" Harriett gave her sister a puzzled glance.

"Ophelia. In that play by Mr. Shakespeare Papa was reading us last month. You know, she disguised herself as a man to win Romeo's love. If she could do it all those years ago, I am sure you can do it now, Harry."

"The Reverend Haversham and Miss Haversham," the butler announced.

Harriett smiled, then remembered Augusta's warning and frowned. A veritable sea of faces seemed to frown back at her. In reality, there were only six other people in the room, one of them Lord Weston, who was staring at her as if she had suddenly grown two heads. Harriett smoothed her moustache nervously.

"How good to see you again, Reverend Haversham," Lord Weston said, after a momentary hesitation. He crossed the room to greet them, looking directly into Harriett's gray eyes.

Again? Again! Alarms sounded in Harriett's head like churchbells rung to warn of disaster. What did Lord Weston mean by "again"? Of course, he had met Papa before, but surely that was some years ago, and Lord Weston would not remember a simple country parson.

"And Miss Haversham. I do not believe we have met before." He bowed over Augusta's hand. Augusta lowered her eyes, then raised them again, glancing coquettishly up at Lord Weston through her long lashes. It was a trick she had learned from Camilla, and one she, at least, would not waste on grooms.

"But are Mrs. Haversham and your other delightful daughter not with you?" Lord Weston asked, turning back to Harriett.

Delightful daughter? Harriett grinned, then frowned, then blushed furiously.

"My sister is ill, and Mama has stayed home to nurse her," Augusta said, firmly repeating the rehearsed lines. "They are both terribly sorry they are unable to attend. Are they not, Papa?" Augusta smiled sweetly as she poked Harriett with a sharp elbow. "Papa?"

"Yes." Harriett growled the word so low in her throat it brought on a violent fit of coughing.

"A pity," Lord Weston observed. "But I do hope you are not feeling ill as well, Reverend Haversham? That's a rather nasty cough."

"No, no," Harriett assured him hoarsely, as she wiped at the tears coursing down her cheeks and into her moustache. "Just something in my throat, is all." Harriett was fast discovering it was one thing to talk about doing something and quite another to actually do it. Especially when a certain gentleman's dark brown eyes seemed to cause a paralysis of the brain.

Lord Weston ushered them into the room. "Let me make you known to my family and guests." He stopped beside an ornate chair carved with dragon heads in the Oriental style.

"My mother, Lady Weston."

The dowager glared up at them. She was a tiny, gray-haired woman who sat at the edge of her chair as if a rod of iron had been placed down the back of her gown or as if she were afraid one of the dragons might suddenly decide to bite.

Harriett bowed low over her hand. "An honor," she murmured, in her low-voiced growl.

"That remains to be seen," the dowager snapped, looking pointedly at Harriett's limp cravat, and snatching her hand back.

Miss Dade and her mother were introduced next. Miss Dade was looking *très elegante* in a gown of sea-green satin with a lace overnet. Harriett made a perfunctory bow. She found Miss Dade a particularly depressing sight.

"Reverend Haversham, how delightful!" Miss Dade offered her hand and simpered coyly up at Harriett, while looking daggers at Augusta. Her mother, having dismissed Augusta as passable but no rival to her daughter, and Reverend Haversham as married and with no prospects in any case, merely nodded.

On the sofa next to the fireplace sat the Misses Prudence and Abigail Smalbathe. Diamonds glittered as Abigail Smalbathe turned her head. The jewels were paste, but no one would know that unless they looked closely. Nor would anyone be aware that the pearls worn by her sister, Prudence, as befit a young debutante not yet out, had been rented for the visit. Harriett followed Lord Weston across the room to be introduced, doing her best to take long, masculine strides without losing her Papa's shoes, stuffed with paper in the toes.

Bowing over Abigail Smalbathe's hand, Harriett felt a sudden, sharp pain in her side. "Ah!" Her eyes widened and her fingers tightened convulsively about Miss Smalbathe's hand for a moment. "So happy to meet you," she gasped, and then sighed as she straightened and the pin that held her trousers to her shirt ceased to dig into her waist.

Miss Smalbathe smiled and fluttered her eyelashes. "Indeed, yes. A pleasure, Reverend Haversham. But I must say, you seem much too young to have a grown daughter, sir."

"Ah . . . older than I look, I expect. Ha, ha." Harriett gave a fake laugh, remembered she wasn't supposed to smile, and lapsed into a flustered silence.

"Ophelia," Augusta whispered at her side.

Harriett nodded. Ophelia. Shakespeare's heroine, the one who'd disguised herself as a man to win Romeo's love. For some reason, she could not remember her father reading that particular part. Perhaps it had been during the first act, when she had left the room to assist Cook with the tea?

"And Miss Prudence Smalbathe," Lord Weston continued, introducing the young woman who sat on the opposite end of the sofa.

112

She was a pretty little thing, about the same age as Augusta, with auburn curls, a sweet smile, and vacuous gray eyes.

Harriett ventured another bow, slowly and carefully this time.

Prudence Smalbathe giggled.

Was something amiss? Harriett raised her head, eyes widened in alarm. Was her moustache drooping, her cravat undone? Had she, all unknowingly, committed some dreadful faux pas? Slowly she straightened, eyes frantically searching out Augusta.

Augusta gave a small shrug and raised her eyebrows in reply.

Fingering her cravat, which far from having come undone seemed to have tightened like a noose around her neck, Harriett frowned and growled out, "A pleasure to meet you, Miss Smalbathe."

"A pleasure," Prudence agreed, giggling again.

"I hope you are enjoying your stay in our part of the country," Augusta said.

Prudence nodded and giggled once more, a hand over her mouth.

Augusta and Harriett exchanged glances. A giggle was obviously the extent of Prudence Smalbathe's conversational skills. Good thing she's a pretty girl, Harriett thought charitably.

"And this is my old school chum, George Reading," Lord Weston said, concluding the introductions with a nod to his friend, who stood, wineglass in hand, observing the proceedings. Augusta gave a small curtsy while Harriett just caught herself from following suit. Ophelia, she told herself. Think of yourself as Ophelia.

"Good to meet you again, Mr. Reading," she greeted him, quaking just a bit. At yesterday's meeting, Harriett had been impressed by the man's acumen. George Reading was nobody's fool and Harriett had not missed the quick look that had just passed between him and Lord Weston.

"Have we met before, then?" George Reading asked, with a look of pleasant inquiry.

Harriett's throat constricted. Now she was in for it. What a clunch she was.

"Oh, dear." Augusta caught her toe on the edge of her gown and with a quick lunge forward managed to tumble into George Reading's arms. The wine flew from his glass, splashing down the front of Harriett's shirt and dripping from the blue waistcoat to the Belgian carpet at her feet. There was a moment of shocked silence. Then—

"The carpet, you imbecile!" The dowager furiously directed a footman who had mistakenly gone to Harriett's aid. Abigail Smalbathe smiled complacently and "tsk-tsked" Augusta's ineptness while Prudence giggled. Augusta and George Reading apologized profusely to each other.

"How dreadfully clumsy I am," Augusta wailed, hands pressed to her cheeks as her brown eyes filled with tears.

"*Au contraire,* it is I who have been clumsy," George Reading corrected. "Are you quite all right?"

"Actually, I'm afraid I'm a bit wet," Harriett answered, though the question had not been directed at her.

Lord Weston stepped forward. "Indeed. We must get you out of those clothes at once," he said. "Your voice already sounds a bit hoarse. We must not have you coming down with a cold, Reverend Haversham. If you will come with me, I shall have my valet find you another shirt to wear."

The suggestion caused Harriett's eyes to all but start from her head and her moustache to nearly come unglued as she unthinkingly bit it sharply with her teeth.

"But . . . but I couldn't—"

"Nonsense, of course you can." Lord Weston quickly ushered Harriett out the door of the parlour. "In fact, I insist, Reverend Haversham, I insist."

Dash it all, now we are in the suds! Harriett thought, blushing furiously.

Six

Harriett had never been in a man's bedroom before. At least, she had been in her Papa's bedroom, but that did not seem at all the same thing. She glanced nervously at the large four-post bed with dark velvet hangings that occupied one end of the room. This is most improper, she thought, shifting her too-large shoes on the woven carpet, and almost losing the left one. If anyone should ever find out, I shall be ruined.

"Here we are." Lord Weston returned from the dressing room with his valet. "James, this is the Reverend Haversham. He is in need of our aid."

James's eyebrows rose slowly as he took in Harriett's wine-soaked waistcoat, too-large jacket, and small, boot-black moustache.

"Indeed, milord," he agreed.

"We must find him a shirt and a new waistcoat, James. Have I anything that will fit, do you think?"

"No, milord. You are hardly of a size."

Lord Weston pursed his lips and turned to consider Harriett. Her face flamed as his dark eyes roamed slowly from her chest to her hips to her legs covered in the revealing trousers. For one brief moment she considered fainting. But that, she decided, would only make things worse. Besides, she had never fainted before and was not quite sure how to go about it—unfortunately. Loss of consciousness held a strong appeal for her at the moment.

"Well, why do you not simply strip down, Reverend, and we shall see what we can find," Lord Weston suggested.

"Strip . . . ah, strip down?" Harriett asked, her voice rising.

"Yes, of course." Lord Weston's dark brows rose. "We do not want you to catch cold, after all."

"Ah, well . . ." Harriett put one hand on her sopping waistcoat. "Actually, there is no need, no need at all," she assured her host. "Why, it is almost dry. Let us just return—" she stifled a shriek as Lord Weston stepped forward and put his hand on the blue waistcoat just over her breast.

"Hmmmmmm." He patted the waistcoat and pressed his lips together, as if considering the matter. "Now I find it quite . . ." he paused to smile down at Harriett, ". . . quite damp still, my good sir. I insist that you change your shirt. I shall not take no for an answer."

117

Harriett swallowed and chewed briefly on her moustache. "I, ah . . ."

"Why do you not step into milord's dressing room?" James suggested, stepping forward. "You may wear one of Lord Weston's morning gowns while I search out something for you to wear."

"Thank you," Harriett said fervently, barely restraining herself from kissing the valet's hands in gratitude.

"An excellent suggestion," Lord Weston agreed. He held open the door to his dressing room. "James will assist you."

Ophelia. What would Ophelia have done? Harriett asked herself, as the door to the dressing room closed, shutting her in with the valet. She backed into a corner. Whatever Ophelia would have done eluded her. Fortunately, James merely stepped to a cupboard, took out a blue silk dressing gown, and laid it over a small gilt chair.

"Will you require any further assistance?" he asked politely.

"No." Harriett's voice was a small, relieved whisper. "I can manage by myself, thank you."

James nodded. "I shall return for your shirt and waistcoat in a few minutes, Reverend Haversham."

Harriett let out the breath she had been holding as the door closed behind him. What a coil! Papa was certainly right about one lie leading directly to another. In fact, that had been part of his sermon two Sundays ago. Why had she not listened? Or rather, why had she listened and then done exactly the opposite?

Whatever would Papa say if he could see me now? Harriett worried. And then told herself that he would most likely say she should get out of that jacket and shirt with all possible speed. Lord Weston's valet would be returning soon, and if he saw her still standing there, he might offer to help again.

Quickly, before she could lose her nerve, Harriett pulled the small gilt chair across the carpet and wedged it under the doorknob. Then, feeling a bit safer, she slipped out of the loose jacket and waistcoat. The cambric shirt was more difficult. Her papa's trousers, which fastened under the foot with a strap, had proved much too long. And so Augusta had pinned them to the shirt, and the shirt, being much too big, had in turn been pinned into a wide pleat in the back.

Removing the pins from the front of the shirt was easily accomplished, and in no time at all, Harriett had a small row of them neatly lined up on the top of Lord Weston's serpentine dressing chest. But removing the pins in the back presented a problem. Harriett had first to unbutton the shirt and pull it partially off before, with a great deal of twisting and turning, she could reach the pins holding the trousers at the back. Once this was accomplished, however, it was the matter of a moment before she could remove the shirt completely and unpin the pleat. With an anxious glance at the dressing room door, Harriett quickly exchanged the sodden shirt for the silk dressing gown and stepped back, shivering slightly.

Not that Harriett was cold. It was the thought of being caught out in such dishabille by Lord Weston that sent a chill of horror down her spine. There was a discreet knock at the door just as Harriett finished tying the cord of Lord Weston's morning gown about her waist, and she heard a muffled oath when the knob would not turn properly.

"A moment!" Harriett cried, and then put a hand over her mouth as she realized she had forgotten to lower her voice. Well, she had more important things to think of just now. Looking down at her feet, Harriett made sure the trousers she still wore under Lord Weston's morning gown were held up by the cord at her waist and not gathered in folds about her ankles, and then dragged the chair back across the carpet, smoothing the marks left by the chair legs with her toe.

The knob turned again and a moment later Lord Weston stood in the small dressing room, smiling down at her. Harriett pulled the morning gown tighter about her throat before she could stop herself.

"Ah, well, you're looking much more the thing," Lord Weston said. "And James has brought us some wine, have you not, James?"

"Yes, milord." James appeared behind his lordship with a silver tray containing a wine decanter and two glasses.

"He has also had the excellent notion of asking Mrs. Peabody, my housekeeper, if she might have something suitable for you to wear. I used to spend my school holidays here, you know. It's possible Mrs. Peabody still has some shirts of mine tucked away in camphor somewhere."

Harriett accepted the glass of wine Lord Weston held out to her, concentrating on the gilt buttons of his jacket. His was much too commanding a presence and the dressing room much too small for Harriett not to feel just a bit overwhelmed. In fact, she was very much afraid that if she looked into his dark eyes and noticed the particular way they seemed to light up when he smiled, she would forget Ophelia and the part she was to play entirely.

Making a show of sipping her wine, Harriett looked idly about the room as she wondered what Lord Weston's reaction would be if his vicar suddenly simpered coyly up at him and fluttered her lashes. Unfortunately, Harriett did not quite have the nerve to put it to the test. For though there might be a good deal of kind understanding and seeming tolerance in milord's countenance at the moment, it was wise to remember the Reverend Smythe's experience.

"I have asked that dinner be held back a few minutes while James finds you suitable clothing," Lord Weston remarked.

"It might be best if I simply went home and changed," Harriett demurred. "It is not so very far and I could join you after dinner. It seems wrong to discommode your other guests in this way."

"Nonsense." Though Lord Weston was smiling, he put a great deal of authority into that one word and Harriett realized that no matter how charming the man might seem, he was used to getting his own way in things. If he said his guests would not mind waiting for their dinner, they would not mind, no matter if they had not eaten in days.

"I shall speak to Mrs. Peabody, milord," James said, removing Harriett's damp garments from the gilt chair. "And I shall see to the cleaning of the Reverend Haversham's shirt and waistcoat with my own hands."

Lord Weston nodded and watched his valet depart, after which he turned back to Harriett again. "So, and how do you find the parish, Reverend Haversham?" he asked, leaning his broad shoulders against the cupboard. "Have you solved the problem with the drainage pipes of which we spoke on my last visit?"

With an air of calm belied by her quivering moustache, Harriett walked past Lord Weston and into the larger bedroom. Drainage pipes? What drainage pipes could he be referring to? She could not remember her Papa ever saying a word about such things. And when had Lord Weston visited last? Surely she would have remembered . . . unless it was when she had gone on a visit to her aunt last year.

She took a quick turn about the room, trying

to resolve the matter. Lord Weston sat casually upon the four-post bed, waiting for his answer. The way a cat might wait at a mousehole, Harriett thought, though the comparison was quite ridiculous. Lord Weston had asked a casual question about the parish as befitted the man who owned most of it. He was not trying to entrap her.

When in doubt, tell the truth . . . it was her mother's maxim, and one Harriett decided to heed. "Things go on well in the parish, milord," Harriett said in her deepest voice, "but I cannot remember any problem with drainage pipes. Are you sure it was at Upper Mourouby?"

Lord Weston smiled, his eyes lighting, as he sat up from his lounging position on the bed. "Ah, well, perhaps I am mistaken," he admitted. Then he raised his wineglass to Harriett in what was almost a salute.

Now, whatever does he mean by that? Harriett wondered. She sat down on a stuffed armchair with cabriolet legs, and twisted her wineglass between her fingers before raising it to her lips.

"I met Miss Haversham in the home woods the other day," Lord Weston remarked.

"She mentioned it, milord," Harriett agreed cautiously. She did wish he would not sit upon the bed. It unnerved her, besides seeming somewhat improper.

"A charming girl."

"Did you think so?"

Lord Weston nodded. "A bit tall, and not in the common way, but charming nevertheless. In fact, she closely resembles you."

A backhanded compliment if ever I have heard one, Harriett thought.

"She is not married, though, nor even betrothed?"

"No. As you say, milord, she resembles me."

"Ah, well, a bit long in the tooth to be considering such things, I suppose. But then, she seems content to devote herself to good works. I believe she is to color Easter eggs for the children in the parish school."

Harriett, still smoldering over the epithet "long in the tooth," could only nod. Dash it all, why was a woman of twenty-four considered an ape leader while a man of the same age or even older, she frowned across at Lord Weston, was considered in his prime? Her fingers tightened around the stem of her wineglass as she fought down a sudden urge to hurl it at the fireplace.

"Mrs. Peabody had a few things which I thought might do, milord," James announced, entering the room after a discreet knock on the door. He carried several garments folded neatly over one arm which he proceeded to lay out upon the bed.

"They reek of camphor," Lord Weston complained, waving one hand before his face and wrinkling his nose.

"Lay not up for yourselves treasure upon earth, where moth and rust doth corrupt,"

Harriett quoted, walking over to inspect the garments.

"Moths would certainly never consider corrupting this lot," Lord Weston answered with a small smile. "In fact, I am afraid the smell will keep away people as well as insects. It will not do, James."

"It is only the coat, milord," James answered. "The shirt was fortunately kept in a chest with lavender."

"He shall still need to dine at another table or put us all off our food," Lord Weston insisted.

"I have sponged off Reverend Haversham's own waistcoat, which is nearly dry," James said, producing that garment with the flourish of an artist. "And he may wear his own coat for now. I merely thought that for the future . . . ?" He frowned as if the thought of Harriett going about clad as she had been in a coat several sizes too large was an affront to his valet's sensibilities. "The garments are several years out of fashion, being worn when milord was considerably younger, of course, but though not in quite the latest mode, quality is always in fashion."

"Yes, James. You may lecture Reverend Haversham on his choice of clothing some other time. Assist him to dress now, if you please, and I shall return to my other guests." He turned to Harriett with a smile that changed quickly to a questioning frown. "Is something wrong?" he asked.

Harriett blinked and shook her head. She would not admit even to herself that she was feeling a bit bereft, now that her tête-à-tête with Lord Weston was at an end. How ridiculous to resent the fact that the man wanted to return to his other guests. Of course he did. He had stayed to talk to her only out of politeness, not because he enjoyed her company. And even if he had . . . Harriett looked down at her father's shoes and sighed. It was not the company of Harriett Haversham that he had been enjoying, but that of her Papa.

Harriett had the dubious distinction of being seated to the right of Lady Weston during supper. Sitting upright, as if her corsets were made entirely of steel, the dowager seemed to regard conversation with those beneath her in the peerage as an unpleasant duty to be dispensed with as soon as possible. After ordering Harriett to serve her with a small portion of oysters in cream sauce, and commenting on the unseasonably cold weather, Lady Weston felt free to ignore her dinner companions and concentrate on her food.

However, emboldened by the unaccustomed glass of wine she had enjoyed with Lord Weston, and the fact that much would be forgiven a vicar that would not be forgiven a young lady, Harriett decided to have a go at cracking Lady Weston's facade. She had sat with enough of her Papa's elderly parishioners to know that people of a certain age enjoyed only one thing more than a discussion of their digestion, and that was to be told how well they looked as compared to their contemporaries.

Harriett turned her head cautiously, the shirt she wore having a rather high starched collar which was apt to jab one's cheek without warning, and addressed the dowager.

"What a lovely necklace, Lady Weston. I have just noticed that the sapphires exactly match your eyes." Harriett eyed the ostentatious jewels hung about the dowager's scrawny neck with every appearance of admiration. "How remarkable. You know, I must confess that I had no idea you were Lord Weston's mother until we were introduced. I was sure you must be his wife. You must have been married remarkably young."

The dowager, who had been married at thirty and only then because her fortune was quite immense, looked up from her oysters.

"I am sure the Marchioness of Tverton looks quite hagged in comparison," Harriett continued, though she had never actually met the lady. "Have you discovered some magical fountain of youth, then, Lady Weston?"

Lady Weston put down her fork. "The Marchioness of Tverton died last year at the age of ninety-two. I should hope I look better than she does. Especially now."

"Oh. Well. Ha, ha." Harriett essayed a smile, remembered she wasn't supposed to, and frowned. "I am sorry to hear that."

"I beg your pardon?" Ice shivered in the dowager's voice.

"I am sorry to learn of her death," Harriett said quickly. "I mean, it's always a pity when one so . . . old dies." Her voice faded away to silence.

The dowager picked up her fork again.

Harriett chewed on the ends of her moustache, which were beginning to droop, and stared down at her curried crab. She would be the first to admit that she had blundered in choosing a name she had only read in her Papa's London papers. Still, she had never considered herself a quitter. I shall try flattery one more time, she decided, and if it fails, I shall resort to digestion.

She glanced at the dowager, who was staring at a piece of tongue in red currant sauce as if it had somehow snuck onto her plate without her knowledge or permission.

It was not easy to find something about the dowager's appearance to compliment. But Harriett continued to stare at her hostess doggedly until, the shirt point biting painfully into her cheek, she fixed upon Lady Weston's emaciated form.

"You are to be complimented on retaining your slender figure," Harriett said, her eyes on the gray silk décolletage that covered Lady Weston's scrawny bosom. "So many women allow themselves to go to fat these days."

The dowager, having hustled the tongue to one side of her plate, allowed the peas in cream sauce she had been about to eat to roll off her knife. Her eyes, a rather watery but still beady blue, narrowed. "Reverend Haversham."

"Yes?" Harriett raised boot-black brows in inquiry, quite sure she had won Lady Weston over.

"Are you not married, Reverend Haversham?"

Harriett nodded, severely abrading her cheek as she did so. "Indeed, I am, Lady Weston. Mrs. Haversham and I have been wed . . ." Harriett did a swift calculation, ". . . twenty-seven years this August."

"Then you should be ashamed!"

"I beg your pardon?" Had the woman taken leave of her senses? Why should one be ashamed of having been wed twenty-seven years?

"A married man casting out lures to me at my own table. It is not to be tolerated."

"But, Lady Weston—"

"I will not share my table with a womanizer!" For all her small size, Lady Weston had a powerful voice when she chose to use it.

Resisting a strong urge to clap a hand over the dowager's mouth and hustle her from the room, Harriett sent a quick, harried glance about the table. All conversation had stopped. Seven pairs of eyes stared at them in horrid fascination.

I could lift the tablecloth and hide beneath its folds, Harriett thought, casting about desperately for some means of escape, and only rejecting the idea when she remembered the cloth would be removed for the dessert course. Or there was always lunacy. Harriett momentarily considered laughing maniacally and allowing herself to be carried from the room, but finally decided on a defense of outraged innocence.

"Why—why, Lady Weston, whatever do you mean?" she asked.

"Don't try to act the innocent with me," the dowager snarled. "A rake disguised as a vicar, that's what you are. Phillip, ring for the footman and have this . . . this *person* shown out at once."

"But . . . but I was only . . ." Harriett stammered to a stop. At the moment she could not remember what she had been saying. Her eyes scanned the horrified faces turned in her direction. Augusta was staring at her, mouth agape like that of a dying fish.

Lord Weston rose from his place at the other end of the table and with measured pace walked to his mother's side. "I shall send one of the footmen for your companion," he said calmly. "You are overwrought, madam. Miss Marshnet shall mix you a soothing draught for your nerves."

"Nerves! I don't have nerves. I have a libertine at my table. I demand that you do something, Phillip. Your father would never have permitted such a thing."

"You supped with my father the few times he was at home, did you not? And yet you

130

speak in outraged tones of libertines and rakes at your table? You seem to have forgotten what your husband and my father was, madam."

The dowager's mouth snapped shut and her body went so rigid, Harriett was afraid she would suffer an apoplexy.

"My lord . . ." Harriett began, only to be waved to silence by a brusque gesture from Lord Weston.

"It is wrong to speak badly of the dead." The dowager ground out the words, but she did not look at her son, preferring to glower at her creamed peas instead.

Lord Weston shrugged, looking amused. "I spoke the same of my beloved father when he was alive. And to his face, as you well know. Now calm yourself, madam, and we shall cease this washing of dirty linen before our guests."

The dowager's fingers curved around her knife as if she would gladly use it to unman her son, did she dare.

"Ah, Miss Marshnet." Lord Weston smiled at the middle-aged woman who sidled into the room, looking about her like a rabbit beset by a pack of hounds. "My mother is not feeling quite the thing and would like to retire to her room. A soothing draught to help her sleep would be welcome, I am sure."

Miss Marshnet nodded but made no move to go to the dowager, who clutched the edge of the table as if they would have to tear it from her grasp.

"Madam?" Lord Weston turned back to his

mother, eyebrows raised. A moment only the dowager hesitated, then with a nasty glare that Harriett could only be glad was sent Lord Weston's way rather than her own, Lady Weston got to her feet and walked slowly from the room, back erect as any soldier's. Miss Marshnet bobbed a hurried curtsy at Lord Weston and scampered after the older woman.

The silence that hung palpably in the air after the dowager's departure seemed not to bother Lord Weston. Without hurry or further apology, he walked back to his chair and resumed his seat. "You were telling me about Mr. Fortesque's new carriage, Miss Dade?" he said, as if nothing out of the ordinary had occurred.

Perhaps it had not, Harriett thought, taking a deep breath to calm herself. Perhaps this was not the first time the dowager had lost control. Harriett tugged at the cravat which James had so expertly tied, and stared down at the curried crab congealing on her plate. Her own mother would never have created such a scene. Nor would her daughters have ever dared speak to her as Lord Weston had spoken to the dowager.

The footmen came to remove the cloth and serve the dessert course. Harriett watched silently while this was done. It seemed as if the others avoided speaking or even looking at her. Though this was difficult to tell, since Miss Prudence Smalbathe was seated to her right, and after the first few giggled responses, Harriett had ceased her attempts at conversation. Now she tried again.

"What think you of Miss Austen's latest novel?" Harriett asked. *Pride and Predjudice* was a favorite of Harriett's, and she knew that the author was admired by both her papa and the Prince Regent.

Miss Smalbathe giggled.

Harriett sighed. "May I serve you with some of the raspberry trifle?" she asked.

Miss Smalbathe nodded and giggled again.

Across the table, Augusta sent her a look of sympathy. She was seated next to George Reading and seemed to be quite enjoying herself. Harriett watched as Augusta tasted her dessert and smiled.

I am glad someone is having a pleasant evening, Harriett thought, hoping it was merely her imagination that everyone was avoiding catching her eye. After all, the dowager's outburst could hardly be laid at her door. She had been trying to compliment the woman, for heaven's sake. Was it her fault that the dowager had gotten her hackles up over nothing?

If you ask me, Lady Weston is . . . is dicked in the nob, Harriett thought, borrowing her vocabulary from their coachman, Old John. She spooned up a bit of the raspberry trifle but found she could not force it past the lump in her throat, though it was one of her favorite desserts, seldom served at the vicarage except when wild raspberries were plentiful.

Dipping her fingers in the bowl of water set out for that purpose, Harriett wiped away the remains of the sticky trifle. She would have liked to splash some water on her face as well, since the room seemed to have become uncommonly warm. I am not used to wearing as many clothes as gentleman do, she decided, glancing down the table at Lord Weston, who was preparing an orange for Miss Dade. He seemed not a whit affected by the heat. Nor did Mr. Reading. Harriett shrugged. She could only suppose that gentlemen became accustomed to such things. They usually wore a great deal more than the ladies, whose gowns were low cut and of the thinnest materials. Harriett patted her forehead surreptitiously, frowning when she noted that the tips of her fingers came away quite black.

What in the world . . . ? Ah, the bootblack. I must have touched my hair, Harriett reassured herself. She dipped her fingers in the bowl of water again, pretending not to notice when the water turned a dark gray. When she looked up it was to find Augusta staring at her, eyes all but popping from her head.

Augusta brushed her cheek with one hand and gave Harriett a fierce look. Harriett's head would have had to be stuffed with cotton wool not to know that something was very much amiss.

Now quite thankful that the other ladies considered her a dissolute libertine whose glance was to be avoided, Harriett put one hand to her cheek while panic galloped *ventre à terre* through her veins. Her face turning scarlet

134

with embarrassment, Harriett looked at her fingers again. Black. Black as bootblack.

Deuce take it, Harriett thought. My hair has begun to melt!

Seven

Since Lord Weston was without a hostess, his mother remaining in her room, the men did not linger long over their port.

Thank God, Harriett thought sending a fervent prayer up to the plasterwork ceiling. She had often thought women's conversations inane. But now, having spent the past fifteen minutes listening to a conversation consisting solely of hunting, pugilistic sports, and the blood lines of some horse called Murphy's Muse, she would have welcomed a few inanities. It had not been at all interesting nor in the least revealing, as Augusta had suggested, except when Lord Weston had started discussing birds of paradise. As an amateur birdwatcher, Harriett had perked up at once, and asked if they were to be found in Lord Weston's home woods and if so, what they looked like. Well, it seemed as if she was never to find out, for both Lord Weston and Mr. Reading had begun coughing quite violently and the subject had not been brought up again.

At least, Harriett did not think it had. She would be the first to admit that after the first few minutes, she had not been listening too closely. No, she had been busy mopping her face with her handkerchief whenever the attention of the two men was occupied elsewhere. She dared not guess what she looked like, and did not wish to know. She only longed for the evening to be over. Not only was the heat and unaccustomed port making her undeniably sleepy, but she now feared she might come down with some infectious disease as well.

Though both Mr. Reading and Lord Weston appeared healthy, these coughing fits that seemed to come upon them so suddenly, causing them to double over and shake with such violence tears came to their eyes, certainly gave one pause for concern. She must see that Mama gave Mrs. Peabody her recipe for mint drops that were so soothing to one's throat. In fact, Harriett would bring the recipe over herself, as soon as she was returned to her normal female state.

Now, walking slightly behind the two men, Harriett entered the drawing room where the waiting ladies looked up from their conversation, their faces wreathed in smiles of welcome. Harriett could certainly understand how some men became puffed up. To walk into a room and be greeted with such effusiveness was a wonderful thing. And the gentlemen did no more to deserve it than smile and bow and take a seat beside the woman they chose to honor with their presence. Harriett, who was used to being unnoticed by most everyone when she entered a room, thought wistfully that being a man might be no bad thing at times.

Choosing a seat in the darkest corner of the room, Harriett sat down and crossed her legs. She was enjoying rather the freedom of trousers. At least, now that she was used to them, and James had fixed things so pins were no longer jabbing into her at every step. But Harriett was afraid she had no head for intrigue. While Augusta might think it great fun to fool everyone, Harriett thought only of what would happen if they were discovered in their masquerade.

Deuce take it, I do wish I weren't so . . . so missish, Harriett thought. I shy away from everything like a nervous horse, while Augusta and Camilla are always so full of pluck. Still, one had to admit it was that very trait in Camilla that had landed them in the briars this time.

Settling back in her chair, Harriett began to calculate how long it would be before they could leave. They must wait for the tea tray, she supposed, but then, surely, they could take their leave of the company and the nightmare would be over. She had never been very good at dissembling. And while Ophelia might be able to disguise herself to win Romeo's love, Harriett was afraid she would never be able to do the same. No. Romeo would simply . . .

Harriett stopped and frowned, considering the matter carefully for the first time.

And suddenly it all seemed rather muddled to Harriett. She knew that both Camilla and Augusta considered her far too practical and not at all romantic. But still, if Ophelia were disguised as a man, and Romeo fell in love with her, or rather, him, how did that help Ophelia? Because Romeo was not really in love with her, but with him. Harriett shook her head. It seemed to her that Ophelia had made a real mull of things. And while Harriett supposed it would all make for a very interesting wedding night, she thought Shakespeare must have had windmills in his head to think it would work.

"Ah, how thoughtful we are, Reverend Haversham." Abigail Smalbathe suddenly hove into view and sat down beside Harriett on the settee. "Are you merely wool-gathering, or are you thinking of serious things I should not interrupt?"

Miss Smalbathe smiled archly, as if it would be quite impossible for any gentleman to consider her presence an unwelcome interruption. "I do hope you were not overset by Lady Weston's outburst. Imagine her declaring a man of the cloth such a libertine!"

"Imagine."

"Why, it is almost as unthinkable as her suggestion that you were flirting with her," Miss Smalbathe said, fingers covering her mouth.

Harriett, who at first thought the gesture due to the buttered eels, realized suddenly that

139

Miss Smalbathe was giggling. It must be hereditary, she decided, noting the distinct resemblance between the two sisters.

"Now I have caused you to frown again, my dear sir." Miss Smalbathe playfully slapped Harriett's arm. "Which was not my intention at all. It is merely that for a woman of Lady Weston's age to suggest that so young and attractive a gentleman as yourself would cast out lures to her . . . well, it is of all things the most ridiculous. Do you not agree?"

"Ah . . ." Harriett looked about the room. She did not like the direction the conversation was taking and was sure her papa would not have approved.

"Of course, you can say nothing, nor should you. Nor should I, for that matter." Miss Smalbathe widened her eyes and leaned closer to Harriett. "For Lady Weston is my hostess, and it is at her invitation that I am here, you know."

"Indeed, yes. I supposed . . . that is, I am here at her invitation as well. Though it was not actually me, but my . . . I mean, my sister . . ." Harriett tugged at her cravat. James had tied it much too tightly, and surely it should not be this warm so far from the fire.

"Ah, I know what you would say, dear sir. That they do you too much honor to have you at Yarwood. But that is not so. Indeed, quite the opposite. You honor us all with your presence. And I, for one, fully appreciate the opportunity to have this little coze with you. I am not like Lady Weston."

Harriett stopped looking about the room and turned to Miss Smalbathe. Though she knew her papa would never have entered into such a conversation, she was beginning to feel more and more like Ophelia. "No, you are not like Lady Weston," she said slowly, and then, throwing caution and her inhibitions to the winds, "No, you are young and beautiful, and your necklace exactly matches your eyes."

"La, sir, but you do know how to flatter a lady," Miss Smalbathe simpered, arching her neck so the diamonds would catch the light.

"I do?" Harriett grinned. Maybe she wasn't as bad at this dissembling game as she had thought. Maybe she could be as full of pluck as Camilla and Augusta, given half the chance. "And you have a superb figure," she said, eyes narrowed as she waited to see how Miss Smalbathe reacted to this particular compliment.

Abigail Smalbathe licked her lips and glanced coquettishly at Harriett from under her lashes. "How very naughty of you to notice. But you really musn't speak to me in this way," she scolded. "At least, not here."

"No?"

"No, you shameless man, for you quite put me to the blush. When we were first introduced, I could tell you were attracted to me by the way you held my hand and by the sudden gasp when you looked into my eyes for the first time." Miss Smalbathe sighed and looked away for a moment as if quite overcome by emotion. "It is an attraction I also feel, but . . . for now we must behave ourselves." She moved apart from Harriett a little. "We must speak only of inconsequential things. It would not do for anyone to suspect that we have such feelings for each other." Miss Smalbathe flicked a significant glance across the room at Lord Weston.

"Lord Stiff Rump." Harriett nodded.

Miss Smalbathe giggled. "Is that what you call him? Well, he is known to be quite proper, of course. But that does not mean he will not do very well as a husband. He has a great deal of money, you know. One could only hope he were not quite so dark nor quite so tall."

Harriett blinked. On the one hand, Miss Smalbathe seemed to be flirting with her, which was quite improper, since she knew full well Harriett was a married man. On the other hand, Miss Smalbathe seemed quite intent on marrying Lord Weston. It was all very confusing. Especially since she didn't see how Abigail Smalbathe stood a chance, with Miss Dade in the running.

"Oh, I know what you are thinking," Miss Smalbathe turned to Harriett, put out a hand and then quickly returned it to her lap. "You are thinking that your hair is dark, too. But you must know that I do not view you with disfavor. It is just that I prefer a pale complexion and someone who is not quite so tall and overpowering. Lord Weston's skin is so swarthy he almost looks . . . well, I should not say it, but one might almost think him Italian rather than English. And his shoulders are much too large. I mean, there is really no need for it, and I do so deplore excess of any kind. Why, one would almost think he shod his horses rather than rode them. I understand he is the despair of his tailor. Then, of course, you will think me indelicate to have noticed . . ." She gave Harriett a questioning look.

"Never," Harriett avowed, her curiosity more than aroused.

"Lord Weston has . . . he has hair upon his hands. Dark, wiry hair." She gave a shudder. "And I don't doubt upon his arms as well. It is not at all the thing."

Harriett gave Lord Weston a considering look. She found his hairiness, his figure, everything about him, in fact, more than attractive. The only thing she did not like was the way he was conversing in so intimate a fashion with Miss Dade.

Lord Weston glanced her way and for a moment their eyes met. He seemed to smile across the room at her, though Harriett knew such a thing was quite ridiculous. It was simply her imagination at work, and nothing more. She was sure he was quite indifferent to her, and in any case, he saw the Reverend Haversham, not Harriett herself.

"You are quite different from Lord Weston," Miss Smalbathe continued.

Harriett nodded. "In many ways."

"Tell me of your marriage. You must have been quite young?"

Shifting uneasily on the settee, Harriett

looked away. She felt awkward talking about such things. "I would prefer not to discuss it," she said.

"I understand. A marriage of convenience." Miss Smalbathe nodded and bit her lip in sympathy. "I, too, shall sacrifice myself upon such an altar."

"You intend to make a marriage of convenience with . . ."

They both turned and looked at Lord Weston. He was conversing with Prudence Smalbathe now, his head bent attentively.

"Of course, it may be that Lord Weston will prefer my sister," Miss Smalbathe observed, not sounding a bit put out by this. "And though she is the younger by two years, I should not stand in the way but wish them happy."

A high-pitched giggle emanated from that corner of the room. Prudence Smalbathe covered her mouth, her shoulders hunched. Lord Weston wore a hunted expression.

"She has an unusually sunny disposition," Miss Smalbathe said of her sister.

"A worthy attribute."

"Yes, for men do not care for serious females. Bluestockings, as they call them. They prefer a woman to be amusing, of a pretty appearance, and a pleasing demeanor. That is all that is important and, in my opinion, all that should concern a woman. Do you not agree, Reverend Haversham?"

Since Reverend Haversham, the real Reverend Haversham, had been known to refer to such women as leeches sucking the blood of humanity, Harriett could not bring herself to agree. "I am sorry, Miss Smalbathe," she said, turning her head and ignoring the stiff point of the collar which dug into her cheek. "I consider that all women, nay, all men as well, have a moral obligation to help others. To be concerned only with one's appearance or amusement is to ignore one's Christian duty."

Miss Smalbathe raised her eyebrows. "Ah, we speak of Christian duty now?"

Harriett blushed, knowing she well deserved the skepticism, for only moments before she had been flirting with Miss Smalbathe, and Harriett was, after all, a married man. "I am sorry," she said. "I'm afraid I have given you the wrong impression. I should not have spoken to you as I did." Harriett had known all that Ophelia-and-Romeo business would only result in a bumblebath, and she had been right. If it took dishonesty to win someone's heart, you had not really won it at all.

"Oh, do not apologize, Reverend Haversham. I quite understand. And truly, I find you even more attractive when you are being all vicarish like this." Miss Smalbathe gave a little giggle. "But if you do not want amusing conversation, what is it that you would discuss? Do men speak of moral obligations over their port? You must know I have been ever curious."

"So have I." Harriett nodded. "But, in fact, men speak of little that would interest you."

145

"Ah, but you do not know that, dear sir. Now confess, do men not discuss the ladies, just as the ladies discuss the gentlemen?"

"Actually, no," Harriett admitted, having been a bit disappointed to find this out herself. "Men discuss things like horses, and sports and . . . and birds."

"Birds?" Miss Smalbathe raised her eyebrows and tittered. "I know your daughter trains rooks, dear sir. And I assure you I do not hold it against you in the least. But I cannot imagine Lord Weston discussing such a thing."

"I do not train rooks," Harriett said. "That is, my daughter does not train them. She merely has been feeding them, due to the hard winter we had this year. And both Lord Weston and Mr. Reading spoke of some duke or other and his interest in exotic birds."

Miss Smalbathe looked suitably impressed. "A duke?" she asked. "What sort of birds is this duke interested in, Reverend Haversham? Certainly not rooks?"

"No. I believe Lord Weston referred to them as birds of paradise. I must confess I have never heard of them, and I doubt that they are native to the area, but—"

"Birds of Paradise! Ladybirds?" Miss Smalbathe went into such a paradoxym of giggles, Harriett was afraid she might injure herself.

"But how droll you are, you naughty, naughty man," Miss Smalbathe scolded as soon as she was able to speak. "But it is quite wrong of you to speak to me of that sort of woman."

She shook a finger playfully in Harriett's face. "In fact, I should really claim to have no knowledge of ladybirds at all. Still, do you remember the name of the duke? It was not Clarence, was it?" she asked, referring to one of the Royal dukes. "I did hear a rumour, though surely he has not—"

The rattle of the tea cart being wheeled in interrupted her. Harriett, hailing its arrival as would the inhabitants of a beseiged castle the arrival of a friendly army come to save them, arose with such alacrity she stepped out of her left shoe and had to stop to retrieve it. Though her only thought was of escape, Harriett hesitated. It would be unpardonably rude to simply walk away and leave Miss Smalbathe sitting there.

"Would you like me to fetch you some tea?" she asked, turning reluctantly back and hopping on one foot as she thrust the other back into her shoe.

"Oh, you need not fetch and carry for me," Miss Smalbathe protested, though she made no move to rise.

"Good." Harriett nodded and moved off, taking Miss Smalbathe's words at their most literal. Not only did Harriett want to put some distance between herself and the amorous Miss Smalbathe, she also truly wanted a cup of tea. Speaking in a low growl was playing havoc with her throat.

Coughing slightly, Harriett smiled in apology as she passed Mrs. Dade, and then quickly frowned as she caught Augusta's censorious eye.

"Are you feeling quite the thing?" Mrs. Dade asked, as Harriett sat down nearby and gratefully sipped her tea. "Your skin looks positively gray, you know."

"It does?" Harriett put one hand to her cheek. Was her hair melting again? She nibbled worriedly at her drooping moustache.

"Not all over, you know, just in sort of . . . streaks." Mrs. Dade peered across her teacup at Harriett and suddenly frowned. "Stick out your tongue, sir!" she commanded.

"What?" Harriett asked, but obediently did as she was asked.

"I knew it!" Mrs. Dade shrieked. "It's the plague! The black death. We're all doomed." Springing to her feet, Mrs. Dade took one tottering step across the room before falling into a swoon at Harriett's feet.

Frozen into a state of immobility, Harriett could only gape at Mrs. Dade's inert form while a babble of voices rose and fell around her. She knew that if she lifted her eyes, everyone would be staring at her, Harriett Haversham, who had never before caused the slightest ripple in the placid life of Upper Mourouby. If only I were a turtle with a shell into which I could retreat, she thought. Or Rusty Brown, so that I might fly away and never return.

"I believe Mrs. Dade has always been a bit high-strung," Lord Weston said, calmly retrieving the tea cup she had thrown to the floor and instructing one of the footmen to mop up the spilled tea. "Are you quite all right?" he asked Harriett. Lord Weston was kneeling to one side of Mrs. Dade's prostrate form, and his dark eyes, on a level with Harriett's own, were so filled with warmth and sympathetic understanding that it was all Harriett could do not to throw herself into his arms and blurt out everything. She gave a little sniff.

"Mrs. Peabody shall fetch some smelling salts for Mrs. Dade," Lord Weston said, taking Harriett's hands. "There is no need for concern."

"I—"

"Yes." He nodded, pressing her fingers. "It has been a dreadful evening for my carpets as well. First the wine and now tea. But I have no doubt you shall both recover."

Harriett rewarded his jest with a watery smile. "Thank you," she whispered, returning his clasp as Abigail Smalbathe plumped down in the chair beside her.

"Whatever was Mrs. Dade shrieking about?" Miss Smalbathe inquired, eyes gleaming as she looked from one to the other. "And why does she think we are doomed?"

Before anyone could answer, Miss Dade joined Lord Weston beside her mother's prone form. Carefully arranging her skirts so that one trim ankle peeped out, she cleared her throat. "Oh, my poor mama," she began, as soon as she had everyone's attention. "How dreadfully she suffers."

"Actually, she seems to be unconscious," George Reading observed, "and probably quite insensitive to any suffering at all."

Ignoring this, after all Mr. Reading had not above five thousand pounds a year, Miss Dade clasped her mother's limp hand to her bosom and bemoaned her mother's fate, allowing a single tear to cascade down her cheek as she did so. "Mama is so delicate. How fortunate she is that I am here to care for her." Miss Dade looked soulfully across at Lord Weston, the picture of self-sacrifice.

"Delicacy runs in the Dade family, does it not?" Miss Smalbathe inquired, in a voice of false pleasantry. "I believe your great aunt, Scrufina, was kept locked in the attic for years due to her great delicacy."

"Aunt Scrufina suffered from a nervous complaint." Miss Dade threw down her mother's hand and sat up, hands on hips. "And if you mean to insinuate that—"

Lord Weston rose to his feet. "Ah, Mrs. Peabody, just in time, as always." He stepped adroitly between Miss Dade and Abigail Smalbathe, and greeted his housekeeper, who came bustling in carrying a small bottle of sal volatile. "I'm afraid Mrs. Dade has fainted. Perhaps one of the footmen could carry her up to her room? And Miss Dade will, of course, wish to accompany her mother." Lord Weston looked down at Miss Dade, who had no choice but to smile and agree.

"Perhaps we should depart as well, Papa."

Augusta stepped forward, smiling nervously. "I can tell by your voice that you are tired and your cold has become worse."

"My cold?"

"Yes, Papa. Your cold makes your voice sound almost as high as my own. Ha, ha."

Harriett clapped a hand over her mouth, looking guiltily over it at her sister. In all the excitement of Mrs. Dade's swoon, she had forgotten she was supposed to growl.

"Now, I usually lose my voice completely when I have a cold," George Reading said kindly. "But I must say, you are looking a bit gray, Reverend Haversham. And we would not want you to be laid low, now would we? Why, I have been looking forward to hearing your sermon this Palm Sunday. And then there is Easter, of course. You will certainly want to be in good health then."

"Indeed, yes." Augusta took hold of Harriett's arm and all but dragged her from the chair. "If you would be so good as to have our carriage sent round, Lord Weston?"

"It is a pity you will not be here for Easter," Harriett said. "For we have quite a lovely service, and Upper Mourouby will be looking its best by then. You are leaving early next week, are you not?" she added, noting the surprised look on George Reading's face.

"La, my dear sir," Abigail Smalbathe broke into the conversation. "We are invited to spend Easter at Yarwood, and would not dream of departing a moment before. Though perhaps

Miss Dade will wish to return home, now that her mother is feeling so poorly. It is a shame, but this sort of mental weakness often runs in families." She glanced at Lord Weston. "A pity, for Miss Dade is certainly an attractive young woman. And yet, who would marry her? For one would always worry that the children might be similarly afflicted."

"Indeed, mental weakness often does run in families," George Reading observed, glancing at Prudence Smalbathe, who was sitting beside the tea cart alternately stuffing cakes in her mouth and giggling.

Sensing that she was the object of his scrutiny, Miss Smalbathe looked up, swallowed, and said, "I, for one, don't see why we are discussing Miss Dade's children, for she hasn't got any that I know of." She paused to suck some icing from her finger. "And even if Mrs. Dade is right and we are doomed, I shall certainly not leave Yarwood beforehand, Lord Weston, for your cook makes absolutely the best cakes ever."

Lord Weston bowed in her direction. "I am pleased that you are enjoying the cakes, Miss Smalbathe, and that we are all agreed that we shall remain past Easter. Indeed, I quite look forward to the egg-rolling on Easter, Reverend Haversham. It is many years since I have seen such an event. Perhaps I can supply some sort of prize for the winner?"

"What a wonderful idea!" Augusta enthused, answering for her sister, who appeared to have been struck dumb by this wonderful news. "I only pray the weather is not inclement, as it was last year."

"There are other things you had best pray for, my dear," Harriett said, moving to the door as the butler announced their carriage.

Indeed, Harriett was praying for a flood of biblical proportions herself. Though Lord Weston, being the type of man he was, would probably row to church, if necessary. Harriett settled herself on the worn squabs of their small, rather shabby carriage and frowned into the darkness.

"Papa will have returned by Easter," Augusta assured her sister, as she arranged her skirts more comfortably. "And we shall say your cold prevents you preaching this Sunday, so Mr. Marsh is taking your place. It will all work out quite well, Harry. Truly it will."

"And what happens when Lord Weston sees Papa in the pulpit at Easter and discovers he is not the same man who shared his supper table at Yarwood? Have you managed to work that out as well, Augusta? You know Papa will never go along with any sort of deception."

The carriage springs squeaked in protest as they rounded a corner and Harriett waited for her sister's answer. It was but a ten minutes' walk to Yarwood using the footpath, but much longer by road, especially while you were waiting for your sister to think of some way out of a disgraceful—no, disastrous—dilemma.

"We shall just have to see that Lord Weston and Papa don't meet, won't we?" Augusta answered airily. "I'm sure something can be contrived, Harry. Do not worry so. What did you think of Miss Dade's dress? I thought it quite grand, but I should have liked a bit more lace about the throat. Of course, they say in London everyone wears—"

"Gusta! How can you not be concerned about the consequences of this evening? If Lord Weston ever learns that we have tricked him, he will . . ."

"Oh, pooh!" Augusta waved a hand in the air. "You seem to forget that Lord Weston is a man, Harriett. And men are easily handled, if one knows how."

"I'm afraid I have not had much practice," Harriett said stiffly. Truth to tell, Harriett had not had any. And considering what a bumble-bath she had gotten into with Lord Weston already, she thought it just might be a good thing to avoid such practice altogether. Except . . . Lord Weston did have a rather endearing way of smiling with his eyes, and he had seemed to understand about Rusty Brown.

"But I must say, I begin to wonder about Lady Weston and Mrs. Dade," Augusta broke into Harriett's thoughts. "Whatever did you say to them?"

"What? To whom?" Harriett asked, abruptly breaking off a promising dialogue in which

Lord Weston was saying he much preferred Harriett's quiet beauty to that of the flashy Miss Dade.

"Whatever did you say to Mrs. Dade and Lady Weston?" Augusta reiterated. "You aren't falling asleep, are you, Harry?"

"No, of course not. And I have no idea what caused them to suddenly erupt as they did. I usually get along quite well with elderly ladies, and I was merely offering Lady Weston a compliment when she suddenly accused me of being improper. Me! Of all people!"

"Yes," Augusta agreed. "You are usually so dull, it quite boggles the mind to think of someone accusing you of impropriety."

Harriett frowned into the darkness of the carriage. Was she really so dull, then? She knew she wasn't vivacious, like her sisters, and she had never gotten into scrapes as they had, but . . . dull? "In any case, I do not know why they acted as they did," she said in a quiet voice. "Maybe there is something in the air at Yarwood that does not agree with them."

The carriage pulled to a halt in front of the vicarage then, and Old John came round to open the door and let down the steps. Helping the two sisters to descend, he could not prevent a slight frown of disapproval from creasing his weatherbeaten face when he saw Harriett.

"The playacting was quite successful," Harriett said to him with a quick smile. "And though I wore trousers to act the part, I am sure not even Lady Weston could find fault."

"Indeed not," Augusta added quickly. "It was all of the most respectable. It is too bad Papa was not here to see. He would have enjoyed it, for he is very fond of Shakespeare."

"Yes, and it was an honor to be asked to play the part," Harriett continued, as they walked to the door. Behind her she could hear Old John grunt as he shut the door of the carriage and climbed into the driver's seat again. If he had thought they were doing anything improper, he would have felt obliged to inform Reverend Haversham.

Turning her head, Harriett watched as the carriage rounded the side of the house. She felt terribly guilty lying to Old John like that. With every lie you dig the trench of your own damnation a little deeper. That had been in one of her Papa's sermons, and it was quite true, Harriett decided, following Augusta inside.

Harriett undressed herself, declining Augusta's help, for Augusta was sure to notice that the shirt Harriett wore was not the one she had pinned in place earlier. And Harriett did not feel up to discussing what had taken place in Lord Weston's dressing room. In fact, Harriett was not sure she would ever feel up to discussing it. She smiled slightly and looked down at the shirt, slowly putting one hand over her breast as she closed her eyes, remembering the warm feel of Lord Weston's hand and the tingling response she had felt. Was that what

156

love felt like, then? Or was it no more than the base response of her flesh?

Snatching her hand away, Harriett sat down quickly on the small stool by her dressing table. She had a horrible feeling it was the latter. "I wonder if that's what Cammie feels for Tom, or if she truly loves him?" Harriett mused out loud. Turning slowly, she faced the mirror, studying the strange image that greeted her there. It did not look at all like the Harriett Haversham she had known for twenty-four years. A young man with dark hair and dreamy gray eyes stared back at her, a thin, drooping moustache slanting crookedly beneath a decided nose and . . .

Leaning forward into the candlelight, Harriett forgot about love and tingling responses as she stared in horrified fascination at her reflection. Not only were her cheeks streaked with gray from the bootblack, but her lips and tongue looked as if she had been chewing on pieces of coal. No wonder Mrs. Dade had accused her of having the plague!

Eight

"Well, well, a blushing vicar, no less," George Reading laughed, and lounged back in his chair, stretching his feet out to the fire.

Lord Weston handed his guest a glass of wine and smiled, taking the chair opposite. "When did you guess?" he asked.

"Guess? You mean when did I know? Almost immediately. All it took was one look at your horrified face to know that something was amiss. And, of course, as soon as I took a close look at Miss Haversham, it was obvious. Don't know why the others didn't catch on. One sees what one wants to see, I suppose. But to try to pass herself off as her father! Perhaps if we had never met and she claimed to be some callow youth . . ."

"Indeed. Her sister seemed much the older and more experienced of the two."

"I found Miss Augusta Haversham to be most charming," George Reading said quickly, eyebrows raised. "Sweet, and innocent. Obviously she was talked into the masquerade by her sister."

Sipping his own wine, Lord Weston glanced at his guest in amusement. "Does the land lie in that quarter, George? You had best be careful, or you will find yourself in the parson's mousetrap before ever I sniff the cheese."

"Nothing of the kind." George Reading sat up and gave his friend an indignant look. "Augusta Haversham seemed an uncommonly attractive girl with a great deal of intelligence and charm, that is all. I enjoyed her company, but I am hardly about to fling myself on my knees before her. Marriage is Horace's responsibility. That's what older brothers are for."

Lord Weston stared into the fire and sighed. "I envy you, George. A nice, tidy estate inherited from your grandmother, well managed by a local, nothing for you to do but visit once or twice a year and spend the rents."

"Dash it all, Phillip. What kind of sapskull do you think I am? As if I didn't know you relished the title and everything that goes with it. Never saw a man more interested in his land and the welfare of his tenants! Saw you just the other day, reading that book on crop rotation and manure and God alone knows what else. Yes, and do you think I don't know we're in Upper Mourouby for Easter because you thought it was time to check up on Yarwood?"

"And here I thought it was because my mother wanted to stretch my neck in the parson's noose." Lord Weston grinned at his

159

friend. "Why else do I allow myself to be surrounded by these bickering hens?"

"Because it amuses you," George Reading answered without hesitation. He relaxed into his chair once more. "And I must say that when Abigail Smalbathe accused Miss Dade of coming from a family of addlepates, it was all I could do to maintain my countenance."

"Yes, I saw you sucking in your cheeks like a stuffed grouse."

"No worse than your coughing spell when Miss Haversham, or should I say the Reverend Haversham, asked where she might go to observe birds of paradise."

Lord Weston chuckled. "I could just see her combing the neighborhood with her bag of breadcrumbs. And then, when the dye in her hair began to run down her face, and Mrs. Dade accused her of having the plague because her tongue was black from chewing on that ridiculous moustache . . ." Lord Weston's chuckle grew to a laugh as he shook his head at the memory. "Still," he sobered suddenly, "I must confess to rather liking Miss Haversham. She has none of the hardness or artificiality of the others."

"Ahhhhh, I see." George Reading gave his friend a knowing look.

"No, really, George. Much as I hate to admit it, Mama is quite right and I must marry one of these days. I am thirty-six, and it is more than time that I started my nursery. And I do begin to think someone like Miss Haversham might do very well for me."

"The older sister or the younger?" George Reading asked, stiffening up a bit.

"The older, George. No need to poker up like that. I refer to Harriett Haversham, not your precious Augusta."

"She is not my—"

"Though you know, if I am not mistaken," Lord Weston interrupted with a puzzled frown, "there is another sister as well. I wonder why she did not take part in tonight's masquerade."

George Reading finished his wine and set down his glass. "I wonder why the masquerade was deemed necessary at all. Do you suppose some sort of wager was involved?"

"Thinking too much like a man, George. No, I am not sure of the reason, but I doubt it was a wager. They are the daughters of a clergyman, after all, and while their upbringing would not necessarily preclude such a thing, I think that is not their reason."

"Then what do you suppose . . ." George Reading let his voice trail off as both men stared into the dying flames. "Do you suppose the parents know what is going on?" he continued after a moment. "They did seem to have free use of the carriage and all."

Lord Weston shrugged and stood up, stretching his long arms to the extent his tailoring would allow. "I have no idea," he said with a yawn. "But I tell you this, George, I mean to find out. Perhaps a little talk with one of my grooms concerning the Haversham coachman?"

"What, ho!" George stood up and slapped his friend on the back. "This Easter masquerade should at least liven things up a bit, don't you think?"

"And here I thought the Easter stakes were enough entertainment," Lord Weston chided.

George Reading followed his friend to the parlour door. "Easter stakes? What do you mean, Easter stakes?"

"I mean the race to snabble my title, my fortune, and my head, George. Miss Dade, Miss Smalbathe, and the Giggler were neck-and-neck for a while, but now, an unknown has entered the race."

"Hmmmm." George Reading picked up his candle from the table. "Well, Phillip," he said as he mounted the stairs, "not that I'm a betting man, but I think I'll place my blunt on the new little filly."

"The Lady Vicar?"

"The Lady Vicar," George agreed. "May she be first to the finish line."

The Lady Vicar herself was up betimes the next morning, having breakfasted by the time Augusta made an appearance.

"Whyever are you up so early?" Augusta complained, a bit grumpy before her morning coffee. "And what are you doing?" She frowned at the paper and ink Harriett was holding.

"I am going to write a letter to Mama," Harriett replied.

"You are not going to—" Augusta cried in alarm.

"No, of course not. I shall say nothing to Mama, or to anyone, for that matter, about last night. At least . . ." Harriett pursed her lips and sat down at the breakfast table opposite Augusta. "It was very bad of you to lie to me like that, Gusta."

"Harry, I did not lie precisely."

"What do you call it, then? You told me Lord Weston was to leave Yarwood early next week, yet he says he has no intention of doing so. I would never have agreed to the masquerade last night, had I known."

Augusta fortified herself with a sip of coffee. "I merely repeated what one of the Yarwood footmen said to Mary. I do not see how I can be blamed for that. And if Mary or the footman misheard and the family is not really leaving until the following week, it is hardly my fault." She gave her sister a wide-eyed look of innocence.

"It won't fadge, Gusta," Harriett said, shaking her head. "You deliberately misled me. It would be better if you simply admitted it. You know Papa is always saying confession is good for the soul."

"I have never found it so." Augusta buttered a piece of toast. "Confession is what happens when they pull out your fingernails with pinchers and force you to say something you would rather not."

"Gusta!"

"Well, it is true, Harry. And besides, I had a famous time last night and you would not have permitted us to go otherwise. Now, confess. Did you not enjoy yourself? And what do you know of Mr. Reading? Is he very rich? Lord Weston is quite old, but I thought Mr. Reading must be younger, even if they are friends. And I think he took a fancy to me, Harry. Truly. Despite the fact that I was in that shabby gown of Cammie's, when I might have been dressed to the nines, if only Papa weren't such a pennypincher."

"Gusta." Harriett sighed and rose from the table. She loved her sister, but there were times when such total self-absorption was more than she could tolerate. "Have you forgotten that Cammie is still not home, that her reputation will be quite ruined if anyone finds out?"

"That is Cammie's fault. I am only sorry that it must reflect so on the rest of us," Augusta replied stubbornly.

"And what of poor Mama, who must nurse a broken ankle among strangers?"

"I am sure I am most sorry for Mama's misfortune." Augusta spoke around a mouthful of toast. "But I believe, and I think I quote Papa on this, that one must make good out of the bad things that occur in life."

Harriett frowned at her sister. These quicksilver changes in the direction of Augusta's

164

thoughts had always left Harriett floundering to catch up. "I am sure that is true," she replied cautiously.

Augusta grinned. "I knew you would agree with me, Harry. We must go shopping at once! I shall direct Old John to bring the carriage round. Though I know you would prefer to walk, there is no telling how many packages we might have to carry." Augusta jumped up, abandoning her piece of toast and heading toward the dining room door.

"What? Where? Whatever are you talking of, Gusta? If you mean to go shopping, I must tell you, I cannot accompany you. And unless you have saved a great deal more of your pin money than usual, I do not know what you mean to go shopping with."

Sagging back against the door, Augusta allowed her eyes to fill with tears. "But Harriett, we must go now. What if Mr. Reading or . . . or Lord Weston should invite us out? I should have nothing to wear."

"Ah, I see what it is." Harriett's fingers curled around the inkjar she held. "You mean to go shopping for that velvet dress you have been coveting while Mama is not here to forbid it. For shame, Gusta. I had not thought even you so self-centered."

"Just because you do not care what you look like, and are not likely to be asked anywhere because you are such a . . . a starchy bore, is no reason to condemn me to such a fate. If

Mr. Reading asks me to go for a drive, I must have something to wear."

"You have any number of suitable dresses."

"Old ones!" Augusta sniffed, pushing away from the door as she defended herself. "Outmoded things. Mr. Reading is from London. He is used to women who dress in the first stare."

"Well, if he expects a woman to wear blue velvet for a drive in the country, his wits have gone abegging." Harriett walked to the door, paper and ink in hand, and waited with obvious impatience for her sister to step out of the way.

Augusta whipped a handkerchief from her pocket and dabbed at her eyes. "You don't—no, you won't understand, Harry."

"No. So you have told me any number of times, Augusta. Both you and Camilla. I wonder that you keep trying to make me do so. Now, if you will excuse me, I must write to Mr. Marsh, asking him to take the service for Papa this Sunday. I shall write a note to Mama as well, asking how she is doing and if she needs anything. Do you wish me to send her your regards, or do you mean to write a letter of your own?"

"I—" Augusta bit her lip and struggled to bring her temper under control. "Please give Mama my regards and tell her I hope to see her home soon." Then, remembering the maxim about bees and honey, Augusta smiled at Harriett and stepped away from the door.

* * *

Sitting down at the small writing table in the parlour, Harriett spread out her paper, placed the ink in one corner, and reached for one of the pens. Then she stared down at the blank paper in front of her, quite unable to write a word. Augusta and Camilla had always been given to outbursts, forever saying things they later regretted, and begging forgiveness.

But sometimes Harriett found it very difficult to forgive. Did Augusta not realize that she might covet a dress of blue velvet as well? Not that it would look like anything on me, Harriett thought bitterly, as a tear dropped to the paper in front of her. I am much too tall to wear such a gown, besides having freckles and red hair and Papa's nose. Still, that does not keep me from wanting such things, Gusta.

Harriett sat for a moment watching her tears drop on the paper, causing it to pucker and stain. Paper was expensive, and she had been brought up never to be wasteful. Still, she could not stop herself from crying. Though I know Gusta does not mean to be hurtful, she told herself. I do not know why I am allowing myself to be so upset. Now it is you who are lying, Harriett chided herself. For in truth, she knew quite well why she was crying. It was because of Lord Weston. Harriett had allowed herself to develop a tendre for the man, it was a simple as that.

Harriett sniffed, and reached for her handkerchief. Giving her nose a good blow, she sat back in the small mahogany chair and acknowledged the truth of it. That was why she had been so willing to participate in Augusta's masquerade. Because she wanted to see Lord Weston again. Because she hoped to find out what he thought of her.

"A bit long in the tooth to be considering marriage . . . content to devote herself to good works." Harriett whispered the words Lord Weston had spoken. She had been angry at the time, but now all she felt was despair.

Putting down her pen, Harriett ran her fingers through her short, thick curls. She had gotten up early that morning to wash the last of the boot black from her hair. And she was back in her skirts again as well, though she rather missed the freedom permitted by her Papa's trousers.

Someday I shall be able to look back on all this and laugh, she told herself. But now, remembering how awful she had looked last night: the gray cheeks, the horrible hair, that wretched moustache, she could only put her hands to her flaming cheeks in embarrassment. I do not see how I fooled anyone, Harriett thought, though no one seemed to suspect. Which was a good thing. To act such a figure of fun in front of Lord Weston! Her face went from red to white as she thought of the consequences if they had been discovered.

Yes, and they were not out of the home woods by any means. Lord Weston must still be told that Reverend Haversham was indisposed and that Mr. Marsh was taking his place. And somehow, once Papa returned, they must contrive to keep him from calling upon Lord Weston. Though how this was to be accomplished was more than Harriett knew, for her Papa was quite meticulous about such things.

And then there is the egg-rolling Easter afternoon, Harriett thought, looking out the long window that faced the garden. Papa always presides over that, and Lord Weston has said he is looking forward to viewing it. They are bound to meet, and then what? Harriett sat up, her tears having dried upon her cheeks, and reached for her pen again. Sufficient unto the day are the troubles therein, she decided, as she pulled the tearstained paper closer.

First Harriett penned a note to Mr. Marsh, explaining that the Reverend Haversham was indisposed and asking him to please take the service on Palm Sunday. Mr. Marsh was a very nice, obliging young man, and since he also was sweet on Augusta, Harriett had no worry that he would not agree.

Next, Harriett wrote to her parents at the inn. There was a great deal of second thought and crossing out in this letter, and in the end, Harriett found it necessary to copy the whole thing out again. Still, she felt quite satisfied with the result. While expressing her concern and hope that Camilla had been found and that her dear Mama was not in much pain, Harriett still managed to suggest that it might be best if they postponed their return for a few days. The roads were rutted from the rain and cold, which would result in much discomfort for poor Mama, and there was no need to hurry, since Mr. Marsh had things well in hand.

Sitting back with her lips pressed together and her brows drawn into a frown of concentration, Harriett reread her letter. Then, with a nod of approval, she folded it, sealed it, and went to fetch Old John. He would find someone from the village who was going in that direction and would deliver it for a few pence. It would be faster and more reliable than the mails.

"Ah, Miss Harriett," Mary called, as Harriett crossed the back hall on her way to the yard. "I've cleaned and pressed that shirt like you said, but what was you wantin' me to do with it?" The maid held out Lord Weston's shirt, neatly pressed and folded. "It's very fine material, miss, but so small it would never fit the Reverend Haversham. Was you wantin' me to store it in one of the chests, then?"

Harriett shook her head. Though she had not been consciously thinking of the cambric shirt, she would admit to not having completely forgotten it, either. Last night, as the shirt had hung like a ghostly form upon the back of her bedroom chair, Harriett had realized with a happy rush of excitement that it would afford an excellent excuse for returning to Yarwood. And for seeing Lord Weston again.

"I shall return it to Yarwood, Mary."

"Return it to Yarwood, Miss? Oh, it was part of that masquerade then?" Mary grinned. "It sounded like ever so much fun. Did anyone guess it was you?"

"No," Harriett said, breathing a silent prayer of thanks.

"Not even Lord Weston, after you borrowed his shirt, Miss?"

Harriett's cheeks flamed. "It was his valet fetched it for me, Mary. And, of course, I did not say that I would be the one to wear it. Now, if you will but tie it up in some paper," she continued, forestalling any more questions, "I shall take it across to Yarwood."

"Yes, Miss, though it does seem a bit strange, you runnin' such errands when you could be sendin' me."

Though she had been growing increasingly irritated, not so much by Mary's comments as by the gaping holes they exposed in the story Augusta had pieced together, Harriett smiled. "I know full well you would like to meet with your footman, Mary. And you have my permission to do so this evening. Only do remind him that in the future he should make sure of his facts before repeating them. I was quite embarrassed to find that Lord Weston and his guests would be remaining until Easter after all."

"Yes, Miss Harriett? But, beggin' your pardon, I don't see as how that has anythin' to do with my John," Mary said, looking puzzled. "Why, he's that quiet he barely says a word, which is fine with me, prattlin' on as I do. But I don't remember him repeatin' anythin' with facts in an' all."

Harriett pursed her lips and tapped her fingers thoughtfully on the letters she carried. "Well, perhaps I am mistaken," she said at last. "In any case, if you will bring me the shirt when it is wrapped, I shall take it to Yarwood myself."

After sending Old John off to the village with the letters, Harriett went to her room and threw open the doors of her wardrobe. She had every intention of selecting her prettiest, most feminine frock to wear when she delivered Lord Weston's shirt. She did not often bother overmuch about what she wore, and so her gowns were hardly on a par with those of her sisters. Still, there was the muslin dress she had gotten last year and hardly worn. It was of a lovely pale canary yellow, which Harriett fancied was quite becoming. And her pelisse, though of a rather dull gray, was new, and trimmed with velvet.

Mary knocked on the door and brought in Lord Weston's shirt, neatly wrapped in brown paper. "Oh, but you do look nice, Miss Harriett," she exclaimed.

"Do you think so?" Harriett asked, frowning at her image in the cheval glass mirror. She always thought the raised waist made her look even taller than she was, and much preferred the natural waistline that had prevailed several years earlier.

"Indeed, Miss." Mary nodded. "And I do think your hair looks ever so nice short like that."

Harriett tugged at a wayward curl. "It is no longer in style, Mary, but," Harriett tilted her head to one side and studied her reflection, "I think I rather like it, too. Which is a good thing, is it not?" Harriett studied herself a moment longer. Vanity of vanities, she thought, but could not help herself. For once she looked almost pretty. No, she told herself firmly, I look quite pretty. And with a giggle to rival Miss Smalbathe's, Harriett turned from the mirror, took up Lord Weston's shirt, and set out for Yarwood.

By the time Harriett had walked through the home woods and across the path that led to Lord Weston's front door, however, her self-confidence had begun to evaporate. Having spent many an evening at the local assemblies sitting alone, Harriett was quite aware that while she might look good enough in her way, beside such beauties as her sisters or Miss Dade, she might as well be part of the wallpaper. At least, as far as the gentlemen were concerned.

It is no use fooling yourself, Harriett, she told herself. Lord Weston is not interested in you, except perhaps as a quaint eccentric whose story he might relate to amuse his guests. She banged the door knocker with a bit more force than necessary and stood back, feeling quite down and just a bit ridiculous. If anyone should find out she had worn her best finery on the chance that she would meet Lord Weston . . .

"Yes?" It was Miss Dade, looking quite splendid in a gown of lavender zephyrine ornamented with little rosettes of ribbon.

Harriett's spirits sank even lower. Next to Miss Dade, no one would know Harriett had taken any special pains with her appearance at all.

"Good morning, Miss Dade," Harriett said politely, though the other woman kept her waiting on the step. "I have come to leave a package for Lord Weston."

Miss Dade's eyes flicked quickly over Harriett. It was quite obvious that she was trying to decide whether or not to direct Harriett to the servant's entrance.

"My father, Reverend Haversham, and my sister were guests here last night," Harriett said, and took a step forward. Though she was naturally rather shy and timid, Harriett could not abide rudeness, and Miss Dade's toplofty manner had sparked her temper. Harriett might not be beautiful or a member of the ton, but she would not be kept waiting on the doorstep. "I believe Lord Weston is expecting me," she said. Which was not true at all, for Lord Weston had said nothing about returning his shirt, and in fact, had appeared to forget its existence.

Miss Dade moved back a pace and allowed Harriett to step into the hallway. "You can give

174

the package to me," she said coldly. "There is no reason to bother Lord Weston."

"Oh?" This time it was Harriett who allowed her eyes to flick quickly over Miss Dade. "Forgive me," she said. "I had thought you one of the guests, not one of the maids whose job it is to fetch and carry." Harriett would ordinarily have said nothing, but meekly handed over the parcel and departed. However, she had decided she did not like Miss Dade overmuch, and if that was a sin, which it probably was, Harriett did not care.

"Do I look like one of the servants?" Miss Dade snapped, glaring at Harriett.

Harriett tilted her head to one side as if she were giving the matter some thought. "Not really," she replied at last, "but then, you did answer the door, and you are running errands for Lord Weston, and . . . your manners are not what one would expect from a gentlewoman."

Miss Dade's small hands curled into fists. "Who do you think you are, to speak to me in this fashion?" she demanded.

"Harriett Haversham. We have met before, Miss Dade, but perhaps you have forgot?"

"Obviously." Miss Dade raised her brows. "At any rate, if you know who I am, you know you may also entrust the package to me. Westie, that is, Lord Weston," she smiled at Harriett in a superior way, "would not mind, I assure you."

No, Harriett was quite sure Westie would not

mind, but she did. She had come apurpose so that she might see him again. It might be foolish . . . well, of course, it was, but—

"Ah, Miss Harriett."

"Mr. Beauchamp." Harriett curtsied to Lord Weston's estate manager, a small, dapper man who looked as if he would be more at home in the city than on a country estate. "How nice to see you. And how are Mrs. Beauchamp and Betsy?" she asked.

Mr. Beauchamp bowed politely to Miss Dade and then stepped forward to greet Harriett, casting a curious glance at the oak door which still stood open to the outside portico and cool spring air. "Mrs. Beauchamp is fussing about having enough dried apples for the Palm Sunday Pax cakes, and Betsy is up and about again after her attack of the rheumatics. She caught a rat out beyond Farmer Greeve's barn, in fact, just yesterday. Like to have played with it all morning, but of course, I wouldn't let her."

Harriett sucked in her cheeks and glanced at Miss Dade from the corners of her eyes.

"A rat?" Miss Dade asked, eyes wide. "Betsy caught a rat?"

Mr. Beauchamp nodded. "Pranced around just like a pup afterward, and here she is, going on ten years or more. Still, she always feels better when the weather turns warm and she can stretch out in the sun."

"I'm sure." Miss Dade's smile was a small one. "Well, I'm afraid I do not have time to be gossiping upon doorsteps. If you will give me the package, Miss Haversham?" She reached forward and all but snatched the wrapped parcel from Harriett's gloved hands.

"Miss Dade!" Harriett fought down a strong urge to grab the package back, but she would not resort to such a brangle. "I would appreciate it if you would see that Lord Weston receives it," she said coldly. "Though I would have preferred to give it to him myself."

"Heavens," Miss Dade tittered. "You don't imagine I would steal it, do you? Why, whatever would I do with . . ." she stopped and toyed with the string that secured the brown paper, ". . . with whatever is in it."

Harriett pressed her lips together. It would be unchristian as well as most unladylike to say what she was thinking.

"I'm afraid Lord Weston is not at home, in any case, Miss Harriett," Mr. Beauchamp said kindly. "I imagine you wanted to ask about using the library while he is here? You need not worry, for I am quite certain he will grant you the use of it. Lord Weston is a most generous man. And when I went up to speak to him in London last year, I mentioned that I had allowed you and Reverend Haversham the use of it. He seemed most happy with the arrangement."

"It was good of you to speak to him of the matter," Harriett said, her eyes still on the parcel held by Miss Dade. "As you know, His Lordship's library is a source of much enjoyment to us."

"Yes, yes, well—ah, my coat." Mr. Beauchamp turned as the butler brought his coat and hat. "Thank you, thank you. I'm afraid it is still a bit chilly. You will tell Lord Weston that I called, then?" he asked, as the butler helped him into his coat. "And my carriage? Ah, yes, I hear it, thank you. Now, please tell your father that I shall call upon him soon regarding the eggs for the children, Miss Harriett," Mr. Beauchamp said, turning back to her again. "Lord Weston relayed your request to me, and I shall see that all is taken care of."

"Thank you." Harriett smiled. She must forget Miss Dade and think of more charitable things. "The children always enjoy the Easter eggs so."

"Indeed, yes." Mr. Beauchamp turned to the large oak door where the butler was waiting. "And when do you expect Reverend Haversham to return, Miss Harriett? I understand he left early this week with Mrs. Haversham to visit an aunt. He shall certainly be back in time for Sunday service, I expect?"

Harriett blushed, her face taking on the expression of a doe cornered by a pack of dogs. "Um . . . he . . . I think . . ."

"But surely Reverend Haversham returned yesterday?" Miss Dade, who had turned away with every intention of slipping off to her room with Harriett's package, stepped back to the doorway. "He was a guest of Lord Weston's last night."

"Oh, well, that's a good thing, then. I shall

call upon him this afternoon, if it's convenient," Mr. Beauchamp said.

"No! I mean . . . Papa is ill," Harriett improvised quickly. "Yes. He is in bed, not receiving visitors."

Mr. Beauchamp frowned. "Must be something in the air. Mrs. Beauchamp is always saying this changeable weather is not healthy. I understand Miss Dade's mother is also not well."

"Ah, but that is some kind of mental condition," Harriett said, before she could stop herself. "Papa has a bad cold, is all." Harriett bit her lip. Her papa would be most displeased with her. Lies, backbiting remarks . . . and the worst thing was, Harriett felt no remorse at all. She stepped outside and paused beside Mr. Beauchamp's carriage.

"May I offer you a ride home, Miss Harriett?" Mr. Beauchamp offered.

"No, it is but a short walk through the woods, thank you."

Mr. Beauchamp nodded. "Do tell Reverend Haversham that I have asked after him, and that I am most sorry he is ill. I am afraid Lord Weston will be disappointed also."

"Lord Weston?" Harriett asked, looking up as Mr. Beauchamp mounted into the driver's seat and took up the reins.

"Indeed, yes," Mr. Beauchamp replied. "Lord Weston was not at home because he had gone to call upon your father."

Harriett heard a bird call nearby, though how

anyone could sing when such devastation had suddenly been visited upon the earth was more than she knew. Lord Weston was calling upon her father? What if the servants told him the truth? What if . . . oh, dear, what if he spoke to Augusta?

Mr. Beauchamp watched in some bewilderment as Harriett suddenly turned and bolted down the path through the home woods.

Nine

It was considered most unladylike to run, as Mrs. Haversham had often told Harriett, when in youthful exuberance her daughter had engaged in such an activity. Therefore it was fortunate that Mrs. Haversham was not there to see her daughter gallop unheedingly down the path, skirts lifted disgracefully high, bonnet hanging down her back, pelisse unbuttoned and whipping along behind.

Her breath coming in short gasps, Harriett rounded the corner near the small meadow where she always fed Rusty Brown. She had brought her bread crumbs, as always, but there was no time to stop. Lord Weston could be conversing with Augusta at this very moment, and who knew what story her sister might invent to satisfy his lordship.

Still, the thought of Rusty Brown waiting hungrily for his breakfast stirred Harriett's sympathetic heart, and she decided the few minutes it would take to run to the meadow and fling the breadcrumbs on the ground could hardly matter.

Slowing down slightly—it would not do to turn one's ankle on a tree root—Harriett veered off the path and into the woods, ducking the tree branches that seemed suddenly intent on poking out her eyes and tangling her hair. It was muddy. She had worn her good slippers, which would be utterly ruined, and drat! her pelisse had caught on a branch, resulting in a most ominous ripping sound. Still, Harriett did not hesitate, but burst breathlessly into the clearing amidst a great flurry of wings.

"Oh!" Harriett exclaimed, dropping her skirts and putting her hands in front of her eyes as it seemed an explosion of feathers was taking place at her feet.

"Miss Haversham."

"Oh." Harriett said again, and stood there panting and quite thoroughly disheveled, staring into Lord Weston's amused eyes.

He rose from the tree trunk upon which he had been seated, looking as impeccable as always in a black cloak and high crowned beaver. Harriett took a deep breath and let it go in a sigh of relief. Lord Weston had not yet called at the parsonage, then. There was no need to hurry. Quickly, and as unobtrusively as possible, Harriett ran her fingers through her curls and straightened her pelisse, thinking all the while that she had never seen Lord Weston look so darkly handsome before.

"Good morning, Miss Haversham." Lord

Weston removed his hat and bowed slightly. "You are certainly out early. Have you come to feed your rooks?"

"Yes, um . . ." Harriett was trying desperately to untie her bonnet strings without appearing to do so. Since they had become quite hopelessly knotted and were threatening to strangle her, it was a rather difficult task. "I . . . um . . . hope Lady Weston is well?"

"So do I, Miss Haversham. But since my mother chose to breakfast in her room, I have not had a chance to ascertain her health. I hope you have recovered from the indisposition that prevented you from attending my dinner party last evening."

"Oh, well . . . um . . ." Harriett stared cross-eyed down at her snarled ribbons.

"May I help you with that, Miss Haversham?" Lord Weston asked.

Harriett looked up, startled to find Lord Weston standing so close she was afforded an excellent view of the silk frog which fastened his cloak.

"You will never be able to unknot those yourself," he continued, putting his gloved hand over hers as it tugged at the knotted ribbons.

Harriett's hand went still, her fingers feeling quite paralyzed, as was the breath in her throat. She stopped staring at the silk frog and tilted back her head to look into Lord Weston's face. His dark eyes smiled down at her and then suddenly stopped smiling and grew darker still.

For a moment they stood thus, and it was as if the world stopped spinning and all grew still.

Then, blushing furiously, Harriett snatched her hand away and would have stepped back. Only she could not. Lord Weston held her bonnet ribbons and she was his captive. Eyes on his gloved hand, Harriett felt herself grow warm, then cold, then warm again. It was quite improper for her to be here in such close proximity to Lord Weston, or to any man, for that matter. Still, there was nothing she could do about it. Lord Weston would not let her go. And he was only trying to help. As he had said, she would never be able to unsnarl the ribbons herself. Besides, there was no one there to see them.

Harriett raised her eyes to the top of Lord Weston's bent head. He had left his hat beside the tree trunk, and Harriett felt a little jolt to her heart at the sight of his thick, dark hair. Clenching her hands at her sides, Harriett fought down the urge to lose her fingers in his black curls, to smooth the strands that had been displaced when he'd removed his hat. Instead, she closed her eyes and stood quite still for a moment, inhaling the spicy, cinnamon scent of him and giving herself up quite utterly to the pleasure of his closeness.

"There." His words whispered against her cheek, and Lord Weston stepped back, leaving Harriett feeling quite bereft. She opened her eyes and blinked. It was like being rudely awakened from a pleasant dream and wanting nothing so much as to fall back to sleep again. But, of course, she could not.

Pressing her lips together, Harriett forced herself to step back as well. "Thank you," she said, bending her head to retie the ribbons beneath her chin.

"You are most welcome." Lord Weston walked back to the fallen tree trunk and retrieved his hat. "I am afraid I have been before you in feeding Rusty Brown." He indicated the empty bag on the ground. "I hope you do not mind?"

"No, of course not," she replied, and then stood there awkwardly unable to think of anything else to say. Fortunately, Rusty Brown was still hungry and began to caw quite loudly from a nearby tree. Harriett smiled.

"Caw, yourself," she told the bird, and turning, reached into her bag of crumbs and threw a handful into the clearing. Not only Rusty Brown, but a bold warbler and several wrens as well flew down to partake of this largesse.

"Ah, I am jealous," Lord Weston said, observing the birds. "My offering was eaten, but not with such enthusiasm. Is it that they know you for a friend?"

Harriett shook her head. "I am afraid the birds resemble their human counterparts too much for that," she said. "No, it is not my friendship they value, but Cook's stale muffins, which contain raisins and nuts. If you but improve your offering, the birds will give you the same enthusiastic greeting."

185

"I shall speak to the cook at Yarwood, who dared give me only the finest bread," he replied with an air of false gravity.

"Yes, but . . ." Harriett turned away, her eyes sweeping the greening treetops that edged the clearing. "Do you think it wrong to feed birds when so many people are without food?"

Lord Weston shrugged. "A piece of bread or two, or even a stale muffin with raisins, will not solve the country's woes, Miss Haversham. For that, one must work in Parliament to see that laws are changed."

"And you . . . ?"

"I do my duty in Parliament, Miss Haversham, and contribute to private charities as well. And I know you also do your part by visiting the poor and seeking to educate their children."

"Yet, the poor are always with us."

"You quote Scripture to me," Lord Weston said with a smile. "I believe it is St. John, is it not?"

Harriett nodded, feeling a certain happiness fill her breast that he had recognized her remark as such. "It is a favorite quotation of my papa's when I lament that what I do seems to make so little difference."

"Your father has taught you well."

"Yes." Harriett looked down at a small patch of wood sorrel blooming at her feet and smiled, bending down to touch one white petal gently with her fingertip. "Papa takes his vocation very seriously. He believes one must live what one professes, and yet . . ." Harriett straightened and frowned slightly, as if she had never considered the matter before. "And yet, Papa never is preachy or . . . or belabors the point, you know?"

"And so will never earn the epithet 'Stiff Rump'?"

Harriett blushed and bit her lip. "No," she said, tilting her chin slightly. "Papa would never be accused of that."

"After last night, I well believe it."

"What do you mean?" Harriett bristled, rushing to her father's defense.

"Merely that he seemed a gracious gentleman, not at all stiff or unbending, Miss Haversham. What did you think I meant?"

"Nothing—that is, I did not know. And I am sure that you are not deserving of such an epithet, either," Harriett finished in a rush.

Lord Weston gave her a small bow. "Thank you, Miss Haversham. And may I, in my gratitude for your faith in me, presume to point out a lovely patch of primrose to your left."

Turning in the direction he indicated, Harriett could not keep a little gasp of pleasure from escaping her lips. The primroses stood in a patch of sunlight filtered by the overhanging trees, their yellow blossoms shining brightly in the ever-greening grass of the meadow. "How lovely," she exclaimed on an indrawn breath. "They look quite like small patches of sunshine themselves, do they not?"

"Yes," Lord Weston agreed beside her. "And

soon we shall be delighted by the sight of wild hyacinths, and the apple orchard behind Yarwood will burst into blossom."

"Spring is my favorite time of year," Harriett said softly.

"My brother Robert died in the springtime," Lord Weston said, a small frown drawing his dark brows together.

"Oh, I am so sorry." Harriett looked up at him, her gray eyes wide in sympathy. "I regret to say I did not even know you had a brother, but I know what a loss I should feel if one of my sisters . . ." Her voice trailed away. They were all so concerned with Camilla disgracing herself, afraid that she would never now be able to make an advantageous marriage, that she would ruin herself as well as the Haversham name. And yet beside Lord Weston's loss, this seemed such a little thing.

"It happened many years ago," Lord Weston said, his voice quiet and reflective. "Robert was eight to my eleven. I was away at school at the time. It was . . . it was so strange, coming home to find him gone, as if he had never existed."

"What happened?"

"He drowned. In the lake, at one end of a small estate that belongs to my mother's family in Sheffield. He wasn't supposed to be there, of course, but . . . we think he fell and hit his head. My father was devastated. My mother . . . well, it is all a long time ago now, as I said." Lord Weston turned and looked down at Harriett. "But I still think of him at springtime because it was Robert's favorite time of year as well."

Harriett nodded. There was little that one could say, after all, and so she reached out and put her hand upon his arm in a gesture of quiet sympathy. They stood for a moment thus and then Lord Weston took her hand and brought it to his lips, the gesture quite without any desire or impropriety, but a simple, silent thank-you.

"There is a blackbird's nest near the turn in the path," Lord Weston said. "Robert was always the first to discover such things, which always irritated me, since I was the elder. Let me show it to you?" He still held her hand between his own, and he pressed it slightly, as if he would persuade her to agree.

"Of course," Harriett said. "If you promise not to disturb it, like some horrid little boys I know."

"Never," Lord Weston vowed solemnly. "In fact, I am quite hurt that you think I might consider such a thing."

Lord Weston released her hand then, much to Harriett's disappointment, and she stopped to empty the remaining crumbs from her bag, before following him to the path.

"I saw it right along here," Lord Weston said, carefully scrutinizing the bushes that grew a few feet from the path. "There, that gorse bush. Do you see it in that little fork? It is made of moss, and the mother bird is sitting upon it, daring us to interfere."

"Yes." Harriett nodded, noting the bright eyes of the mother blackbird staring at them in disapproval. "But I would never have noticed it unless you had shown it to me."

"Now that we have shared this, there is a bond between us, Miss Haversham."

"Is there?" Harriett asked, glancing up at him shyly. Why was he speaking so intimately to her? Was he merely teasing, flirting with her?

Lord Weston looked away and suddenly stepped back, putting a space between them so that Harriett felt the cool breeze she had not noticed before. "Yes." He answered her question rather brusquely. "There is always a bond between people who share a love of nature."

Harriett pressed her lips together. There was a tightness in her throat, and for some reason she felt suddenly close to tears. "Yet you reside much of the year in London, do you not?" she asked, her tone that of a polite stranger.

"My mother prefers it. Most of her friends are in residence during the Season, and she enjoys the round of parties and social events. I always try to oblige her by acting as her escort, since I am there when Parliament is in session, in any case."

It was almost as if he were emphasizing the difference in their social standing, Harriett thought, with a small frown of resentment. Well, the Havershams might not be peers of the realm but they were of good family. Her father was related by marriage to the second son of the Duke of Argyle, and they were distant cousins of Sir Reginal Freemantle. Lord Weston had no right to speak to her in so condescending a manner, as if she had no knowledge of society.

"I'm afraid I must be going, Lord Weston," Harriett said, tilting her chin ever so slightly and busying herself with straightening the strings of her reticule.

"Yes," Lord Weston agreed. "I should not have kept you here talking when I know you must be anxious to return home with your father so ill."

"You have called at the parsonage?" Harriett asked, her heart suddenly lurching in her breast. "I don't suppose . . . you didn't talk to my sister, did you?" There was just a chance Augusta had still been abed.

"A charming girl," Lord Weston said, dashing her hopes. "But obviously quite upset at this sudden change in your father's condition."

"What sudden change?" Harriett demanded. "That is, has Papa taken a turn for the worse?" Oh dear, Harriett thought. That sounded quite as if they expected poor Papa to expire at any moment.

"All I know is that your sister looked quite grave and your mother dared not leave his side to speak to me."

"Yes, Papa's cold has, ah . . . settled in his chest. I have only left for a few minutes to . . ."

Good heavens, what possible excuse could there be for leaving when Augusta has made Papa sound so desperately ill, Harriett wondered.

"A bit of fresh air after having sat up with him all night?" Lord Weston supplied.

"Yes, of course," Harriett agreed, quickly.

"And you so recently recovered yourself." Lord Weston shook his head and sucked in his cheeks as if he could not bear the nobleness of it all.

"And I so recently recovered," Harriett repeated, frowning over the words as she tried to make sense of them. "I'm afraid my fever must have affected my memory."

"Only yesterday you were too ill to attend my dinner party," Lord Weston told her, "and it was necessary for your mother to remain behind to care for you. Did they cut your hair because of the fever?"

Harriett nodded, one hand going up to the wispy curls that escaped from the brim of her bonnet. "Do you like it?" she asked.

"Most becoming," he assured her.

Harriett smiled, her dimples appearing enchantingly beside her mouth. "Thank you," she said simply. "But I had really best be going now. I must find out what Augusta is up to. I mean, concerning Papa, of course."

"They may need you," Lord Weston said gravely.

"Yes." Harriett turned away and then turned quickly back. "Lord Weston?"

"Yes, Miss Haversham?"

"I would not have you think that my family is usually beset by illness like this. We are rarely sick at all."

"It is the plague, Miss Haversham," Lord Weston agreed. "I understand it is going around just now."

Augusta was lounging upon the settee in the parlour, eating chocolates and frowning over a picture in *The Lady's Magazine*, when Harriett arrived home. "You know, I do not like this fringed shawl at all," she told Harriett, as soon as her sister entered the parlour. "I do not care if it is the fashion, I shall never wear the like."

"I am gratified to hear it, Augusta. But perhaps we might speak of something else, such as Lord Weston's call?" Still clad in her pelisse and bonnet, Harriett sat down on the chair opposite. "Exactly what did he say, and what did you tell him?" she demanded.

Augusta sucked a bit of chocolate from her finger before replying. "I simply told Lord Weston that Papa's cold had become worse, and that Mama was nursing him. Do you think Mama will notice that I have eaten several of her chocolates? I did not mean to, since it is still Lent and we are supposed to forgo such things, but she will leave the box upon the table."

"Augusta, you have convinced Lord Weston

that Papa is gravely ill. What a bumblebath this will cause when Papa returns."

"Well, I did consider telling Lord Weston that Papa had been shot by highwaymen on the way home last night," Augusta offered. "But then I thought better of it."

"Good," Harriett said, absently reaching for a chocolate herself.

"Yes, for this works out much better, you know, and will quite explain why our cousin must conduct the service this Sunday."

Harriett gasped, choked on the chocolate, and began coughing quite violently. "Cousin?" she managed in a hoarse voice. "What cousin?"

"Our cousin the curate," Augusta said, frowning at Harriett. "Are you quite all right? Your face is all red and your freckles are showing most unbecomingly. And don't you think you should take off your pelisse?"

"I may not be staying," Harriett told her. "I may have to leave the country, in fact. Augusta, as far as I know, we do not have a cousin who is a curate."

"No, but that is not to say we never will. There is Cousin Isholm, after all."

"Cousin Isholm is three," Harriett pointed out.

"But you must admit, a rather solemn child."

"That is beside the point, Augusta. I have been away from the house no more than," Harriett glanced at the mantel clock, "no more than an hour or so, and I find that you have

quite landed us in the briars with your out-
landish tales."

"I?" Augusta looked quite amazed by her sister's accusations. "Really, Harriett, I should
think you would thank me for having such
presence of mind. Lord Weston called and
asked to speak to Papa. What would you have
had me say? Certainly not the truth?" She
looked at Harriett with eyebrows raised.

Harriett lowered her eyes. "No," she agreed.
"It is just that now Lord Weston thinks Papa
is gravely ill with the plague, and I do not see
how your saying we have a cousin who is a curate will do anything to improve matters."

"Well, I only said it because of this," Augusta
said defensively, reaching beneath the chocolate
box to retrieve a folded note. "It is from Mr.
Marsh," she explained, as Harriett unfolded it.
"That is, it is not precisely from Mr. Marsh,
for he is not at home, which is most unfortunate, seeing as how we had been depending
upon him for the Palm Sunday service. But
that cannot be helped now, and in any case, he
is not at home and will, in fact, be away until
Easter."

Ignoring her sister's prattle, Harriett unfolded Mr. Marsh's note and read it for herself.
What Augusta said was quite true. Mr. Marsh
was away visiting relatives.

"It does seem an odd time to be gone, don't
you think?" Augusta asked. "For Mr. Marsh
usually assists Papa at Easter."

"Yes." Harriett read the note over once

again, but the words, written in the unformed letters of the curate's housekeeper, gave no further information. "Perhaps one of his relatives is ill," she hazarded a guess.

"The plague?" Augusta asked.

"I hardly think—oh, you are funning me. I am sorry, Augusta. I know you think me a prosy dragon, but I cannot help but be worried. Mama left me in charge and with every falsehood, we seem to need three more to explain the first."

Augusta turned a page of her periodical. "Ah, now, that is much more the thing. Do you not think so, Harriett? I should look quite stunning in such a gown."

"Augusta, have you not heard a word?"

Augusta sighed and slouched down on the settee. "Yes, of course, I have. But I told you. I have taken care of everything. I do not see why you are carrying on so, Harriett. The curate shall conduct the service tomorrow, if Papa does not return. And when or if Lord Weston and Papa do meet, we may say Papa looks so changed because of his illness. It shall all work out quite well. Would you like this chocolate? I really cannot abide the caramel centers."

"Well, I suppose . . ." Harriett took the chocolate without thinking and began to chew on it. "But who is the curate you have asked to conduct the service tomorrow? Do I know him? And why have you said he is our cousin? Surely, that was not necessary, Augusta."

"I thought it necessary to explain the resemblance. Would Mama let me wear a gown with such a décolletage, do you think?"

"No. What resemblance, Augusta?" Harriett asked, not quite sure that she wanted to hear the answer.

"The resemblance to Papa. Everyone remarks on how much you take after him."

Harriett nodded. "I am the curate," she said, as if she had always known it.

"Of course," Augusta agreed with a smile.

Lord Weston sat down opposite George Reading, thankful that no one else had decided to join them for the cold collation set out for their nuncheon. "I tell you, I came close to declaring myself," he told his friend. "When we stood there looking at the blackbird's nest and she had this look in her eyes, both tender and curious, it was all I could do not to ask her if she would do me the honor. I could not, of course. I must speak to her father first."

"And we are not sure where he is." George Reading said the words as a statement of fact rather than a question.

"No. I could find out easily enough, I suppose. But I am sure he will be returned by tomorrow. It is Palm Sunday, after all, and Reverend Haversham was never one to shirk his duties."

"Hmmmm." George Reading cut himself a piece of meat pie and sat back. "You know, Phillip, if I didn't know better, I would almost say you were head-over-ears in love with the girl."

Lord Weston stopped with a piece of ham halfway to his mouth. "In love? I never said that." He continued eating the ham, chewing thoughtfully for a moment. "I find her attractive, mind, but love? I mean, I am hardly mooning about like poor Riverton when he first became attached to that Nedwick chit. I am not like that, George. It is just that I feel Harriett Haversham will make me a suitable wife, is all. A conformable, suitable marriage partner who will be able to manage my household, see to my comfort and be a good mother to my children."

"Not knocked all cock-a-hoop at all," George agreed.

"No. Did I tell you what she said when I told her about Robert?"

"Twice."

Lord Weston nodded. "It meant a lot to me, knowing that she understood how I felt—how, in fact, I still feel. And the flowers, did I tell you how excited she got about the patch of primrose?"

"Her whole face lit up." George reached over and helped himself to some of the ham, looking bored.

"Try talking about primroses to someone like Miss Dade," Lord Weston suggested. "She won't know what you're talking about, or else she'll say she has a gown that exact color which is most becoming."

"I understand her mother intends to leave."

"Says we're all doomed," Lord Weston agreed. "Only wish the daughter would go with her."

"Tsk, tsk. And here I thought you appreciated the beauties of nature," George Reading chided.

"Pitching it much too brown, George. Do you intend to eat that entire meat pie by yourself?" He pointed across the table with his knife.

"I thought I'd make the attempt, yes. And then, if you promise not to prose on about your lady love, I will allow you to take me fishing."

"Maybe we can catch something for dinner," Lord Weston agreed, cutting himself another piece of ham.

"Or at least, enjoy a comfortable doze until tea." George Reading dug into the remains of the meat pie.

"And I do not prose on about my lady love."

"Of course not." George lifted his glass and washed down the meat pie with a bit of home brew. "In any case, you have quite convinced me she is not your lady love at all, but merely an agreeable acquaintance."

Ten

Harriett steadfastly refused to consider Augusta's plans for yet another masquerade.

"It simply will not do, Gusta," she said, as they sat down to their dinner of boiled cod. "It was one thing, and a rather foolhardy thing, now I think on it, to pretend to be someone else for a dinner party. But I will not masquerade as a curate for worship services. It would be—it would be beyond anything wrong."

"You are worried that the villagers would recognize you." Augusta nodded. "But I have had the most famous notion! We could—"

"No, Augusta. It is not merely a matter of being recognized, though I do not see how someone like Mrs. Micklewaithe could fail to know me, when I have called upon her several times a week this past month and more."

"People see only what they want to see," Augusta observed. "After all, Lord Weston had met you before, had he not? And yet he believed you were Papa because that is who he was expecting to see. Now, if you were to dress like Mr. Marsh and wear Papa's vestments and—"

"No, Augusta!" Harriett said for the second time, putting down her fork with a decided thump. "I have told you, it is not just being recognized that bothers me. I could not conduct a worship service, it is quite impossible. There are the Pax cakes to be given out, and Papa always celebrates Holy Communion on Palm Sunday. You know I could not do that."

Augusta pushed a bit of boiled cod around her plate and frowned. "I suppose not," she said regretfully. "Though it does seem a shame, when I had everything planned out so well. I do not know what we shall do if Papa does not return this evening, which he is unlikely to do. For even if he does find Camilla, Mama will not want to travel with her broken ankle. And everyone in Upper Mourouby knows Papa would not remain abed on such an important day unless he were deathly ill, so we shall have everyone wondering and gossiping and sending offerings of food and such."

At this thought Augusta sat up and smiled. "Someone from Yarwood might even send some of those chocolate biscuits we had with tea. What an excellent notion. They were quite delicious. Did you have one, Harriett? When Mr. Reading saw how fond of them I was, he made sure I had the last two, which quite put Miss Dade's nose out of joint. So you see, Harriett, it does not do to sink into a fit of the dismals. Everything will come right in the end. One day's evil is more than sufficient. Isn't that what Papa always says?"

"Something like that," Harriett agreed, though she was not able to dismiss her own worries quite so easily. When she had walked by the church earlier, she had stopped to peek inside and had seen Mrs. Beauchamp and some of the village ladies decorating the altar with spring flowers and catkins. Two potted palms, doubtless borrowed from Lord Weston's forcing house, had been placed on either side of the chancel in honor of the day as well. Yet without Mr. Marsh or Papa there could be no Palm Sunday service.

Still, it was silly to be worrying over something that she could do nothing about, Harriett told herself firmly. Augusta was right about that. And after supper, she would go to the church to dust the lectern and make sure everything was in place as usual. Ever since she was a child and had followed her mother about, dustcloth clutched in one small hand, chest puffed out with importance, Harriett had considered this her responsibility. As if the service could not take place the next day without me, Harriett thought with a smile.

Nodding to Mary to serve the pudding, Harriett stared down at the tablecloth, remembering her father's first church in Leister, when she was little more than a baby, and then turning her thoughts to the church at Upper Mourouby, which she had first seen when she was seventeen. She had fallen in love with the small, gray stone building and its tall, square tower almost at once, though it was not the most beautiful church she had ever seen. There were, in fact, only two windows that still had stained glass, the others having fallen to Cromwell's soldiers and never been replaced. But the two remaining windows were a particularly lovely shade of yellow, and even when it rained and the sky was overcast, it seemed as if the sun was shining inside. Harriett had spent many days sitting quietly in one of the pews with her eyes closed, letting the peace and tranquility of the little church wash away the hurts and slights endured by a young girl only passably pretty.

And so, after the pudding had been finished and the dishes cleared away, Harriett walked down the lane to the church, a dustcloth in her hand and a frown upon her face as she worried about what the next day would bring. It was easy to tell yourself not to worry, but a difficult thing to do, Harriett found, for she was the sort of person who took everything to heart. If only she could be like Augusta, who was once more looking longingly through her fashion plates, as if she had not a care or concern beyond the length of her skirt or the feathers on her bonnet.

Walking through the churchyard, where a few sheep stood silently grazing like so many woolly gravestones, Harriett pushed open the small oak door that led into the south aisle. Directly opposite was the raised pew where Lord Weston and his guests would sit tomorrow. She shivered slightly. It was cold in the church, or perhaps . . . Harriett brightened suddenly, perhaps an ague was settling in her chest? How fortunate that would be. To have an excuse to stay in bed tomorrow and not have to face Lord Weston or the villagers! Harriett walked up the aisle to the chancel, firmly resolving to sleep with an open window so that the harmful night air would have a chance to do its work.

She set to work immediately, vigorously dusting the ornate walnut carving that surrounded the pulpit. The figure of a small cherub was carved in the center panel, and Harriett smiled as she carefully removed dust from each wing. Then, humming the tune to "All glory, laud, and honor," the hymn which would be sung tomorrow, Harriett worked her way around to the steps leading up to the pulpit. The outside light was fading fast, so Harriett gave the balustrade no more than a cursory swipe with her cloth. She would have to leave soon or light some of the candles, which she was reluctant to do.

Stepping back, Harriett took a final look around the chancel. The potted palms shone like dark-fingered shadows in the gathering gloom, and the vases which Mrs. Beaumont and the other women had filled with catkins of the early flowering willows stood with their wild primrose companions beside the altar. Many a young couple from the village would have gone apalming today, gathering the early willows, which they called English palms, to bedeck their hats or to make crosses which they would keep for luck throughout the year.

I should have remembered and gathered some for Mrs. Micklewaithe, Harriett thought suddenly, and some primroses, too. But perhaps there will be time tomorrow. Yes, and I shall bring her some of the fig pie Cook has baked.

"Harriett."

Startled, Harriett turned, peering across the dimly lit nave to the south aisle. A man stood beside the opened door, his figure wonderfully familiar to Harriett and more than welcome.

"Papa!" Harriett cried, and ran quickly down the aisle to his side. "I am so glad to see you," she said, flinging herself into his arms.

"I must say, I find my reception quite gratifying," Reverend Haversham said. "First Augusta, and now you, so inordinately glad to see me, it makes me wonder what you have been up to."

Harriett felt a guilty blush suffuse her face as she pulled back and looked up at her father's face. Should she tell him about the masquerade? Not now, she answered herself, there were more important matters to discuss.

"Is Mama with you?"

"Yes. Though her ankle still pains her, she insisted she would be much better once she was home. I'm afraid she is feeling quite overset just now, however. The roads were rough, and her ankle jostled about more than was good for it. Not that your mother complained, of course. She never does. Just pressed her lips together and smiled whenever I asked if she was all right. I have sent Old John for the doctor. Your mother will take no laudanum if I prescribe it, but perhaps she will listen to Dr. Bruden."

"And Camilla?" Harriett asked, her breath catching in her throat as she feared what the answer might be.

Reverend Haversham sighed. "Camilla, thank the good Lord, is safe with your Aunt Penniwort. She had no intention of eloping with Tom Watkins, it seems, and merely used his name because she knew he was leaving that day to take some horses to Fairfield. In fact, Tom is sweet on one of the village girls and intends to get married in August. No, Camilla left a note saying she had eloped so we would not know she had gone to London. She said she intended to write as soon as she had established herself."

"Established herself as what?"

"Your sister Camilla had intended to apply for a position as governess to a family in London."

"Camilla?" Harriett blinked, thinking she had not heard right. "But Camilla can barely do her sums, and she . . . well, she doesn't hate children, precisely, but she has never shown any interest in the church school or in helping with any of the children's activities. Whyever would she want to be a governess?"

Reverend Haversham did not reply at once, but walked down the south aisle to the nave of the church, where he stood for a few moments looking toward the chancel and the altar. Then he sighed and turned back to Harriett once more. "It is not an easy thing to raise a child," he said, as Harriett joined him. "What you think is best is sometimes not the best at all. Camilla wants desperately to go to London, to see the sights, go to the parties . . ."

"Camilla wants a Season," Harriett said flatly. "She has always wanted a Season, as has Augusta."

"Yes." Reverend Haversham nodded. "And your mother and I have decided it would be best if they both had one."

"What?" Harriett was sure she had not heard correctly. "You would reward Camilla after what she has done? After what she has put you and Mama through?"

Reverend Haversham shrugged his shoulders. "I must confess that my first thought upon finding Camilla, after I had thanked and praised the Lord for her safety, was that she should be confined to her room on a diet of bread and water for a month. But she truly wants this, Harriett, and she was most repentant, never having considered the consequences of her actions. You know how Camilla is, how headstrong and heedless she can be, yet how loving."

"She cried." Harriett nodded. Camilla was even better at shedding crocodile tears than Augusta.

"As I said, she was most repentant."

"And you believed her, Papa?"

Reverend Haversham moved to sit down in one of the pews. "What you are really asking is, was I taken in by Camilla's wiles once again? And you know the answer as well as I. Even when one is quite aware of what your sisters are up to, they can be difficult to resist."

"Yes." Witness my agreeing to attend Lord Weston's dinner party in disguise, Harriett thought ruefully.

"And Camilla is to remain with your Aunt Penniwort until June. That will be punishment enough."

"For her, or for Aunt Penniwort?" Harriett could not keep from asking.

Her father gave her a look of reproof. "I have always admired your lack of jealousy or ill-feeling toward your sisters, Harriett. I know it has not been an easy thing."

"I am not jealous," Harriett said, crossing her fingers behind her back. "It is just that you are always saying there is no money to spend on fripperies while people are hungry. How can you now justify a Season for Camilla and Augusta?"

"It will mean the strictest economy for your mother and me, as well as for you, Harriett.

And I am afraid I cannot justify it. In fact, you know I deplore the very things your sisters declare they cannot live without." Reverend Haversham frowned at the wooden back of the pew in front of him. "Still, I feel this will be for the best. Sometimes, we want something so badly it all but consumes us, yet when we possess it, we find it does not matter so much, after all. I am hoping that will be the case with your sisters. If I did not feel this, I could not countenance such a thing."

Harriett stared down at her hands. She had not worn her gloves, and her pale skin shone softly in the gathering dusk. "When I was six," she said at last, in a small voice, "I ate a whole box of sweetmeats Mama had left out and forgotten about. I remember being violently ill. But I still eat sweetmeats, Papa."

"Moderation in all things," Reverend Haversham replied absently, as he patted her hand. "That is the important thing. I myself become quite ill if I eat too many oysters. Now, as I have explained to Camilla, it is too late to be thinking of a Season this year, and she quite understands that this sort of thing takes a great deal of planning. Also, as your mother pointed out, if we wait until next year, we may bring Augusta out as well. It hardly seems possible, but Augusta will be eighteen in the fall." He smiled fondly as he thought of his youngest daughter. "This trip to London will be good for her. Though I hate to think on it, Augusta is of an age to be married, and neither she nor

Camilla is likely to meet any eligible gentlemen in Upper Mourouby."

"I suppose not," Harriett replied, swallowing hard to keep back the tears that were making her nose tingle unpleasantly.

"Your mother thinks it would be best if she traveled to the city several weeks before the start of the Season so that Augusta and Camilla will have time to order gowns and such."

"And me?" Harriett asked in a small voice. Why did no one ever consider what she might want?

"You will remain at home to take care of the household in your mother's absence. I do not know what we would do without you, Harriett. It is a relief that at least one of my daughters has not given herself over to the lures of the social whirl. I am glad you are different, my dear."

Actually, I am not so very different, Harriett thought. At one time I, too, wished for a Season and pretty gowns, and a chance to see the sights of London.

"Well, now, it's time and more that we were getting home," her father said, getting up. "Everything looks to be in order for tomorrow. I imagine Mrs. Beauchamp has made the Pax cakes as usual?"

Harriett nodded.

"Good, good. Let us be off, then. It is almost dark outside, your mother will be worried."

Nodding, Harriett rose obediently to her feet and walked to the pew in the south aisle where she had left her cloak and dusting cloth. I will not say anything more, she promised herself. And I will try to be happy for Augusta and Camilla. But it will not be easy.

As she walked back to join her father, Harriett's eyes fell on the ornately carved pew at the back of the church. Tomorrow Lord Weston would be sitting there with his family and friends. What possible explanation could be offered for the change in Reverend Haversham's appearance? And whatever would her papa say when he found out that not only had he supped with Lord Weston, but Lady Weston thought him a womanizer and Mrs. Dade was convinced he had the plague?

I shall definitely sleep with my window open tonight, Harriett decided.

Palm Sunday dawned bright and cheery, which was a pity, in Harriett's estimation. She had been hoping—nay, praying—for rain. Not just rain, but a squall, the sort of thing that would make members of the ton decide not to venture forth. It was, however, a lovely day: the birds were singing cheerfully, the sun was shining, and the trees were bursting with green buds.

"Drat it all," Harriett said, leaning out her window. "Why couldn't it at least be overcast? Is that too much to ask?" She shut her window and stood scowling down at her bare feet.

Harriett turned from the window and walked

over to peer in the mirror over her dressing table. As if the beautiful weather were not bad enough, Harriett herself was looking remarkably well. "It simply isn't fair," she declared to the room at large. "I left the window open, I did my best to get a chill. Why must I be so disgustingly healthy?"

Feeling quite betrayed by nature, Harriett rang for Mary and then washed and dressed in one of her newer gowns of pale green gros de Naples ornamented with satin bands of a darker green.

It was one of her most becoming gowns, chosen because Harriett felt she was going to her own funeral this morning and wanted to look her best. Lord Weston was sure to be at church. And what he would say and think when he saw Reverend Haversham was something Harriett did not wish to dwell upon. It was true, as Augusta had said, that the Weston pew was at the back of the church. But even so . . . And would Lord Weston come forward to receive one of the Pax cakes? I am as doomed as if I *did* have the plague, Harriett thought.

"There you are, Miss." Mary finished buttoning the last button of Harriett's gown and stood back. "Would you like me to brush your hair, now?"

Harriett shook her head. "There's very little to brush," she said, gazing morosely at her head of wispy curls. "Besides, Augusta will be wanting your assistance, too. Is Mama awake

212

yet? I did not get a chance to see her last night."

"She's still sleepin', Miss. That laudanum the doctor dosed her with eased the pain she was feelin' and she dropped off almost at once. Reverend Haversham said as how we wasn't to disturb her, no matter what."

"Yes." Harriett frowned. "Papa told me it was a very difficult journey for her." Harriett picked up her pelisse and turned from the mirror. "I shall just peek in on Mama for a moment before I join Papa downstairs. Do see if you can hurry Augusta along, so we are not late. Otherwise we must walk through that gauntlet of eyes, which I quite dislike."

Harriett hurried down the hall to her parents' bedroom and after a perfunctory knock, opened the door. The room was silent except for the soft sound of breathing coming from the invalid in the large bed. Tiptoeing across the carpet, Harriett looked down at the sleeping form of her mother. Mrs. Haversham's lace cap was askew and a few auburn locks escaped beneath the edge. It was easy to see from whom Augusta and Camilla had inherited their beauty. They should have a Season, Harriett told herself. They are both so pretty and full of life, and will enjoy it so much. While I would spend my time sitting in a corner, feeling horribly embarrassed and wishing I could escape through one of the windows.

"At least, that's how I feel when I go to the assemblies," Harriett whispered to her mother.

"And I know everyone there. I mustn't be envious of Camilla and Augusta. But it would be nice to go to the theatre and see Hyde Park and the Tower of London and . . . and everything." Harriett sighed, and leaning over, touched her mother lightly on the shoulder. "Anyway, I'm glad you're home, Mama. And that Cammie is all right. I have a great deal to tell you when you're feeling more the thing. If I can get up the courage. I—I'm afraid I made quite a mull of things while you were gone. And I feel I must confess our masquerade to Papa because I am almost certain he will be meeting Lord Weston today."

Harriett leaned against the post of her mother's bed, the pelisse in her arms drooping almost to the floor. "But I am so reluctant, Mama, because I know he will be disappointed in me. And the worst part is, I am such a . . . a prosy prude, I did not even enjoy myself overmuch. Cammie would have thought it a wonderful lark and not given a whit for the consequences. I wish there were some way to silence a conscience that will continue to prattle on at one."

The small clock over the fireplace mantel struck the hour, and Harriett realized she must hurry if she wanted to see her Papa before he left for church. "I'll bring you back some primroses," she promised her mother, and gathering her pelisse across her arm once more, she quickly left the room.

Reverend Haversham was in the parlour, reading over his sermon.

"I've chosen number thirty-eight," he told Harriett. "I used it four years ago. Do you think anyone will remember? What with one thing and another, there's been no time to compose something new."

Harriett smiled for the first time. There was always one thing and another in her father's life, and most of his sermons were repeats or embellishments of earlier ones. Still, since most of the parishioners slept through parts of the sermon anyway, Harriett had never seen any harm in using them again. "I'm sure it will be fine, Papa," she said, refraining from adding, *As usual.* "I looked in on Mama. She seems to be resting quite comfortably."

"Do you think so?" A look of relief spread over Reverend Haversham's face. "I must admit I was a little worried. But the doctor says everything should be fine, as long as she does not attempt to stand or walk on that ankle for the next month." He picked up the pages of his sermon, folded them, and put them in the pocket of his coat. "Well, I'd best be going now. You know," he looked up at Harriett, a strained expression back on his face, "this will be the first Palm Sunday in twenty-seven years that I have looked out upon my congregation and not seen your mother sitting there."

"She will be fine, Papa. I shall bully and coerce her into behaving. You know how fearsome I can be."

"As fearsome as a spring lamb," her father agreed with a smile. "You may unhappily resemble me in appearance, Harriett, but quite fortunately, you have inherited your mother's disposition. Which is much the better thing, my dear. As some young man will discover to his great benefit one of these days."

"Yes, Papa." Harriett agreed because it was the thing to do, not because she believed him. "I . . . um, there is something I should tell you before you leave."

"Yes? If it is about Augusta, I think I can guess what you would say."

"No, it is not about Augusta. I mean, you know I am not one to carry tales, but Lord Weston is in residence and—"

"Is he, now? There was some rumour that he might be coming for Easter. Ah, I wish I had known. I would have spent more time on my sermon." He patted the pocket of his coat where the copy of number thirty-eight now resided. "Well, well, I am sure he has not heard it before. He is not often here for Easter week, after all. Now, I had best be going, it would not do to arrive after the family."

"But Papa, I have not told you what happened. And it was not Augusta, it was me."

"Yes, yes, I know my dear. And there is nothing to worry about. What you did is not so very serious. You would never do anything wrong, my dear. Our little angel daughter, your mother and I used to call you, because you never seemed to get into any trouble," Reverend Haversham patted her cheek, lifted his eyebrows at the clock, and turned to go. Then, frowning, he turned back. "Have you done something different to your hair, Harriett?"

"I've cut it, Papa."

"Yes, ah . . . well. Do not be late, now."

Harriett sighed at her father's departing back. Well, she had tried to warn him. Not that she had tried very hard, she supposed, but— "Oh, do be quiet," she told her conscience, suddenly frowning. "I'm getting tired of being told what to do all the time and never having any fun. Why can't you be more like Augusta's conscience?"

"My what?" Augusta swept into the room, looking quite splendid in one of her sister's pink muslin gowns. "I borrowed it, because I knew Cammie wouldn't mind," she said untruthfully. "And, oh, dear. Was that my stomach making such a noise? I do hate fast days, don't you? At least Lent will soon be over. It is such a dreary season. And while we are on the subject, dear Harriett, I want you to know that I confessed all last night."

Harriett blinked. "You did?" This was a surprise, since Augusta usually was unaware there was anything to confess.

"Yes," Augusta said. "And Mama was quite understanding and quite forgave me. She said she might very well have done the same under the circumstances."

"She did?" Harriett knew she was behaving like the automaton on top of their mother's music box, but she could not believe what she was hearing. "And does Papa know as well?"

Augusta nodded. "He was not quite so forgiving. You know how he is. And, I'm afraid—I did not mean to implicate you," Augusta continued in a rush, "but it just sort of came out."

"Was Papa very disappointed in me?" Harriett asked.

"Well, he did say he could not believe that you had followed my lead, but he was not disappointed, exactly. It's just that Papa cannot really understand because he would never do anything like that himself."

"Yes. Well." Harriett took a deep breath. "I must say I am glad you confessed, Augusta. I did wonder when Papa seemed to know what I was talking about this morning. I had meant to say something to him myself, but I am afraid I had not your courage. It is a relief to have it done and over with. Thank you."

Augusta grinned. "You are most welcome, dearest sister. I surprised you, did I not? You think me such a scatterbrain, I would not realize that what we had done was wrong. And I must admit that while I do not think something so very enjoyable can be so very bad, I knew Papa, at least, would consider that we should not have done it."

"Yes." Harriett glanced at the mantel clock and picked up her pelisse. "We had best be going, Gusta. But you know, I am surprised Papa did not make more of it."

Shrugging, Augusta picked up her reticule

from the table where she had dropped it earlier. "Usually Papa makes you feel so truly guilty just by the way he looks at you, that I hate to confess even the smallest of sins. But I think he is preoccupied by worry over Mama. And the only reason I said anything at all is because I was sure he would find out anyway."

"He was bound to," Harriett agreed, buttoning her gray pelisse.

"And also because I did feel terrible when Papa told me about Cammie and how we are to have a Season and everything, despite her having run off like that. Oh, Harry!" She reached over to hug her sister. "Is it not wonderful?"

Harriett swallowed and smiled at her sister. "Most wonderful," she said, knowing she must not spoil things for Augusta by acting the hangdog. And while Harriett might not feel quite as her sister did about the proposed Season for obvious reasons, it was a wonderful relief to have their masquerade off her conscience. Now she could face the service with some equanimity, at least.

And it was most agreeable to find that their papa had not been quite as overset as she would have expected by what they had done. Maybe I have been making mountains out of molehills, Harriett thought. Maybe our masquerade looms large only in my own conscience. Though they must still face Lord Weston. When Papa told him what they had done, as he was bound to, Lord Weston might prove less forgiving.

Harriett and Augusta walked to church down the little pathway that led through a white picket fence surrounding their herb garden and across a small hill. Augusta, now that she had a clear conscience and was free to think of other things, began at once to chatter excitedly about the proposed Season in London.

"It is above everything, Harry!" she exclaimed, her blue eyes sparkling in anticipation. "I know we must wait until next year, but to think that I shall have a Season after all. And here was I, all bedazzled by the mere thought of a dinner at Yarwood. Why, I shall soon be attending a thousand such dinners!"

Harriett nodded, the blue ribbons of her bonnet blowing about her face in the spring breeze. She was trying to enter into Augusta's enthusiasm, truly she was, but she found she could not speak for the awful lump of jealousy lodged in her throat.

Which is a terrible thing, Harriett thought, looking up at the square tower of the church as they drew near. Today is Palm Sunday and Papa will give out the Pax cakes in token of peace and good neighbors. I shall probably choke on mine.

Pasting a smile upon her face, Harriett entered the church with Augusta still prattling on beside her. The Haversham family always occupied the first pew immediately under the pulpit. They were, by their attentiveness, to serve as an example to the villagers. Mrs. Haversham always managed to do this, sitting up straight and looking thoughtful, as if her husband's sermon was of great import. Harriett knew that her mama was often merely doing the household accounts in her head, but at least Mrs. Haversham looked as if she were paying attention.

Which was more than could be said for Augusta and Camilla, who spent most of the service naughtily casting sheep's eyes at visiting curates or handsome village lads. Though Harriett could hardly censure their behavior. Not that she spent the time peeping coquettishly under the brim of her bonnet, at least she did, but only in her thoughts. For while Harriett was incurably shy around men, she was quite bold in her imaginings. Often, while her Papa spoke eloquently of the sins of the flesh, Harriett was sitting in front of him, mentally indulging in them.

Nodding and smiling now, Harriett and Augusta made their way to the front pew. They were early, the Haversham family was not allowed to arrive late, and so they needed to explain the absence of their mother only to the few villagers who were already there.

"Yes, Mrs. Armitage," Harriett said, stopping to speak to one of the farmers' wives. "It is true that Mama broke her ankle stepping from the carriage. She is still in some pain, but we expect she will be able to attend Easter services. I shall give her your good wishes." They continued down the aisle, the buzz of whispered conversation following them.

Sitting in their pew and doing their best to look as saintly as possible, the two sisters suddenly became aware of a hush that fell over the villagers like a great wave crashing upon a beach.

Augusta, having no qualms about displaying her curiosity, turned around. "It's them," she whispered to Harriett, who was staring straight ahead, her lips pressed together. "Lord Weston has arrived with the rest of his house party. Miss Dade is wearing the most stunning dress. I shall get a closer look at it after the service."

"And Lord Weston?" Harriett whispered back. Was he frowning? Was he upset? Would he ever forgive her?

"Lord Weston?" Augusta looked back at her sister in surprise. "He is wearing a blue frock coat and pantaloons. Whyever does it matter?"

"No, no. I mean, how does he look? Is he . . . is he angry?"

Augusta turned her head around again, almost poking out Harriett's eye with one of the artificial flowers upon her bonnet. "I don't really—oh!"

"What? What?"

"He is staring at us, Harry. And I'm afraid he is frowning."

Oh, dear, Harriett thought. Papa has spoken to him already. Or else . . . she lifted her eyes to the chancel where Reverend Haversham now sat, having entered from the little side door by the pulpit. Or else, Papa has not spoken to him and Lord Weston is wondering about the identity of the strange vicar presiding over the Palm Sunday service. What a dreadful muddle!

Eleven

The Pax cakes handed out at the end of the Palm Sunday service were a custom of long tradition, though not until after Reverend Haversham arrived was it practiced at Upper Mourouby. Still, it was such a fine custom that the villagers took it to their hearts, and Palm Sunday service now saw the church as crowded as it was for Christmas or Easter.

It was not just the prospect of the cakes, however, nor the free cider provided to wash them down that brought people out in such numbers. No, it was the fact that the ancient custom was also a gossiper's delight. The cakes were supposed to be shared between people who had quarreled that year, with the expectation that the argument would now be forgiven and forgotten. And everyone watched avidly to see who did and who did not share one of the Pax cakes together.

After the conclusion of the service, during which sermon thirty-eight had been quite well received, Reverend Haversham walked to the back of the church and stood at the door, handing out the cakes with the words, "This is a token of peace and good neighborhood." And often adding the injunction, "See that you share it now and make up old quarrels." Out beyond the churchyard, Mr. Beauchamp was serving the glasses of cider, surrounded by eager partakers and a general air of joviality, quite in contrast to the somber Lenten mood of previous Sundays.

Harriett, who usually helped her mother and Mrs. Beauchamp with the cakes, was dawdling about inside, straightening hymnals, checking to make sure the palms did not need water, and picking up bits of willow that had fallen to the stone-flagged floor.

"Come along, Harry," Augusta urged. "We are missing everything. I want to see if Nan Braidwaite shares a cake with Tim Wilmot. You know how they quarreled last week. And Tom Watkins is back from taking the horses to Fairfield. I want to ask him about Cammie."

"Have Lord Weston and his guests left yet?" Harriett asked, looking toward the back of the church nervously. "I find I am not so anxious to encounter them. I am sure Papa has spoken to Lord Weston about our masquerade, for I swear I could feel the earl's eyes on the back of my bonnet the length of the sermon. And I am—well, I am a bit of a coward, Gusta. I just do not know what to say, or how to excuse our behavior, or—"

225

"You mean you told Papa about our going to supper at Yarwood?" Augusta interrupted, eyes wide in horror. "And about your wearing his clothes and everything? Oh, Harriett, what did he say?"

Harriett, who had been bending over to pick up a catkin that had strayed under a pew, straightened and looked at her sister with sudden apprehension. "What do you mean, what did he say? You're the one who told him about it."

"Not me," Augusta replied ungrammatically, sitting down in one of the empty pews. "I was hoping Papa would not find out. You know what a stickler he is about such things. He will be terribly upset, Harriett. And of course, you are right. He will tell Lord Weston. He will consider it his duty to do so." She put her hands up to her face. "I shall never be able to face Mr. Reading again. I shall have to join Cammie at Aunt Penniwort's."

Bending back the brim of her bonnet, which she felt must be interfering with her hearing, Harriett sat down next to Augusta. "Augusta," Harriett spoke very slowly and very clearly, "you told me not more than an hour and a half ago that you had confessed everything to Mama and Papa."

"About the chocolates," Augusta said. "I told Mama we had eaten some of her chocolates, even though it was Lent and we were supposed to give up such things until after Easter. I knew she would find out anyway, because the box is now half empty. I would never have told them about . . . about the boot black and your wearing trousers and everything. I am not such a ninnyhammer. Papa would have a fit."

"Then he does not know?" Harriett asked.

"Well, I certainly did not tell him, and if you did not tell him, either, then—oh, what a relief!" Augusta put one hand to her bosom and sighed. "My life is not ruined, and I need not go into exile at Aunt Penniwort's." She rose to her feet, all smiles once again. "Thank heavens for that. Now, let us go and get a Pax cake. I want to share it with Tom Watkins and worm out of him everything that happened."

"But Augusta, what about Lord Weston?"

"Lord Weston will doubtless share one with Miss Dade, or no, it is probably Miss Smalbathe that will snare him. Let us go and see who is successful."

"But Augusta, are you forgetting that Lord Weston will know immediately that Papa is not . . . not Papa? Yes, and so shall everyone else in his house party. Whatever shall we say?"

Augusta was halfway down the aisle already, but she turned back and waved a gloved hand at her sister. "Oh, pooh. You worry too much about these things, Harriett. I tell you, people see what they want to see. But if you like, I shall go and stand by Papa and see that all is well."

Harriett slowly rose and followed Augusta to the door of the church. If her sister could talk her way out of this bumblebath, Harriett would acknowledge that she more than deserved her Season in London.

"Ah, there you are, my dears," Reverend Haversham greeted his daughters, as he dusted crumbs from his hands. "We barely had enough Pax cakes this time. That is what happens when your mother is not here to supervise."

"That is what happens when people hear there are to be free cakes and cider," Augusta replied pertly.

"Naughty, puss." Reverend Haversham gently tweaked Augusta's nose. "Now, I am just going over to greet Lord Weston and give him your mother's excuses. The two of you must come along, and make your curtsies as well." Grabbing their arms, he steered them toward the churchyard where Lord Weston and his guests stood sipping cider.

We're in for it now, Harriett thought, walking beside her father while her heart pounded sickeningly in her ears. Perhaps she would be fortunate and lightning would strike her down, or one of the gravestones would topple and crush her beneath its cold stone.

"Lord Weston, how good to see you again," Reverend Haversham greeted the earl with a bow. "And especially so, since I take it you are to spend Easter week at Yarwood?"

Lord Weston bowed in return. "Reverend Haversham?" he asked. And if a man could be said to frown and smile at the same time, that is what Lord Weston was doing. "I am glad to see you looking so well. The last time we met, you were looking rather gray, and it must have been a trick of the lighting, of course, but I could have sworn your hair was not red."

"Yes, Papa is much better," Augusta answered, quickly insinuating herself into the conversation. "It is worry over our mother that has so changed his looks. She broke her ankle stepping down from the carriage, you know."

"Indeed." Lord Weston's eyebrows rose. "I did not know. But I thought she did not dare to leave her poor, ill husband's side even for a moment."

"She had gone to fetch the doctor, of course."

"Gone to fetch the doctor?" Reverend Haversham expostulated. "Whatever are you talking about, Augusta? Why—"

Harriett tugged at his arm. "Papa, you have not greeted Lady Weston yet, I believe. She will be thinking you quite rag-mannered."

Leaving Augusta to explain things to Lord Weston, Harriett dragged her father away, her cheeks growing warm from fighting down the panic bubbling up in her throat. Any moment now she would begin to laugh hysterically or . . . or scream. How Augusta thought they could possibly talk their way out of such a situation, Harriett could not imagine. In fact, it might be a good idea if both of them went on a visit to Aunt Penniwort after this. An extended visit.

The dowager, standing stiff as a fence post, viewed Reverend Haversham's approach with something akin to revulsion on her face.

"Lady Weston?" Reverend Haversham bowed and smiled down at her.

She frowned and curled her lip at him. "How dare you sully the pulpit with your presence," she hissed. "You should remove the stick from your own eye, before pointing it out to another."

"I beg your pardon?" Reverend Haversham cupped one hand around his ear and leaned closer.

"Keep your distance!" Lady Weston commanded.

"Indeed, yes," Mrs. Dade chimed in. "You may look better, that is, you don't look better, precisely, but you do look different. However, there is no saying but that you're still contagious. Stick out your tongue, if you please."

Reverend Haversham stared at Mrs. Dade. "Have you quite lost your mind, madam?" he asked.

"It's my life that I'm worried about losing," Mrs. Dade replied, her voice beginning to quaver. "Anyone so changed by disease as you must represent a threat to us all."

"Disease? What disease is this, if you please?"

"The plague. It's as plain as the nose on your face. First the gray skin and black tongue, now

230

the color leaching from your hair. We must leave at once, Laurenda," she cried, turning toward her daughter. "I do not care if he does have thirty thousand a year. What good will that do us if we are dead?"

"I think perhaps you should sit down, madam." Reverend Haversham took a step forward. "You seem quite overset by—"

"Stand back!" Mrs. Dade swung her reticule at him. "Keep away. Oh! I feel a fainting spell coming on." She tottered and collapsed backward. Fortunately, George Reading happened to be standing nearby and was able to catch her before she fell to the ground.

Reverend Haversham stared thunderstruck at her prostrate form. "Has everyone taken leave of their senses?" he asked Harriett, who was chewing nervously on her bottom lip.

"Ah, I think, ah . . ." Remembering the supper party, Harriett was struck with sudden inspiration. "I think it runs in the family, Papa," she said firmly. "A pity, but I believe Mrs. Dade's sister suffered from just such a nervous condition and had to be locked in the attic to keep her from harming herself."

"I can well believe it." Reverend Haversham watched as Miss Dade waved some smelling salts under her mother's nose. Then, suddenly becoming aware of the unnatural silence that hung heavy as a thunderstorm in the spring air, he looked up. The avid eyes of fifty villagers looked back, glasses of cider and half-consumed Pax cakes suspended halfway to their mouths.

Not knowing what else to do, Reverend Haversham raised his hands and gave the traditional blessing of dismissal. "And I hope I shall see you all in church tomorrow for evening prayer," he added. The villagers, most of whom had intended to spend tomorrow evening elsewhere, immediately turned away, quite unable to meet his eyes.

"Has she had another fit?" Abigail Smalbathe, coming up to the small gathering, viewed Mrs. Dade's body with casual interest. "A pity." Her sister, Prudence, peering over Harriett's shoulder, covered her mouth and giggled.

"I must say," Miss Smalbathe continued, with a frown at Prudence, "that I quite adored your sermon, Reverend Haversham. There is something so . . . so commanding about a man standing in a pulpit. Mrs. Haversham is not here?"

"No, I'm afraid my wife has broken her ankle and could not attend services today."

"Good." Miss Smalbathe smiled and linked her arm through his. "Why do we not take a stroll through the graveyard and have a little coze?"

Reverend Haversham found himself being propelled along quite without regard to his own wishes. "I take it you have something of a serious and confidential nature to discuss with me? Perhaps we should go into my church office instead?"

"What an excellent idea," Miss Smalbathe agreed.

"And I am sorry, but I do not believe I was given your name," Reverend Haversham apologized, leaning closer.

Miss Smalbathe looked around at the villagers, who were staring at the pair from the corners of their eyes. "How clever you are," she whispered back, "pretending you do not know me. I must admit, when I saw you this morning, I was startled by the change in your appearance. But unrequited love will do that to a man, I told myself. Sleepless nights age one, add lines to the face, and whiten the hair quite overnight."

"My hair is red," Reverend Haversham pointed out.

"Or turn it red." Miss Smalbathe nodded. "People react in different ways to this sort of thing."

Reverend Haversham gave one backward glance of appeal to Harriett, who watched heartlessly as her papa was led away to slaughter. Aunt Penniwort's will probably be lovely this time of the year, she told herself.

Harriett took some of the primroses that had been used to decorate the church, and brought them home to her mother. They were already

233

beginning to wilt a little, but she knew her mother would enjoy them anyway.

"You must put a copper penny in the water, Harriett, and the flowers will soon revive," her mother instructed with a smile. "I do enjoy primroses, my dear. Thank you for thinking of me."

Harriett nodded, feeling guilty, which was how she always seemed to feel these days. "I intend to bring some to Mrs. Micklewaithe later today, with perhaps a few catkins. And some fig pie, if there is any left over." Fig pie was a traditional dish on Palm Sunday in the Haversham household, Mrs. Haversham's grandmother having come from the Midlands, where they were eaten in memory of the barren fig tree cursed by Christ.

"You are so thoughtful," her mother said. "I am sure Mrs. Micklewaithe will appreciate it. Now you must tell me all about the service. Was Lord Weston there? And were there enough Pax cakes? I always worry about that, you know. And where is your papa? Should he not be home by now?"

"Ummm." Harriett looked down at the coverlet on the bed, trying to decide what to tell her mother. "Lord Weston was at the service with some of his guests. The dowager was there as well, and they all seemed very appreciative of Papa's sermon."

"Ah. Which one did he preach?"

"Number thirty-eight."

234

"I always like that one," her mother said with a nod and a smile. "And the Pax cakes?"

"Barely enough. Papa said that is what happens when you are not there to oversee things. Does your ankle still pain you?" Harriett added, desperate to change the subject.

Mrs. Haversham looked down at her foot, which rested on a pillow under the blue coverlet. "It is much better. I am sure it was just all that jostling about yesterday that made it ache so. I shall get up this afternoon. Easter week is no time for a vicar's wife to be lying abed."

"No, Mama. But I have already asked about extra eggs from Yarwood, and I had planned on decorating them on Wednesday, if that is all right with you."

Her mother nodded. "Cook has been saving onion skins and you must see what other plants and flowers may be gathered to color the eggs. Some gorse flowers make a lovely yellow, if you can find any, and of course, the leaves of the pasque flower can be used for green. Perhaps Mrs. Micklewaithe has some old fabric scraps we may use. You must remember to ask her."

"I will, Mama, and Madame St. Germaine promised that she would save some scraps for us as well."

"It will be good fun," her mother said with a smile. "I always enjoy decorating the eggs. I only wish I had not so stupidly broken my ankle like this." Mrs. Haversham sighed and frowned, and to Harriett's horror, two small tears slid slowly down her cheek.

"Mama? Mama, is something else the matter? I haven't seen you cry since grandmother died."

Mrs. Haversham sniffed. "Would you hand me a handkerchief, Harriett? It is of no matter, really. I am just being silly, but oh, my dear, you do not know what a relief it is to know that Camilla is safe and has not disgraced herself! Did your Papa tell you about it?"

"Only that Camilla had some idea of becoming a governess and had not run off with Tom after all."

"No." Mrs. Haversham blew her nose. "Tom was taking some horses to Fairfield for Mr. Beauchamp, and Camilla asked him to take her to one of the inns where she might get a coach to London. It was he, in fact, who told us where she was, for he thought it quite strange that she should be traveling alone. Such a good boy. I feel quite terrible when I consider the awful thoughts I had of him. But it is over now, and Camilla is safe, and your Aunt Penniwort has promised to have a long talk with her, for it was quite unfair to involve Tom Watkins like that. Still, Camilla knows how foolish she was and is most remorseful."

"So Papa said," Harriett replied in a small voice, not looking at her mother.

"And Camilla did not think you would mind that she took the garnets, for she says you never wear them, and though she had been saving her pin money, she was not sure how much a

236

ticket to London would cost. Such a flea-wit."
Mrs. Haversham sighed and wiped her cheeks.

"I cannot imagine how she thought she could
be a governess, Mama."

"Oh, that was to be only temporary, Harriett.
Camilla intended to marry a duke or viscount
within the week, and then she assured me she
would replace your garnets with something you
would like much better. I am sure she quite
expected you would thank her, though you may
be sure I have told her how very wrong it was,
and I have the garnets safe in my jewelry box
once more."

Harriett nodded. "I am happy to hear it, but
Camilla was right, you know. I rarely wear the
eardrops, for there is little occasion in Upper
Mourouby. Perhaps it would be as well to sell
the garnets and use the money for the Season
Camilla and Augusta are to have."

A frown of pain that had nothing to do with
her broken ankle creased Mrs. Haversham's
brow. "You are upset that your sisters are to
have a Season while you did not," she said,
noting the touch of bitterness beneath Harriett's generosity.

"Do you blame me, Mama?" Harriett asked.
"I know I should be happy that Camilla is safe,
and I am. But it seems so very unfair for her
to have a Season while I must remain at home."

"Yes." Mrs. Haversham reached out one
hand to her daughter. "But you know, my dear,
you are . . ." She hesitated and looked across
the room at the faded rose wallpaper for a mo-

ment before continuing, ". . . you are twenty-three and would be considered an antidote in London. And even if your father and I had had the resources to give you a Season when you were eighteen, you would not have taken, Harriett. You would have been quite miserable, truly you would."

"I know, Mama." Harriett swallowed her chagrin and did her best to smile. "I know that being as tall as I am and with little else to recommend me as well, it would be most unlikely that I should make a match. But I should still have liked to see London."

Leaning back on her pillows, Mrs. Haversham nodded. "Perhaps one of your sisters really will marry well and have a house in town. You could go for a visit then."

"Yes." Harriett rose from her chair and put the small vase of primroses she had been holding on the bedside table. "In any case, Papa will need someone at home while you are gone, will he not? And even though I am not pretty, at least I may be useful." She said the words lightly, though that was not the way she felt. "Shall I have some nuncheon brought up to you, Mama, or do you wish to be carried downstairs?"

"If your Papa or Joseph could carry me to the parlour, it would be most enjoyable. I find myself lying here redecorating the room, and that will never do. But Harriett . . ."

"Yes, Mama?" Harriett turned back from the door.

"I did not say anything at first, Harriett, but . . . your hair?"

Harriett raised her chin just a trifle. "I decided to cut it," she said. "I have decided not to be an antidote, but an eccentric, instead."

A covered dish containing some fig pie swung in a string bag beside her reticule as Harriett walked down the path to Mrs. Micklewaithe's cottage. She remembered that Lord Weston had pointed out a patch of primroses in the little meadow, and she thought she would stop to pick a few, and bring her birds some scraps of toast as well.

Harriett peered nervously around the edge of the clearing when she arrived. She did not want to meet Lord Weston. That is, she did, actually, but she had not had a chance to speak privately with Augusta, and so was not sure what she had told him. A few catkins and the remaining primroses from the church were wrapped in paper and rested beside the fig pie in her bag. She would pick some fresh flowers to add to her bouquet, feed the birds, and then be on her way. It would take but a minute. There was little chance she would meet Lord Weston.

Still, when Harriett left the home woods some five minutes later with Rusty Brown's caws echoing behind her, she was conscious of a distinct feeling of disappointment. Of course, she had not wanted to meet Lord Weston. She would have had no idea what to say. And despite Augusta's assurance that people saw only what they expected to see, Harriett was uneasily aware that Lord Weston was no one's fool. He might very well put two and two together and find the sum of four not to his liking.

And while I can no longer think of him as Lord Stiff Rump, Harriett thought, I should still not care to be his enemy. For all the kind humor in his dark eyes, I am afraid Lord Weston is a man to be reckoned with.

Harriett walked along the path that led between hedgerows to the edge of the village. She walked briskly, her muslin skirt swirling about her ankles. It was not so when she wore her Papa's trousers. Then she had been able to stride along quite unhampered. It is a good thing I did not wear my disguise any longer, she thought. I was beginning to enjoy the freedom to walk as I pleased and use language most inappropriate for a young lady.

"Dash it all, anyway," she whispered experimentally, and then grinned. "The devil, you say!" she told a bird singing lustily on a branch. Yes, it might be fun to be a man. Though I could never wear pantaloons, she decided. They are much too revealing. Still, a generous length of limb is considered a good thing in a man, and a face that is more interesting than conventionally pretty, or handsome, she corrected herself, is not seen to be a disadvantage in a man. Witness Lord Weston. His was not a truly handsome face, and yet . . .

Harriett stopped for a moment and stared unseeing at the hedgerow . . . and yet Lord Weston was most attractive.

"And it is not just his fortune that makes him so," Harriett told a branch of budding crab apple that hung over the hedge. "Lord Weston could be a common farmer and I would still . . ." Harriett bit her lip. And you would still what, Harriett Haversham? she asked herself. Harriett shook her head, not liking the answer. And in a moment she continued on her way, walking more briskly than ever.

Mrs. Micklewaithe's small cottage on the outskirts of the village soon came into view. Opening the little gate in the hedge, Harriett stepped into the yard and walked up the stone-flagged path to the door. She was surprised not to see George, Mrs. Micklewaithe's elderly tomcat, peering out the window as he usually did.

I do hope nothing is wrong, Harriett thought, hurrying her steps a little. It might just be that George was enjoying his dish of milk a bit earlier than usual, of course. But still . . . Harriett knocked on the cottage door and waited anxiously for Mrs. Micklewaithe to answer.

The door opened and Lord Weston stood there, his broad shoulders almost touching the doorframe on either side. He looked as elegant as usual, except for a plethora of orange cat hairs on his otherwise immaculate coat of blue superfine, and the fact that he cradled a purring George in one arm.

"Ah, Miss Haversham. How good to see you once more."

Harriett stood there, her mouth agape, until Lord Weston reached over and closed it with a finger under her chin. "You are surprised to see me." He stated the obvious fact with a slight smile. "I know I have become the most notorious of absent landlords, but I do occasionally call upon my tenants, you know."

"Yes." The words came out as a hoarse whisper, and Harriett had to clear her throat and repeat the word once again. "Yes. I am sure you do."

Lord Weston's smile broadened, causing his dark, rather formidable face to soften. "Do come in, Miss Haversham. Mrs. Micklewaithe and I were just about to enjoy some tea."

Harriett nodded, and stepped past him into the cottage, her face almost the color of her hair. Mrs. Micklewaithe sat in her favorite upholstered chair by the fire, a welcome smile on her face.

"Come in, come in, my dear. How fortunate I am to have two guests for tea. Lord Weston, would you fetch another cup from the cupboard, if you please?"

Harriett sat down abruptly in one of the hard wooden chairs opposite, her eyes following Lord Weston as far as her bonnet brim would allow.

"A fine figure of a man," Mrs. Micklewaithe observed. "A girl could do worse."

"Yes, um . . . yes, I am sure you are right."

"And look at you, your face as bright as a bear-berry. Well, it would be a fine match, and there's no mistakin' it."

"Mrs. Micklewaithe!" Harriett turned her head and saw to her embarrassment that Lord Weston stood behind her, a cup in his hand and what could only be called a grin upon his face.

"Would you like me to pour?" he asked Mrs. Micklewaithe, though his eyes remained on Harriett.

"Nay, nay. I can pour tea just fine," the old lady protested. "And I've got me a cane from Henry Bronton down the lane, so I can hobble about more. In fact, I've been thinkin' as how I just might get to church on Easter. If'n somebody is willin' to take me up in their carriage, of course."

The hint was as broad as any Harriett had ever heard, and she looked up at Lord Weston to see how he would receive it. She found his eyes warm upon hers as he assured Mrs. Micklewaithe that a carriage would be sent for her.

"An' then there's old Mrs. Blytenton lives down the road. She has a bit of trouble walkin', too."

Lord Weston turned to Mrs. Micklewaithe with a smile. "And Mrs. Blytenton as well. Is there anyone else you would like us to take up in the carriage?"

"No." Mrs. Micklewaithe chuckled. "But I would like you to make as big a show of it as possible. Right up to the front door, an' all. No sneakin' around the back."

"Right up to the front door," Lord Weston agreed.

"Well, now, then." Mrs. Micklewaithe turned back to Harriett and eyed the string bag she had put beside her chair. "Here's your tea, my dear. An' what have you brought me this time?"

Harriett explained about the fig pie and then showed her the flowers and catkins. "And I brought a copper penny to put in the water for the flowers. Mama says they will perk up at once."

Mrs. Micklewaithe nodded and directed Harriett to the cupboard and a glass jar which would serve as a flower vase.

"Well, now," she said, once the primroses and catkins had been arranged to her satisfaction and placed upon the table. Her shrewd eyes twinkled mischievously as they traveled from Harriett to Lord Weston and back again.

Harriett bit her lip and tried desperately to think of something to say to forestall the embarrassing comment she was sure hovered upon the old lady's lips. "Ah, Griffie Wortleburt was in church today, and Bertie Mortwent. Papa was careful to give them a Pax cake to share together so they might make up their quarrel over the apple trees."

"Good, good. And you, Lord Weston?" Mrs.

Micklewaithe turned to the earl, "did you share a Pax cake with anyone?"

"With my mother," Lord' Weston replied. "We have many quarrels to mend between us."

"Ay, a good thing to do when a man is contemplatin' tyin' the knot," Mrs. Micklewaithe observed. "Keeps old quarrels from flavoring the new vegetables in the pot."

Lord Weston raised his eyebrows slightly but made no comment beyond wishing George's nails were not so sharp. The old cat was lying upon his lap, purring noisely as he was stroked, his claws kneading Lord Weston's elegant fawn-colored pantaloons. "I'm afraid James will never forgive me," Lord Weston said, looking ruefully down at the pale threads that now bristled from his knee.

"I named George after the Prince Regent," Mrs. Micklewaithe said proudly. "Ay, he's a grand cat."

"Indeed," Lord Weston agreed, and then winced as George dug in his claws before taking a flying leap onto the table, where he batted at a suspicious looking catkin with one paw.

Harriett, seeing this diversion as a chance to escape, put her cup down and picked up her reticule. "I'm afraid I must be going now, Mrs. Micklewaithe. But Mama wanted me to ask if you had any fabric scraps we might use for dying the Easter eggs."

Mrs. Micklewaithe nodded. "I've been savin' them, as usual. Keep meanin' to make a rag rug for myself," she explained to Lord Weston.

"But seems as if I never do get around to it."
Picking up the cane beside her chair, she hobbled into another room and came back a moment later with a round basket. "Take whatever you like," she told Harriett. "But mind you don't take them all. George likes to nap there sometimes, and he wouldn't like it if he couldn't make a little nest."

Selecting some of the more brightly colored scraps, Harriett stuffed them into her now empty stringbag, and after thanking Mrs. Micklewaithe, stood up to take her leave.

"It is time I was leaving as well," Lord Weston said, standing beside her. "I shall escort you home, Miss Haversham."

"But—"

"And I shall see that something is done about your ill-fitting windows, Mrs. Micklewaithe," Lord Weston continued, ignoring Harriett's protest.

"An' the carriage," Mrs. Micklewaithe prompted.

"It shall be here bright and early Easter morning with as much pomp and show as I can muster," Lord Weston promised, before turning to look down at Harriett. "However, I'm afraid I did not bring my carriage today, Miss Haversham. Still, I know you enjoy a brisk walk, and this will give us a chance to have a little talk."

"A talk?" Harriett asked, swallowing nervously.

"A talk," Lord Weston reiterated, his eyes no

longer smiling. "After speaking to your sister this morning, I find there are some things we must discuss."

"Oh," Harriett said, and pulled her bonnet brim as low over her face as possible as she mulled over ways she might divert the conversation from a particular topic she wished very much to avoid.

Twelve

"That was very bad of you, Phillip."

"No, how can you say that, George?" Lord Weston grinned at his friend across the chess board.

"You deliberately let Miss Haversham think her sister had revealed their masquerade to you, and kept her on tenterhooks as long as possible, I've no doubt."

Lord Weston's hand hovered over the board. "Her dilemma was of her own making. She had only to tell me the truth of the situation. I am not above cutting a lark myself—"

"As I know too well," George interrupted.

"Just so," Lord Weston agreed, "but I believe in pound dealings, as you also know. I am no dragon whose fire Miss Haversham must fear. Surely she must know this." He gave George a questioning glance. "Dash it all, I want to marry the girl. But I must know that she truly wants me, George, that she trusts me enough to admit the truth. I will not have a marriage where nothing is shared but a house and name. That is the sort of wedded bliss my parents had because neither really wished for the match."

"But you do."

"Yes." Lord Weston glared down at the playing board, causing George Reading to wonder if he were about to finally win a match from his friend.

"She is not beautiful, you know."

"Is she not?" Lord Weston picked up his rook and stared across the room at the fireplace, absently rubbing the chess piece against his chin. "To me she is everything I have ever looked for in a woman. There is a sweetness about Harriett that attracts more than the sharp wit or fragile beauty of those endowed with both."

"You will have people saying you could have done much better."

Lord Weston shrugged. "I care not what others may say. I know only that when I am with Harriett Haversham, I am the happiest of men. She may not be as beautiful as some on the marriage mart, but then, beauty is no more than a marketable commodity hawked on every street corner in London. My Harriett has more than mere beauty to recommend her."

"Well and truly caught." George Reading shook his head.

"Well and truly caught," Lord Weston agreed.

"She might not have you."

"She will have me," Lord Weston said firmly. He moved his rook and sat back, reaching for the decanter of wine by his side.

It was late, and they were the only ones still awake at Yarwood. At least, Lord Weston supposed James was still somewhere about, waiting to assist him. The valet steadfastly refused to retire until every article of the earl's clothing had been properly attended to. Besides, James had been so horrified by the state of Lord Weston's mangled pantaloons earlier, he would doubtless have great difficulty sleeping, in any case.

"Is Mrs. Dade still determined to leave in the morning?" George Reading moved his knight in what he considered a brilliant maneuver, and now tried to distract his host from the game.

"As determined as her daughter is to stay," Lord Weston answered. "Would you care for some more wine, George?"

George Reading nodded and accepted the decanter from his friend. "What I cannot understand," he said meditatively, after filling his glass, "is why no one but you and I saw through Miss Haversham's disguise. And how can they not realize that Reverend Haversham is not the same person they supped with?"

"It is quite simple, really," Lord Weston replied. "I knew Miss Haversham on the instant because she has the most beguiling gray eyes of anyone, male or female, I have ever met. But since I did not denounce her, everyone assumed Miss Haversham was the person she pretended to be. Just as they now assume her father is the same Reverend Haversham who shared a meal with them earlier. If I do not question it, why should they?"

"Because it's quite obvious to anyone with a bit more between their ears than vacant space."

"And what tipped you off to Miss Haversham's disguise, George?" Lord Weston asked, casually studying the board.

"I knew the moment—"

"Yes?"

"The moment I glanced at your face and saw that look you get when there's something smoky afoot. I suppose if I had not been standing opposite you when Miss Haversham entered the room, I might not have noticed anything either. After all, I had never met the vicar before, and the idea of one of his daughters disguising herself as a man is so preposterous, it beggars the imagination. Still . . . I say, Phillip, what do you think you are doing?"

"Capturing your knight with my bishop."

"But you can't do that!"

"I've just done it. The real question here is, why did they do it?"

"Do what?" George Reading asked testily, as he frowned down at his captured knight.

"Why did they feel it was necessary for one of them to attend the supper party disguised as the vicar? Where was Reverend Haversham that evening? And why do his daughters want no one to know about it?"

"Maybe he really did have the plague, as Mrs. Dade maintains."

Lord Weston smiled. "If you move that rook, you leave your queen defenseless."

Dropping his chess piece as if it were a hot coal, George Reading stared down at the gameboard in disgust. "Does your future bride play the game?"

"Of chess? I don't know, I shall have to find out. I believe I have you in check, George."

George Reading threw up his hands in a gesture of surrender. "I have not a mind for this tonight," he defended his play. "The thought of losing another bachelor friend to the parson's noose destroys my concentration. So," he looked up at Lord Weston, "when may I wish you happy, Phillip?"

"I shall speak to her father early this week, and then to Harriett herself. Do you intend to help with the egg decorating at the vicarage this Wednesday?"

"Why? Don't tell me you intend to pop the question over a boiled egg, Phillip?" For the first time since he had known him, George Reading saw his friend blush uncomfortably.

"I did have something of that sort in mind, yes," Lord Weston confessed. "I read somewhere that in certain countries decorated eggs are given as tokens of love, and you know how women adore that sort of flummery. So I thought it would be romantic to write a short verse on one of the eggs. Tell Harriett how I feel about her. You know—" Lord Weston stopped and cleared his throat. "Something like . . .

> *"My dearest heart, when we're apart,*
> *I think of you—"*

"When on eggs I chew?" George interrupted, his expression one of innocent interest.

"George! This is serious business. And if you are going to laugh like that, you will do yourself an injury."

"I do apologize, old boy. And you may be certain I shall be at the vicarage on Wednesday. I would not miss watching the dashing Lord Weston wax eloquent on a boiled egg for anything. Will it become all the rage, do you think?"

Harriett searched out her egg-decorating gloves from the bottom drawer of her bureau. They had once been white, but were now splotched with dabs of red, green, and a lovely brown onion-skin color. She had on one of her oldest dresses: a lime green muslin with dropped waist which she never wore anymore but for working in the garden or helping Cook with the preserving or some such task.

"Are you sure you want to wear that gown?" her mother asked, eyeing the green muslin with some disfavor, as Harriett walked into the parlour.

"I will be coloring eggs for the children and

those who are invalid and cannot get about anymore, not going to a dance," Harriett replied a bit stiffly. "At any rate, Lord Weston and his guests might not come. It is hardly the sort of thing they are used to doing."

Mrs. Haversham settled her foot more comfortably on the stool in front of her chair. "We hardly decorate eggs every day either, my dear."

"No, but . . . you know what I mean, Mama. Miss Dade is used to having any number of servants about. I would not be surprised to find that she thinks the hens lay eggs already decorated at Easter time."

"That is unkind, Harriett," Mrs. Haversham said, though she could not forebear to smile. "And probably untruthful as well. Just because Miss Dade is unusually beautiful does not mean she is deserving of such remarks."

"No, Mama."

"Not that I do not understand, Harriett."

Harriett glanced at her mother and then down at the basket into which she was emptying the bag of fabric scraps she had collected from Madame St. Germaine earlier in the week. She wanted desperately to confide in her mother, to tell someone how she felt about Phillip Sinclair. For that is how she thought of him: not as Lord Weston, and certainly not as Lord Stiff Rump. Harriett smiled to herself, remembering their first meeting and Rusty Brown.

"They must be pleasant thoughts, my dear," Mrs. Haversham remarked.

Harriett nodded. "Mama?" She pleated a small scrap of blue satin between her fingers and hesitated for a moment, biting her lip. "Mama, how did you know you were in love with Papa?" she asked finally, all in a rush.

Her mother smiled and looked across the room at a ray of sunshine that seemed determined to fade the carpet. "I knew the moment I looked into your father's eyes," she said softly. "They were so kind and . . . and honest." She looked at Harriett again. "You know I have always thought that is one of the most important things two people can have. The first mad rush of love quickly fades, but honesty . . . an honest friendship, in fact, is something truly to be treasured."

An honest friendship, Harriett thought. I have not even that, though it might have been possible once.

"You look very sad, my dear."

"No. It is only that I wish . . ." Her voice faded away and she found herself blinking rapidly to keep away the tears.

"You only wish for Lord Weston?" her mother asked.

Harriett sniffed. "Am I so obvious, then?"

"You are my daughter. I know you better than anyone, and it is not so strange that he should have caught your fancy. He is handsome and worldly and—"

"Nice, Mama. He is also very nice," Harriett

said. "We have always called him Lord Stiff Rump, because that is what Reverend Smythe named him. But he is not like that at all. You should have seen him with Mrs. Micklewaithe's cat. He was—" All of a sudden Harriett burst into tears, and in a moment found herself on her knees, her head buried in her mother's lap.

"Oh, Mama," she said, as soon as she was able. "I am afraid I have gone and done something very stupid."

"You have fallen in love with Lord Weston."

Harriett nodded, looking up at her mother over the handkerchief that had been thrust into her hand.

"And does he return your affection?"

Swallowing the lump in her throat, Harriett squeezed her eyes shut and shook her head. "How could he?" she whispered, her voice ragged. "I am plain, sensible Harriett Haversham. And Lord Weston might have anyone."

"You have always given yourself short shrift, Harriett. The right man will appreciate you because you are plain and sensible and loving and honest."

Harriett's face was already red and streaked with tears, but it turned even redder now. "You do not know, Mama," she said. "But I'm afraid Gusta and I have done something very bad, and I have not been honest with Lord Weston at all. Quite the contrary, in fact."

Mrs. Haversham smiled, and cradled her daughter's face between her hands. "It cannot be so very bad if you are involved," she assured

Harriett. "Now, why do you not tell me of it, and you will feel better. A bad conscience is a very heavy thing to carry around, as your Papa would say."

Blowing her nose rather fiercely, Harriett nodded. "I should like to tell you," she admitted, "but you will be very disappointed in me, Mama."

"I could never be disappointed in you for telling the truth, my dear." She settled back in her chair. "I take it this does not involve the raid on my chocolate box to which Augusta has already confessed?"

"This is much, much worse," Harriett said. "And I do not blame Augusta because I am the elder and should have known better. Only I did want to see Lord Weston again and perhaps find out what he thought of me. So when Gusta suggested I play Ophelia, I was quite agreeable and—"

"Ophelia?" Mrs. Haversham interrupted.

Harriett nodded. "Ophelia disguised herself as a man to win Romeo's love."

"She did?" Her mother looked at her in surprise.

Harriett nodded again. "You must have missed that passage when Papa read it too. But anyway, I thought maybe such a thing would work with Lord Weston, and so . . . I dressed like a man and pretended to be Papa and went to a supper party at Yarwood with Augusta!" The last was said in such a rush, Mrs. Haversham was certain she could not have heard correctly. It was only by dint of many questions and much repetition that the whole story finally came out. And even then Mrs. Haversham could not quite believe she had truly grasped what Harriett had said. "You dressed in your Papa's trousers?" she asked Harriett for the third time. "Not Augusta, but you?"

Looking miserable, Harriett explained, "Gusta was too short. And though she was too kind to say it, she is too pretty as well. No one would ever mistake her for a man."

"I cannot imagine anyone mistaking you for one, either," her mother replied. "Was everyone quite foxed?"

"Foxed, Mama?"

"Had everyone been drinking, Harriett?"

"No. Well, of course, there was some wine before dinner. And then, I did share a glass of port with Lord Weston and Mr. Reading, after the ladies had withdrawn. You know, I must say, Mama, I was quite disappointed to find that gentlemen do not discuss anything at all interesting over their port."

"Oh? Ah, exactly what do the gentlemen talk about, my dear?"

"Horses and birds, mostly. It was really quite boring—except, well, you know, it was rather nice to be one of the fellows and to find out what Lord Weston is really like."

"And what is he really like?" Mrs. Haversham prompted, knowing this must now be a subject dear to her daughter's heart.

Harriett sighed and looked dreamily down

at the handkerchief she was twisting between her fingers. "Lord Weston is everything a woman could want in a man. He is handsome and kind, intelligent and caring, not at all stuffy or high in the instep, as we had thought. I do not know why people call him Lord Stiff Rump."

"Actually, I don't think anyone does, Harriett. I know you children thought it quite funny when Reverend Smythe called His Lordship by that name and have ceaselessly repeated it, but your father always thought it quite wrong of Reverend Smythe to name him so."

"Oh." Harriett frowned for a moment. "You know, I must say that I cannot imagine Lord Weston being such a stickler for propriety as Reverend Smythe made out, but . . ."

Mrs. Haversham shifted restlessly on her chair. "I am sorry to say that I never cared for Reverend Smythe," she admitted. "And though we never discussed it, you should know that he was removed from the living because he had been drinking and drove his curricle so recklessly a small boy was killed."

"I see." Still frowning, Harriett rose slowly from her kneeling position. "So I was quite wrong to call Lord Weston, Stiff Rump."

Mrs. Haversham gave a little shrug. "I never think it wise to nickname any person unkindly, my dear. But as to whether the epithet fits, I must say, I barely know the man. We have met only once, and that several years ago. Lord Weston is not a frequent visitor, but—"

"Beggin' your pardon, ma'am." Mary stood at the parlour doorway. "But the folks from Yarwood is here for the egg decoratin'. I was goin' to show 'em into the parlour, but Lord Weston said as how he saw the tables an' such already set up in the yard and so they would go there."

"We cannot have Lord Weston in the chicken yard, Mary," Mrs. Haversham protested.

Harriett quickly straightened her gown and reached for the basket of fabric scraps. "We will be coloring eggs, Mama. You know how messy that is, and you never allow us in the house, not even last year, when there was a downpour."

"Last year Lord Weston was not here."

"All men are equal under God, Mama."

Mrs. Haversham pursed her lips and shook her head. "Sometimes I think reading sermons can be more dangerous than reading novels. He will think us terribly rag-mannered, Harriett. I am sure your Papa would say it is only proper that such guests be entertained in the parlour."

"You do not even approve of the sun being in your parlour, Mama. What would happen if Lord Weston should spill some of the dye upon the carpet?"

Mrs. Haversham hesitated. "Very well, Harriett. But at least make sure the chickens are locked in their pen. And that the gate to the yard is closed. I do not want to hear of Bessie stepping on the toe of some influential member of the ton. Your sister would never forgive us."

"Her life would be ruined." Harriett smiled, and then grew serious for a moment, biting her lip. "Mama? What should I say to Lord Weston? Should I . . ." She took a deep breath. "Should I tell him about my masquerade?"

"I have told you that to me, honesty between two persons is the most important thing they can share. But you must come to your own decision on this, my dear."

Harriett nodded, cradling the basket of fabrics to her chest. "He need never know," she said, half to herself. "He could go back to London and never know, and it would make no difference in his life."

"But would it not make a difference in yours?" her mother asked.

Harriett sighed. "Being a vicar's daughter can be very difficult."

"Indeed, my dear, but I have every confidence that whatever decision you make will be the right one." Mrs. Haversham smiled and pulled her satinwood work table closer, lifting the hinged top and reaching into the well for some thread. "Now go and play hostess for me while I finish hemming these towels, and Cook sets the water to boiling for the eggs."

"Yes, Mama."

"And when you bring our guests inside for refreshments later, would you mind using the side door? It seems that your Papa has developed a bit of an aversion to one of the young ladies who is coming this afternoon, a Miss Smalbathe?"

Harriett nodded.

"It is rather odd, for your Papa is usually the most understanding of men, but he seems to think Miss Smalbathe is a bit . . . well, dicked in the nob, were the words he used. So if you could make sure he is not disturbed, my dear?"

"I do not think that will be a problem, Mama, for I heard him tell Mary he was locking himself in his study this afternoon."

Mrs. Haversham raised her eyebrows. "Sometimes being a vicar's wife can be a bit difficult, too," she murmured, as Harriett left the room.

Three trestle tables had been set up in the side yard of the parsonage. A large bowl of eggs was on each, along with a collection of herbs and a large pile of onion skins. Harriett hesitated just inside the kitchen doorway, surveying the scene. Miss Dade, talking animatedly with Lord Weston by one of the tables, was wearing an elegant blue silk dress with a little apron tied in front trimmed to match the pink bows on the hem of her gown. Harriett brushed one hand down the skirt of her faded green muslin and gritted her teeth, refusing to give in to the melancholia that seemed to engulf her whenever she was in Miss Dade's presence.

Instead, Harriett turned her eyes to the

chicken yard, where Abigail Smalbathe and her sister stood giggling over the hens as if they had never seen one before except on a dinner table. Surprisingly, Augusta was also standing nearby, conversing with George Reading. Augusta never helped with the egg decorating, declaring it much too messy and complaining that the steam from the hot water ruined her skin.

Raising her eyebrows slightly as she wondered what her sister's presence might import, Harriett gripped the basket of fabric scraps in her arms as if it were a battle shield, and stepped into the yard.

Augusta rushed up at once.

"Dear Harriett, do let me help you with that," she cried, snatching the basket of fabric scraps from Harriett's arms. "I was just telling Mr. Reading what truly cunning eggs we make for the children."

"Oh?"

"Yes." Augusta smiled at George Reading. "With imprints of leaves and flowers, and all in the most wonderful colors."

"Indeed." Harriett nodded. "But since the children either eat them at once or take them to the egg roll, where they are quickly smashed, they must be content with merely having their names writ on each egg in candle wax."

"But we do decorate some with leaves and flowers," Augusta insisted, giving Harriett a meaningful look.

"For the invalids," Harriett agreed. "Would you like to be in charge of those, Augusta'?"

Augusta beamed. "I am very artistic," she assured George Reading. "What would you have me do, Harriett?"

Harriett showed her how to place leaves or flower petals on the egg. "Sometimes they will stick by themselves," she said, demonstrating this, "but if they will not, there is a bit of golden syrup in that jar to make them stay in place. Then you may wrap the eggs in scraps of fabric, tie it all in place with string, and place the whole in boiling water where the color of the fabrics will adhere to the eggs. Or, if you prefer, you may place the eggs in the water with onion skins. That gives a rather lovely brown effect which is quite pretty with the leaf and petal outlines."

Since the women all considered themselves artistic, or at least, wanted to impress the men with their skill, they all gathered round and began to stick bits of leaves and flowers to the eggs and snatch at the basket of fabric to find their favorite color.

"Designs may also be sketched on the egg shell with a pen knife," Harriett told George Reading, who was watching Augusta carefully sticking flower petals on the entire surface of one egg. "They look quite pretty when dyed in the onion peeling."

"Ah, I am afraid I have no such skill," he replied. "No, I am here merely to fetch and carry and assist where I may."

Harriett nodded. "Then perhaps you will not mind helping Cook and Joseph bring in the pots of boiling water," she said, blandly accepting him at his word. "Though one does tend to get a bit wet in the process."

George Reading accepted the implied challenge, and as good as his word, was soon fetching pots of boiling water to the ladies who were so intent on being artistic that Harriett was afraid only a dozen eggs would be colored by nightfall.

Shaking her head, Harriett walked to the table that contained a bowl of eggs and several candles. She would write the names of the children on the eggs and color them simply, with onion peelings and some green herbs in the water. Picking up one of the eggs, she began to carefully letter the name "Alicia."

"I will assist you with the children's eggs if you will but tell me what to write," Lord Weston said.

Harriett almost dropped her egg, not having realized he was standing so close by. "Yes, thank you," she replied, a little breathlessly. "I am afraid I am not at all artistic, and so this has always been my job."

Lord Weston smiled but did not reply, merely picking up a bit of candle and one of the eggs.

"I—I have a list of the children's names so I will not forget anyone," Harriett said. And putting down her own egg, she fetched the list from her pocket and put it on the table.

Lord Weston nodded. "Why do I not start at the bottom of the list and you may start at the top, and we shall meet in the middle," he suggested.

"Yes." Harriett picked up her egg and bit of wax and took a deep, steadying breath. She found standing so close to Lord Weston unnerving, and her hand was shaking a little as she finished printing "Alicia" on the egg. Doubly unnerving was the fact that they seemed to be quite isolated from the others at the moment, and if she was going to confess the masquerade to Lord Weston, this would be the ideal time. Provided she could summon sufficient courage to do so. Honesty, she told herself: it is the most important thing between two people. But there is nothing really between Lord Weston and me anyway, she answered herself. There is no need for him ever to know what Gusta and I have done and—"Lord Weston?"

"Yes?" He looked up from his egg and smiled politely across at her.

"I . . . there is something I must tell you." The words were out before she had time to reconsider, almost as if her too-vocal conscience was determined to confess whether the rest of her agreed with the decision or not.

Lord Weston waited silently, his brows raised in polite inquiry.

"At the supper party, I . . . um, my parents were away from home, and Augusta desperately wanted to attend, so I . . . I disguised myself as Papa and went in his stead."

"I know," he said quietly.

"It was unforgivable of me, and I am very sorry. We did not want you to know that Papa had gone after Camilla because we believed she had run away with your groom, but it seems she did not and so it makes no difference. And besides, now that I know you better, I am sure you would have understood in any case." Harriett stopped, the spate of her words having been blocked by sudden comprehension. "But—you knew?"

He nodded. "How could I not?"

"But everyone else was taken in." Harriett turned to look at the others, her face turning so bright a red her freckles disappeared. "Weren't they?"

"None of them guessed," Lord Weston quickly assured her. "But I . . . how could I not know it was you?"

Harriett swallowed. He was looking at her in such a way that Harriett thought he wanted either to strangle her or kiss her. Was it possible?

"La, here you are!" Miss Dade insinuated herself between Harriett and Lord Weston. "Well, what are we doing? Writing names on eggs? I shall certainly help, for I dearly love children, you know. Shall I take the first name, Westie? And you may take the second."

"I have already written Alicia's name on several eggs," Harriett said, her voice a dry croak. "But Andrew's name is next."

"Oh, yes." Miss Dade smiled up at Lord Weston and daintly picked up an egg and piece of wax. "Oh, dear, I'm afraid this wax needs a sharper point to it. Could you cut it with your pen knife, Westie?"

Harriett stood to one side, biting her lip to keep back tears, as she silently wrote "Bertram" on several eggs. Miss Dade had turned so that her back was to Harriett, quite shutting Harriett off from any converse with Lord Weston. Not that it matters, Harriett thought.

I have confessed, and he already knew what I had done. All this time, he knew. What must he think of me? Harriett's face grew warm and her fingers tensed on the bit of wax she was holding. If only I could have explained, told him how it was most unlike me to have done such a thing. Not that it would have helped to let him know how staid and dull I am, she thought. Not that it would have made any difference.

"Does the child prefer 'Thomas' or 'Tom'?" Lord Weston asked, stepping behind Miss Dade to stand at Harriett's other side.

"Tom," she said, sniffing back her tears.

"Is something wrong, Miss Haversham?" he asked.

Harriett shook her head. "It is merely the boiling water." She indicated the pot of water George Reading had fetched moments before. "It makes my eyes water."

"I see." He was silent for a moment, and then Harriett felt him suddenly press something into her hand. It was an Easter egg, one that had been decorated with a pen knife design and had a short verse on one side. She turned it over, admiring the delicate color.

Lord Weston took a step closer and cleared his throat. "Miss Haversham, would you—"

"Oh!" Miss Dade screeched suddenly, and dropped her egg into the pot of green dye, spattering her gown.

"How clumsy." Abigail Smalbathe suddenly materialized nearby. "You must have been concentrating too much on trying to write the alphabet," she purred. "It is difficult for some, I know. Does a lack of mental acuity also run in your family, Miss Dade?"

"You jarred my arm!" Miss Dade turned furiously to face Miss Smalbathe. "You deliberately jarred my arm so I would drop the egg and ruin my gown."

"You musn't blame others for your own clumsiness," Miss Smalbathe observed calmly. "It is quite tedious, like a child who can never accept the consequences of his behavior."

"I am not a child!" Miss Dade raged, and stamped her foot.

"No?" Miss Smalbathe smiled.

Lord Weston stepped between the two women just as Miss Dade grabbed an egg and raised her arm. "It is time for tea, is it not, Miss Haversham? I have no doubt your mother will be waiting in the parlour for us. May I escort you inside, Miss Dade?"

"You may certainly escort me," Miss Smalbathe said, snagging his arm. Miss Dade, never one to give up the field, grabbed his other arm, and Lord Weston, like a prize bone between two snarling dogs, escorted both ladies inside.

Harriett watched them for a moment, as with some difficulty the narrow doorway was negotiated. Then she turned, dropped the egg she was holding in her pocket, and began to mop up the grccn dye with a cloth. Looking at the bowl of eggs, she thought sadly that they were supposed to be a symbol of rebirth.

"But I feel as if I have quite died inside," she whispered.

Thirteen

It was not until everyone had left and Harriett was outside in the yard once more, finishing the children's eggs, that she remembered the one Lord Weston had handed her. Curious, she took it from her pocket. It was a lovely thing, a mottled golden color, with a heart drawn on one side and a verse inscribed on the other. Harriett read the verse once, and then, unbelievingly, again, while her heart soared within her like one of the birds she loved to feed.

> *My dearest heart, when we're apart*
> *My thoughts of you are never free.*
> *Please say that you will marry me.*

Did that mean—? Harriett sat down on the bench beside the trestle table and bit her lip. Then, taking a deep breath, she read the verse a third time. The letters were tiny and a bit hard to make out where the egg curved at the end, but there was no mistaking the words. It was both love poem and proposal, and Lord Weston had given it to her.

Was it some sort of cruel jest? Harriett put one hand to her mouth as if to silence the thought. Certainly she had learned early on that men could be cruel. Perhaps everyone was waiting to see what she would do, waiting to laugh at her and . . . but surely not. Surely everything she knew of Lord Weston told her this could not be so.

And if it were not a jest, then it must mean . . . Harriett's lips curved into a smile beneath her gloved fingers, a smile that soon became a grin. Lord Weston loved her. Loved her, and wanted to marry her. And she had been honest with him, had told him about disguising herself as Papa, had admitted her hoydenish behavior. And it had not mattered. Lord Weston had known in any case. Had known, in fact, when he had made the egg for her.

Able to sit still no longer, Harriett sprang to her feet, twirling around the tables, her happiness bubbling joyfully to the surface. And then, grasping her precious egg close to her breast, she stopped and stared unseeingly at the chickens clucking in their pen.

I cannot believe this is happening, she thought, as two hens cocked their heads and stared at her suspiciously. That someone as wonderful as Phillip Sinclair, Earl of Weston, is in love with me. With me! Tall, plain, Harriett Haversham.

Harriett wanted to go to him at once. Tell him that of course she accepted his proposal, of course she would marry him, and then ask what it was that had made him fall in love with her. Harriett could tell him quite clearly why she had fallen in love with him. It was not just that he was the most attractive man she had ever met. No, it was the way his eyes lit when he smiled, and the kindness he had shown to Rusty Brown, and . . . oh, a dozen things or more! Including the fact that he had known about her masquerade and had kept that knowledge to himself. Some men would have gotten great pleasure in exposing her for the entertainment of their guests. But Harriett didn't think Lord Weston would have done that even if he hadn't loved her. He was much too kind and nice and . . . and wonderful. Harriett sighed, kissed her marvelous egg, and put it in her pocket for safe keeping.

I wonder when Lord Weston first knew he loved me? she mused, reaching to throw a bit of feed to the hens. I think I fell in love with him almost at once. Harriett wagged her fingers through the chicken wire at the hens, admonished them not to be greedy, and then turned . . . to find herself face-to-face with Abigail Smalbathe.

"You seemed so lost in thought, I did not wish to interrupt you, Miss Haversham," she said. "I knew you must be concerned with something of import to be concentrating so. Or else must have an extraordinary interest in chickens. Do you train them, too? Or were you merely planning a new masquerade? How did you plan to disguise yourself this time, Miss Haversham? As the butler, perhaps?"

Harriett swallowed the bile that suddenly rose to her throat. "I am afraid I do not know what you mean," she said.

Miss Smalbathe gave her a tight, humorless smile. "La, my dear, you must not imagine you can deny it. I have heard the whole story. What a strange creature you are, to be sure. For who would think so quiet and plain a woman would dare to disguise herself as a man and come to a supper party, given by an earl no less?"

Her face burning, Harriett blindly gripped the chicken wire behind her, until it cut through her gloves into her fingers and the pain took away the sense of unreality she was feeling and the sickness that settled cold as a March frost in her stomach.

"I knew at once, of course," Miss Smalbathe continued, tittering. "Still, it was quite amusing for me to pretend that I did not and to flirt with you as if you really were the Reverend Haversham. It is a droll tale I should quite enjoy telling. But of course, I will not. I could not be so cruel. No, my dear Miss Haversham, your secret is quite safe with me. I shall tell no one, and I should advise you to do the same. The gabblemongers would love to feast on such a tasty tidbit as this."

Harriett walked over to the bench beside the table and sat down, staring at her hands, still in their gloves of many colors but now scored with the marks of the wire. "Did everyone know?" she asked, her voice a small, tight knot of sound.

Miss Smalbathe sat down next to her and patted her hand. "No, the others are not so discerning. Miss Dade, for instance, did not suspect a thing. Silly widgeon. I do not know what Lord Weston sees in her. But men would ever care about a pretty face without thought to the empty mind behind it. I had thought Lord Weston different, but I see now I am mistaken. He shall doubtless marry the silly chit, and they are welcome to each other."

"Do you think he will marry her?" Harriett made an effort to speak normally, as if her world had not just been felled by Miss Smalbathe's ax.

"La, my dear. If you could have seen the way Lord Weston stared at Laurenda Dade in the carriage! Why, it was almost indecent. I would not be at all surprised to find that he had already gone on bent knee to her, for there was quite the smell of April and May about them."

"Perhaps because it is now April," Harriett said, in a toneless voice. "And it will soon be May. They used to be my favorite months of the year."

"Indeed? I have always preferred the winter, when one may remain indoors and not be forever sloshing about in the elements and pretending to enjoy it. At any rate, I am sure we will soon see an announcement in the paper. It is all quite distressing, for I could have remained in London and not bothered with all this rustication. Ah, well, I shall begin pursuit of Lord Burnleigh as soon as I return. He was next on my list, and shall do as well, I suppose, though he is not quite as rich and I had hoped for more than a mere viscount."

"A pity."

"Yes, but in actual fact, Lord Burnleigh is more to my liking. Yes, I am sure he will do very nicely. Well, I must be going, my dear, the carriage is waiting. I only returned because I had left my—" Miss Smalbathe hesitated, looking around for something she could claim to have left behind. Finding nothing, she merely smiled. "I shall see you at Easter, I expect. I am so glad I could help you with decorating the eggs. It was a novel experience."

"One usually reserved for your cook, I expect?" Harriett said, lifting her chin a trifle.

"Of course." Miss Smalbathe shrugged. "But I must admit that charitable work does make one feel so . . . charitable, does it not? Until Sunday, then, Miss Haversham."

Harriett nodded and watched as Miss Smalbathe, carefully lifting her skirts, crossed the yard and rounded the side of the house. Harriett remained sitting on the bench, not even offering to walk with Miss Smalbathe to the carriage. "Which I know is quite rag-mannered of me, but I do not think I care," Harriett told the hens, who were staring at her through the chicken wire.

Removing her gloves, Harriett reached in her pocket and slowly brought out Lord Weston's egg. With one finger, she traced the words scratched into the shell. Why had he given it to her when he intended to marry Miss Dade? What did he mean by it? She read the words softly aloud, trying to puzzle out the mystery of Lord Weston's intentions.

> *My dearest heart when we're apart*
> *My thoughts of you are never free*
> *Please say that you will marry me.*

It was true that Lord Weston had not mentioned her by name in the verse, but it was certainly to her that he had given the egg. Harriett closed her eyes and frowned, trying to remember exactly what Lord Weston had said. Then she opened her eyes and took a deep breath of relief. He had mentioned her name. She remembered it now, could once again hear his deep baritone saying, "Miss Haversham, would you . . ." And then he had given her the egg and Miss Dade had screamed and—

Harriett bit her lip. Miss Dade. Laurenda Dade had been standing next to her. Was it not possible . . . no. Was it not probable that Lord Weston had been going to say, "Miss Haversham, would you give this egg to Miss Dade?"

Of course. Harriett swallowed. Of course. It had not been meant for her at all. What was it Miss Smalbathe had said? Men would ever care about a pretty face. Not plain, tall, tongue-tied, prosy Harriett Haversham. Not that odd woman who feeds rooks and wears her papa's trousers to dinner parties. Not Harriett Haversham. No one would write verses of love to her. Not when they might have an Incomparable.

"Well, I shall have to see that Miss Dade receives her love token, shall I not?" Harriett asked the hens. "It is the Christian thing to do. I must not keep it, for I am sure Miss Dade will want it. I know if it were mine I should treasure it always."

Harriett looked down at the egg, at the lovely golden color, and the small heart etched on one side, and the verse . . . she could no longer read the verse for the tears that now obscured it. "Still, I must take it to Miss Dade, for it was never meant for me. I must take it to Miss Dade and wish her every happiness."

Cradling the egg in her hand, Harriett got slowly to her feet. The egg was still slightly warm from having been in her pocket. For a moment still she held it and then suddenly whirled around and with all her might dashed the egg upon the ground. "The devil I will!" she cried, and ran into the house.

Harriett was not herself. Everyone said so. She was too quiet, and she seldom smiled. And most surprising of all, she had never finished decorating the Easter eggs. Mary had gone into

278

the yard to fetch Harriett for supper and found the trestle tables still with their bowls of eggs and only a dozen or more of them decorated. It was not like Harriett to leave a job half done. Usually she was the one who remained behind to finish things after everyone else had left. It was most unlike her.

Mrs. Haversham, who could still hobble only a few feet with the aid of a cane, watched her daughter move silently about the parlour. It was Good Friday, and Harriett had assisted Cook with baking the traditional hot cross buns, and then taken some to Mrs. Micklewaithe.

"How is Mrs. Micklewaithe?" Mrs. Haversham asked, looking up from the devotional she had not been able to read. "And George?"

Harriett smiled for the first time in days. "George is fine, Mama, and I am glad I was wearing gloves, or I would have a fine scratch to prove his mettle. And Mrs. Micklewaithe intends to go to church on Easter. Lord Weston has promised to send a carriage for her."

"Indeed? Did you know that he called yesterday? And today? And asked very specifically to speak to you?" Her mother waited, hopefully, to see how Harriett would receive this news.

Harriett shrugged and looked down at the sermon she was reading for her father. "Yes, I knew," she replied in an indifferent voice, and made a notation in the margin.

"I am sure it is no concern of mine," Mrs.

Haversham tried again, "but it did seem as if he was anxious to speak to you. Do you not think, perhaps, you might go to Yarwood to find out what he wanted?"

"No, Mama," Harriett said, not looking up, "I am sure it was only a courtesy call of no import."

Mrs. Haversham pressed her lips together. She would say no more, she would—"Harriett, do not be a clunch!" she begged her daughter all at once. "No one calls twice and asks specifically to speak to a person out of courtesy. Especially not an earl. Now, you must go up to Yarwood and speak to Lord Weston. Not to do so would be considered quite uncivil."

"I thought you said it was no concern of yours," Harriett said, her eyes quite without their usual smile but filled with a reserve that Mrs. Haversham found quite off-putting, and quite unlike Harriett.

"Of course it is my concern," Mrs. Haversham said. "I am your mother, after all." She frowned. Harriett had never spoken to her like that before. For all her daughter was quiet and a bit shy, she was no dissembler and had always been very open in her feelings. "Are you not feeling well, Harriett?"

"I am fine, Mama." Harriett dipped her pen in the inkwell.

"You seem quite out of sorts, and while I know this is Good Friday and one should not be dancing about, it is unlike you to be so hangdog and mopish. That is more like Camilla or Augusta."

Harriett sniffed and bit her lip. "I am sorry, Mama," she said, in a thick voice which warned Mrs. Haversham that further probing would result in tears.

Mrs. Haversham sighed and went back to her devotional. It was sermon number ninety-three, and Reverend Haversham was wondering whether to include it in the book of devotions he was planning to publish. What did Mrs. Haversham think of it? Mrs. Haversham was afraid she could not make sense of it, though this was no doubt due more to her own state of mind than to the quality of the sermon.

It had been exactly four days since Lord Weston had called and requested a private audience with Reverend Haversham. Four days in which to gloat and indulge in the surely pardonable sin of a mother's pride. To think of Harriett as wife to an earl! Not that it was Lord Weston's title that was of first consideration, of course. No, had he been other than a fine, upstanding man, his offer would not have been entertained for a moment. But he was all of that and more, and Mrs. Haversham could have sworn, if a vicar's wife was allowed to do such a thing, that her daughter was head over ears in love with Lord Weston.

In fact, had Harriett not confessed that to her only a few days ago and in this very parlour? What had gone wrong? Mrs. Haversham was almost certain the earl had intended to propose to Harriett on Wednesday. Had something happened? Had Lord Weston changed his mind? And why was Harriett so unhappy? Mrs. Haversham sighed and tried to read her husband's sermon again. She would be glad when Lent was over and she had her husband's attention and her box of chocolates available to her once more.

Thankfully, Augusta soon came bouncing into the parlour to show her mother a fashion plate in *Ackermann's Repository* and thus dispel the gloom that hung as heavy as the winter draperies which had not yet been removed from the windows. The print was of a long wrapping coat of dark blue cloth lined and trimmed with ermine. "And see, Mama, she holds a muff of ermine as well." Augusta's voice was hushed by the beauty and extravagance of it all. "I shall die if I do not have one exactly like it," she informed her mother.

"Then it is fortunate that your Papa may perform the funeral service and it shall cost us nothing," Mrs. Haversham replied, without a shred of sympathy.

"Mama! If I am to be dressed in rags, I would rather not go to London." Augusta sniffed, and after a moment's concentration, allowed a few tears to slip down her cheeks. "Do you not see how important it is for me to be fashionably dressed, so I may make a suitable match? I daresay no one but second sons or mere gentlemen will make me an offer otherwise." Augusta pressed her lips together and looked suitably woeful. "And it is not as if I ask for myself, Mama. Once I am rich, I shall make my husband give a great deal to the parish."

"If you are to be dressed in ermine, he shall not have a great deal to give," Mrs. Haversham pointed out. "And should you not be reading devotions, since it is Good Friday, rather than wasting your time with *Ackermann's?*"

"Yes, Mama." Augusta looked suitably meek. "Not that *Ackermann's* is a waste of time, exactly, for there is a great deal to read concerning the arts and literature, you know. Still, I am sure you are right." She sat down on the settee and tried to look suitably chastened, but Augusta could never keep silent for long.

"Are you correcting Papa's sermon for tonight, Harriett?" she asked. "I hope it is shorter than last year, when Mr. Sternwort started snoring in the middle. It was most embarrassing."

"I shall give Papa your advice," Harriett said, with a small smile. "But I have already eliminated the page where Papa speaks of the pigs in the churchyard."

"Pigs in the churchyard?" Mrs. Haversham asked.

Harriett nodded. "You remember last fall, when there were a great many acorns in the churchyard and Farmer Morley's pigs wandered in to eat them and overturned one of the gravestones?"

"Your father was quite upset. I remember it

well. But what has that to do with Good Friday?"

"Nothing," Harriett acknowledged. "But Papa feels he should mention it, and so has been putting it in every sermon since. I keep taking it out because I think it would embarrass Farmer Morley, but I suppose one of these days Papa will simply speak of it anyway."

"I should not want my grave stepped upon by a pig," Augusta said. "Especially since I intend to have a very large monument with an angel on top." When no one replied, Augusta got up and went to look out the window. It was raining. It seemed always to rain on Good Friday, which quite dampened her spirits. Turning, her glance fell upon Harriett, who was frowning over the page she was correcting. Her sister looked so sad and pale, Augusta's heart gave a little flipflop of concern.

"Harriett?" Augusta walked up to the desk and spoke her sister's name softly.

"Yes?" Harriett looked up, her gray eyes quite dull, as if she had a terrible headache but was trying not to show it.

"I am sorry you are not going to London with Cammie and Mama and me," Augusta said. "I did not know at first that Papa meant for you to stay at home. Are you very upset? I know it is most unfair, and almost as if you were being punished. If anyone should remain at home, it should be Camilla. Would you like me to speak to Papa about it?"

Harriett bit her lip, and the eyes that had

been dull before were now shining with tears. She got up and slowly walked around the desk to put her arms around her sister. "Thank you," she whispered. "It is very sweet of you to be concerned, Gusta, but a Season in London means little to me now. Besides, you know very well I should not take."

"I know nothing of the kind," Augusta said in a firm voice, pulling back to stare up at her taller sister. "Why, I am sure there are any number of men who like freckles and red hair and who think decided noses are quite the thing."

"Now you are telling a bouncer, Gusta. Men want pretty women for their wives. They may talk to the rest of us and consider us quite sensible and agreeable, but they would never think to make a plain woman an offer."

"What about Liddy Estlefop?" Augusta declared, with an air of triumph. "She has spots and lank brown hair and is fat besides, and she married a viscount!"

"Liddy Estlefop has a dowry of twenty thousand pounds," Harriett replied conclusively.

"Well," Augusta frowned, "well, I am sure there are men to whom money or a pretty face is not as important as the fact that you are nice and . . . and good."

"Lord Weston, for instance," Mrs. Haversham said. She had been watching her two daughters and doing her best to refrain from being an interfering mother, but found she could not help pushing things along a bit.

"Lord Weston strikes me as the kind of sensible man who would appreciate a woman's true worth."

"But Lord Weston is so old," Augusta protested.

"No older than Mr. Reading, whose praises you were singing just yesterday," her mother replied.

Harriett turned and began to rearrange the inkwell and pens upon the desk. "It hardly matters what his age," she said in a tight voice. "Lord Weston is going to marry Miss Dade."

"He is?" Both Mrs. Haversham and Augusta spoke at once.

"Well, I must say I would not have thought it," Augusta said. "For though she is very beautiful, Miss Dade is not very agreeable. When I asked her where she had gotten that blue silk frock with the white lace, she did not reply, but looked at me as if I were a . . . a worm or something."

Mrs. Haversham, who had remained silent as she thought over the matter, finally said, "Are you quite sure of this, Harriett? I do not think Lord Weston had any intention of offering for Miss Dade earlier this week. I mean, I do not know, of course, but it did seem to me that he looked, that is—"

"I am quite sure, Mama," Harriett cut through her mother's ramblings. "He all but told me so himself when we were decorating the children's eggs."

Distracted from her nasty thoughts of Miss

Dade, Augusta asked, "Did you ever finish them? I decorated one that was very beautiful, Mama, all covered with flower petals. At least, I think it would have been beautiful, but I did not get a chance to finish it. Would you like me to help you some more, Harriett?"

"I had planned on coloring them tomorrow," Harriett replied, glad for the change in subject. She was dangerously close to tears, and that would never do, for it would mean even more questions she had no wish to answer. As far as decorating the eggs, well, truth to tell; Harriett wished never to set foot in the yard again for the unhappy memory it held. Still, the eggs must be finished by Easter. "Thank you, I would appreciate your help, Augusta," she accepted gratefully. "I'm afraid things were left rather at sixes and sevens."

Augusta nodded. "Mary told me that one of the eggs got broken. She said it must have rolled off the table and gotten smashed, and then Bessie stepped on it. Mary said it was ever such a lovely golden color and looked like it had a verse on it. I wonder who did it? Mr. Reading said he wasn't much of an artist, so perhaps it was Lord Weston who—is something wrong, Harriett?"

Without a word, Harriett turned and rushed from the room, leaving her sister and mother staring after her. "Well, for heaven's sake, what is the matter with Harry, Mama?" Augusta asked. "I mean, it is a pity the egg got broken when it was such a nice one, but it was only an egg, after all."

"Well, and so when do you mean to pop the question?" George Reading asked that afternoon. "I want to know when to offer my commiserations."

Lord Weston glanced up from his *Gazette*. He and George had been friends for more years than he cared to remember, but at the moment he strongly felt like strangling him.

"Don't tell me you can't get up the nerve? Nothing to it, old boy. You merely throw yourself down on one knee, promise the chit your life and fortune, and kiss your freedom good-bye."

George Reading got up to pour himself a glass of port from the decanter on the sideboard. "Have you broken the news to your mother yet? No, of course you haven't," he answered himself. "Should have heard her carrying on clear through the county, if you had. Especially since she considers Reverend Haversham a worthless womanizer who should be removed from the living. Wonder how she ever got that idea? Must say, Reverend Haversham seems a decent enough sort to me. Still, I suppose a woman sees these things differently."

"George?"

George Reading raised his eyebrows in question.

"Did anyone ever tell you how irritating your prattle is?"

"Yes." George Reading sat down in the upholstered chair across from his host and smiled. "You did. Just yesterday, as a matter of fact. Which makes me wonder why your nose is out of joint. You only bite my head off when you're feeling down about something else. What's the matter? Won't your Miss Haversham have you?"

"I don't know," Lord Weston confessed.

"What? You must be joshing me. You mean you made the chit an offer and she didn't snap it up at once?"

Lord Weston folded his paper and put it to one side. "That's the problem, George. She didn't say yes or no."

"But—but she must have said something," George Reading protested. "You make a girl an offer, she doesn't just stay mum about it."

Lord Weston's face darkened. "Harriett did."

"I don't believe it." George Reading smacked the arm of the chair he was sitting in with his hand. "You're bamming me, Phillip. Must be. I can think of scores of females who would give their eyeteeth for the chance to be Lady Weston."

"Apparently not Miss Haversham," Lord Weston replied.

"Now, there you're wrong, Phillip. I would be willing to wager that the girl's smitten. She's always looking at you, you know, and her face lights up like a candle flame when you speak to her. In fact, she looks almost beautiful. Were I a ladies' man, I would quite envy you."

"There's nothing to envy. I'm afraid she won't have me."

"But you still haven't told me what she said when you proposed."

"Nothing," Lord Weston replied testily. "I tell you, she said nothing."

"But she must have said *something*," George Reading persisted. "Now, you went down on one knee and said, 'Miss Haversham would you do me the honor,' or some such thing, and she replied . . ."

Lord Weston scowled down at the tips of his gleaming Hessians. "Thing is, George, I didn't exactly propose in words. That is . . . I wrote it on an egg."

George Reading blinked, then broke into a roar of laughter. "Wrote it on an egg? No wonder she didn't say anything! Poor thing probably wasn't sure whether you were offering her a proposal or supper. Must say, I thought better of you, Phillip."

"I thought it exceeding romantic, George. Just the sort of thing that would appeal to a female. I even sent to London and had a gold locket made in the shape of an egg and engraved with our initials to give to her when she accepted. I feel the complete fool. Worse."

George Reading nodded. "You're in love with the chit."

"Yes. But I'm afraid she doesn't return my feelings."

"Can't know until you ask her. Have to put it to the test again, Phillip," George Reading advised. "Go over to the parsonage and ask her plain out."

"Don't you think I've tried?" Lord Weston snapped. "She always seems to be out on one of her blasted visits. I've been trying to see Harriett Haversham for the past two days now, and she is never at home."

"Avoiding you."

Lord Weston glared at his friend and got up, restlessly pacing to the window and back. "Her father was quite agreeable to the match. I suppose I could talk to him about it, though I wouldn't want Harriett to feel forced in anyway."

"Doubt that the father would do that. Doesn't seem the sort. But you know, Phillip . . . you don't suppose Miss Haversham feels she can't accept you because of that business with the trousers?" Noting his host's blank expression, George Reading continued. "You know, when she disguised herself as her father. Maybe she feels a bit odd about that. Does she know that you know about it?"

Turning from the window where the dismal rain seemed to match his mood, Lord Weston nodded. "Told her I knew from the start. Actually, she confessed the masquerade to me first, told me her reason for it."

"Which was?"

"I'm not a gabblemonger, George. Besides, though the reason seemed sufficient to her at the time, I must admit her version of it was a bit too convoluted for me. Not that it makes any difference. Harriett is too good and kind and . . . decent a person to do anything really wrong. I had thought to discuss the masquerade with her later, because she seemed so distressed by her part in it. But now—"

George Reading put down his glass of port and stood up. "You're bound to see her at church tonight, Phillip," he counseled his friend. "Insist that she talk to you, give you your answer. Surely even she realizes she cannot keep you on tenterhooks like this."

Lord Weston nodded. "I shall speak to her tonight or else track her down tomorrow. If she is not at home, I know where she probably will be. The thing is, George, what if her answer is not the one I want to hear?"

"Then you shall marry her by proxy and I shall be Miss Haversham's substitute. How do you think I should look in muslin?"

"Resistible, George, quite resistible. You had best pray that Miss Haversham will have me."

Fourteen

Harriett walked slowly down the path that led from the parsonage to the road. Ordinarily, she would have taken the shortcut that led through the meadow, but Harriett had decided that way lay too near Yarwood, and she would not chance meeting Lord Weston or one of his guests.

Walking along the grassy verge, Harriett allowed her eyes to wander around the green hedgerows, looking for bird's nests or anything else that would take her mind off Yarwood. Well, not Yarwood, precisely, she acknowledged to herself, but Lord Weston. He had been at the Good Friday service last night. Though she had not looked at the Weston pew, had done her best not even to think of it, she was as aware of his presence as if he had walked up to her and said good evening.

Harriett sighed and shifted the basket she carried to her other hand. She was bringing a few things to Mrs. Micklewaithe, and while the basket was not heavy, she had burned her fingers while coloring the eggs earlier that morning, and they were still a bit painful.

Not painful enough to make her forget Lord Weston, however. And every thought of him was so distressing that she had to stop, put down her basket, and search in her reticule for her handkerchief. "I don't know what is wrong with me," she said to herself. "I never used to be such a watering pot." But now, the slightest thing could set her off. Coloring the eggs this morning, for instance. All she could think of was the way Lord Weston had offered to help with the children's eggs, how kind she had thought him, and then . . . then he had handed her that awful egg for Miss Dade.

"How could he?" she asked the hedgerow at large. And then, "how could he not? For she is so very beautiful. I daresay, if I were a man, I would offer for her myself." Harriett sniffed, picked up her basket, and walked on, scuffing her feet on the grassy verge as she went. It was not just the proposal to Miss Dade that hurt, however. That Harriett could try to understand. But to think Lord Weston had actually told Miss Smalbathe about her disguise! Harriett's cheeks burned all over again to think of it.

Miss Smalbathe had said she would not repeat it to anyone, but Harriett was sure everyone must know. How could she ever face them again? And how could Lord Weston have so betrayed her? I trusted him, she thought, her eyes beginning to blur with tears once more. Even though I knew he could never love me, I trusted him, thought him a true gentleman. He seemed so kind and nice, and he understood about Rusty Brown. Why, he even showed me the bird nest and said there was now a bond between us. Obviously, those were no more than words to Lord Weston, without meaning or thought behind them. Harriett sniffed and gritted her teeth. She would not cry again. A man who would so betray her was not deserving of her tears.

Or so Harriett tried to convince herself, repeating the words like a litany as she neared Mrs. Micklewaithe's stone cottage. George was in his window, watching the road, his meow alerting Mrs. Micklewaithe that she had a visitor.

"Come on in, then," Mrs. Micklewaithe called. "I've not shut the door but once, the day bein' so fine an' all."

Harriett stepped inside and stood blinking for a few moments. The sun outside was so bright, she had to wait for her eyes to adjust to the dim interior. But after a moment Harriett could see the rough table and chairs, Mrs. Micklewaithe's ample form in her rocking chair, and the shining Hessians of Lord Weston.

Harriett blinked again and took an involuntary step backwards. Lord Weston?

"Ay, it's not often I have so many visitors. But I was tellin' Lord Weston here, that I was sure you'd be comin' today, seein' as how you didn't come yesterday nor the day before."

"Yes, I'm sorry," Harriett apologized automatically. "I'm afraid I've been very busy, what with Easter and all. But, I . . . um . . ."

Mrs. Micklewaithe put her cane to the floor and hefted herself up from her chair. "Lord Weston has put the kettle on and I've just to get an extra cup an' we'll have our tea. What's in the basket, then?"

Without looking in Lord Weston's direction, Harriett uncovered her basket with trembling hands. Surely this was not happening. Surely this was only a bad dream. What would she say to him? He would want to know what had happened to the egg he had given her. Why she had not given it to Miss Dade. For surely he must know by now that she had not. How could she tell him she had thrown it to the ground in a fit of jealousy, and then Bessie had stepped on it and the chickens pecked at what was left?

It had been a lovely egg, too, and had doubtless taken Lord Weston a long time to make. Especially with that verse. Harriett thought back to the way she had felt when she'd first read it, the happiness that had filled her and caused her heart to soar like one of those huge balloons that carried people up and far away beyond their usual humdrum lives.

And all at once, to her horror, Harriett felt her eyes fill with tears again.

"Somethin' wrong then, Miss Harriett?"

"No. I mean, I just have something in my eye, is all. I shall be fine in a moment." Blindly, Harriett tore open her reticule and began to search for her handkerchief.

"Allow me, Miss Haversham."

Lord Weston spoke behind her, as if her thoughts had suddenly materialized at her side. "There is no need. I am—"

Placing a hand on her shoulder, he turned her to face him. "It seems to me there is every need," he said softly, and began to wipe away her tears.

His gentleness only made her tears flow more copiously, and Harriett knew she must look a sight. She was not like Camilla or Augusta, who could cry prettily. No, when Harriett cried, her nose got pink and her eyes became red and her lashes stuck together in clumps. Still, the more she tried to stop, the more she cried, until suddenly she found herself sitting down in Mrs. Micklewaithe's rocking chair with a hot cup of sweet tea in her hand.

"Drink that, sweetheart," Lord Weston said. "And tell me what is wrong. I am sure it cannot be anything so very bad, and whatever it is, I shall do my best to rectify the matter. Is it about Camilla? I spoke to your father about your sister, and I am sure there will be no scandal attached to her name. Surely that is not why you have been avoiding me? You were not so foolish as to think you must refuse my offer because of your sister, were you?"

"It was . . . it was . . ." Harriett hiccupped, took a gulp of her tea, and then blurted out every thought she had had about Lord Weston in the past three days. "It was Miss Dade," she confessed. "You gave me that beautiful egg to give to her and instead I smashed it, and Bessie stepped on it, and I am sorry, but you should never have told Miss Smalbathe about my masquerade, because even though she says she will not tell anyone, I do not believe her, and it was very bad of you, and I thought you a man of honor." Harriett stopped, took another gulp of her tea, and then said, "but I wish you happy anyway. I am sure Miss Dade will make an admirable Lady Weston, and I am very sorry about . . . about everything."

Harriett looked into the dregs of her teacup, where a few leaves slowly settled to the bottom, and then, when Lord Weston remained silent, stole a furtive glance upward. He was frowning down at her, his brows drawn together over his dark eyes. He looked puzzled and hurt and angry all at the same time.

"The egg was meant for you," he said finally. "I had thought you might want to keep it— might, in fact, treasure it and the words I took such pains to scratch upon the shell. But now that I know your true opinion of me, I can see how you might think it worthless, deserving of no better fate than to have your cow crush it into nothingness beneath her hoof. Still, the sentiments were sincere.

"As for telling Miss Smalbathe about your

disguise, I did nothing of the kind, nor would I. The only one who knew about it was George Reading, and he would certainly not have said anything. I do not know how Miss Smalbathe learned of it. She has a habit of eavesdropping, perhaps she was standing nearby and heard us talking. I do not know. Nor does it really matter now, for if you could think me capable of doing such a thing, your avoidance of me for the past few days becomes understandable. I withdraw my suit, Miss Haversham, and I bid you good day."

Harriett sat frozen in Mrs. Micklewaithe's rocking chair, unable to move or speak for the shock of Lord Weston's speech. She watched unbelieving as he donned his hat and, with a short nod to Mrs. Micklewaithe, strode out the door without another word.

"Well, an' who would have believed it?" Mrs. Micklewaithe said softly, her eyes gleaming.

"I . . . um . . ."

Mrs. Micklewaithe limped over to a chair, narrowly missing George's tail with her cane. "And what's this about a disguise now, eh? And an egg? What egg might that be?"

"Ah, Lord Weston was helping to decorate the eggs and one rolled from the table to the ground. It was very pretty, but I have brought you these instead," Harriett said. With quick resolve she walked over to the table, and took out the decorated eggs she had brought. "Now I am afraid I must be going, Mrs. Micklewaithe. I have some urgent business to attend to."

"As long as you promise to invite me to the weddin'," Mrs. Micklewaithe said with a chuckle. "Be off with you, now, and tell Lord Weston not to forget to send the carriage tomorrow."

Harriett ran through the meadow, stopping breathlessly to glance at the little clearing where she usually fed the birds. Lord Weston was not there. He must have gone straight to Yarwood, Harriett thought, her heart singing to rival the birds overhead. "The egg was meant for you." The egg was meant for *me!* The words repeated over and over in her head as she ran, heedless of appearances down the path that led through the home woods to Yarwood.

The butler answered her knock on the door, his eyebrows rising as he took in her disheveled appearance. "Miss Haversham, is something wrong?" he asked, stepping back so she could enter.

"No, no." Harriett stopped to catch her breath. "But I must see Lord Weston. It is very important."

"I'm afraid Lord Weston has not returned. But if it is important, perhaps you could see Lady Weston?"

"No!" Harriett said at once. She had no desire to see the dowager. "It was just . . . I . . ." she glanced down at her hand, which still held the handkerchief Lord Weston had used to wipe away her tears. "It is just that I wished to return Lord Weston's handkerchief, is all."

The butler nodded. "I shall see that milord receives it, Miss Haversham." The butler took the bailed, damp piece of linen between two fingers. "Was there any message?

"No. I mean, yes. That is, there is no message, but is Mr. Reading at home?"

"I believe Mr. Reading is in the library at the moment. Shall I announce you?"

Harriett nodded. "If you please."

George Reading put down the *Gazette* he had been perusing with all the concentration of someone who couldn't care less about the country affairs reported but had nothing better to do, and rose to his feet. "Miss Haversham, how nice," he said.

Harriett could see that George Reading was wondering why she had come but was much too polite to ask. Had Lord Weston spoken to him about her? Did he know that Lord Weston had made her an offer?

"Yes, Phillip told me he had made you an offer and that you had not only given him no answer but had, in fact, been avoiding him," George Reading answered her unspoken question. "I do not know why this should be so, but if there is anything I can do to convince you to have him, I shall do so. Phillip and I have been friends for a very long time, and I am sure that he most sincerely cares for you, Miss Haversham."

Harriett smiled. "Does he?" she asked. Though normally very shy and reticent about her feelings, Harriett was quite desperate by now. "I find that I care most sincerely for him as well," she said, "but, I am afraid—oh, Mr. Reading, I am afraid I have made a terrible mull of things!"

Pressing her lips together, Harriett turned away for a moment, concentrating on the embossed titles of the books lining the library shelves until she had her emotions under control again. "You see, I accused Lord Weston of telling Miss Smalbathe about . . . about my masquerade," she continued in a strained voice. "He was terribly offended and said that he withdrew his suit. Only I don't want him to withdraw his suit, for I love him quite dreadfully, and . . . please say you will help me, Mr. Reading."

George Reading nodded, his face flushed with embarrassment. "Of course, I shall. But I must confess," he paused to take a deep breath, "I must confess that it was not Phillip but I who set the cat among the pigeons. Didn't mean to, of course. I was merely engaging in a bit of dalliance with your sister while she was tying some leaves or such around an egg. Had no idea Miss Smalbathe was anywhere around."

"Oh." Harriett sat down suddenly in one of the padded ebony armchairs that stood near the doorway. "Lord Weston said that Miss Smalbathe was a bit of an eavesdropper."

"Makes a career of it," George Reading

agreed, looking down at his boot-clad feet for a moment. "Still, that's no excuse. Shouldn't have allowed my tongue to run along as it did. Fact is, I told your sister I knew she'd been cutting a wheedle and did she think some of us couldn't tell the difference between fathers and sisters? Well, the next thing I knew, Miss Smalbathe had me backed into a corner of the chicken yard and was prying out the details." He looked up at Harriett again. "I am terribly sorry, Miss Haversham. Would you like me to speak to Phillip? Try to smooth things over?"

"No, I . . ." Harriett frowned, her fingers curling and uncurling around the strings of her reticule. She could hear the clock in the hallway ticking away and could feel the slight pain from the place where her gloves rubbed against her burned fingers, but her thoughts were busy elsewhere. "No, I think I have a better idea," she said at last.

Some twenty minutes later, Harriett stood once again in the large entrance hall of Yarwood. She was not smiling, precisely, but she certainly felt much better than she had before. George Reading had his hand upon her shoulder in a gesture of reassurance. "Not to worry," he said. "It shall all work out, and it's the least I can do after making such a cake of myself and causing all this trouble in the first place. Just make sure your aim is true and we shall have the parson's noose snug around Phillip's neck without fail."

"The parson's noose?" Harriett asked. "Do you compare marriage to a hanging, then?"

"Well, I did not mean that, of course. I meant—"

"The parson's mousetrap," Harriett supplied. "Am I the cheese, or the bar that snaps off his neck?"

George Reading smiled. "Definitely the cheese, my dear, a good Havarti, I think. Now you are to leave things to me, I shall see that everything is arranged."

"But what if Phillip—I mean, what if Lord Weston, will not do as you ask?"

"He will, my dear. You see, Phillip is quite right. The pig in the church pew was my idea. Now run along and do your part and leave me to do mine."

After gray skies and the threat of rain, the sun broke through the clouds and the churchbells rang out to welcome Easter to Upper Mourouby. The villagers gave a sigh of relief that their new clothes would escape a downpour and everyone turned out in force for the Easter service. Not only was it a holy day of obligation, but there had been quite delicious rumors circulating about Lord Weston and one of the Haversham daughters, and everyone wanted to see if they were true.

Harriett's face burned as she and Augusta

walked down the center aisle to their pew at the front. She had tried to hurry her sister along, but Augusta had a new bonnet of rose-colored lutestring with a garland of roses around the crown, and had wanted to make sure everyone noticed. Their mother had arrived earlier, an invalid chair having been procured for her, so that she sat a little to one side of the nave, where she could smell the evergreens with which the church had been decorated as a symbol of eternal life.

Her eyes glued to her papa, Harriett did her best to concentrate on the sermon, but found her thoughts drifting time and again to the ornately carved pew at the back of the church. He must be there, of course. Lord Weston would not miss the Easter service, no matter what his feelings might be regarding the vicar's daughter. The final hymn was sung at last and Harriett, her hands feeling clammy inside her gloves, closed her book. With quick resolution she entwined the strings of her reticule about her wrist and went to stand beside her mother.

There was a chance Lord Weston would simply leave without saying anything to anyone, but Harriett did not think so. And George Reading had said he would do his best to steer his friend in the right direction. Nervously, Harriett watched as Lord Weston paused to speak to a few people and then started down the center aisle in the direction of the chancel. He was coming to speak to her mother. This must be her chance to explain things to him, and if that should fail . . . well, then there was the egg-rolling, as she had explained to George Reading.

"Mrs. Haversham," Lord Weston bowed over her hand. "I hope you are feeling better."

"Dr. Bruden thinks I may be able to get about with a cane next week, but I am afraid I must miss the egg-rolling today."

"A disappointment," Lord Weston agreed, "but one I share with you. I will be leaving for London later this morning, though my mother will remain for the rest of the week."

"Leaving for London?" Harriett broke into the conversation, her gray eyes wide with dismay. "But you cannot—"

"Cannot, Miss Haversham?" Lord Weston asked politely. "And why is that?" He waited a moment for her reply, and when Harriett just continued to look at him, continued, "Do you know something about the condition of the roads that I do not? Or is there some other reason I should stay?"

Behind him, Harriett could see George Reading staring at her intently as if willing her to speak. What was she to do? Declare her love for Lord Weston in front of half the congregation? Harriett took a deep breath. She had always been shy and self-effacing, but if it was necessary, she would do just that. Yes, she would shout it from the pulpit, and the bell-tower too, if she must.

Mrs. Micklewaithe watched these goings on with a frown. She had enjoyed being the first with a bit of gossip for a change. Not getting about much anymore, things were always second- or third-hand by the time she heard them. But not this time. She had been so sure that Lord Weston and Harriett would make a match of it that she had begun to spread the rumour almost before they were out of her cottage door. And now look at them! Hemming and hawing about like two moonlings. Well, she would soon put things to right.

Hefting herself out of her seat in the second pew, Mrs. Micklewaithe hobbled over to assist things along. "Let's get on with it now!" she scolded, in a voice that could be heard throughout the church. "You'll have people sayin' I'm no more'n one of them gabblemongers who makes things up out of whole cloth. Now," Mrs. Micklewaithe stopped and thumped her cane on the floor, narrowly missing the gouty toe of Mr. Whitfoot, who had hurried over to make sure he didn't miss anything. "Let's stop all this flummery an' you tell her what your feelin's are," she directed Lord Weston.

Lord Weston's eyebrows rose, and for a moment George Reading was afraid he was going to give the old lady one of his setdowns. Instead, Lord Weston smiled. "Was the carriage to your liking?" he asked politely.

"Well sprung an' no mistakin'," she told him. "All spit an' polish, too. Bit of George's hair on the seats now, of course, but I didn't think you the sort to mind that."

"My staff will enjoy removing them," Lord Weston assured her.

"But now, you're tryin' to put me off the scent, milord," Mrs. Micklewaithe scolded. "And what I say is, you should—"

"Mrs. Micklewaithe?" Lord Weston interrupted. "I am sure whatever you might have to say would make very good sense. However, I shall be leaving this afternoon, and if anyone wishes me to remain longer, they need only say so."

They both turned to stare at Harriett, who looked back at them, her wits gone suddenly abegging. Whereas a moment ago she had felt quite able to shout her love for Lord Weston from the belltower, she now felt her tongue stuck to the roof of her mouth as she faced the crowd of villagers all waiting expectantly to see what part she would play in the melodrama.

Harriett swallowed. She had once lost her voice completely when she was supposed to recite a poem for founder's day, and she now felt her throat tightening up again. "I . . . um, hope you will stay for the egg-rolling this afternoon," she managed to whisper, before fleeing out the side door, cheeks burning.

"Heavens! Whatever is the matter with Miss Haversham?" Miss Smalbathe asked, stepping inside from the churchyard. "Her face was most unbecomingly red, as if she had a fever."

"Ay, there's some call it a fever in the blood," Mr. Whitford said with a cackle. "But I've always thought the fever was a bit below that me-self."

"Mr. Whitford!" Mrs. Micklewaithe thumped him with the head of her cane and gave him a look of reproof which slowly changed to a sly smile. Mr. Whitford was a widower of some years, and while Mrs. Micklewaithe had always thought the old gentleman quite a dead limb on the tree of life, she was beginning to change her mind. "Do you like cats, Mr. Whitford?" she asked, giving him a coquettish look from under her bonnet rim.

Harriett's tongue still felt quite tied into knots as she stood, later that afternoon, hand-ing out the decorated eggs to the parish chil-dren atop Meyer's Hill. I have never been good at this sort of thing, she thought. I shall make a mull of it as usual. And I am sure everyone is staring at me. Why did I ever listen to George Reading? It will never work. Lord Weston is leaving for London today. He is prob-ably happy to have the opportunity to withdraw his suit. But then . . . he did say he would re-main in Upper Mourouby if someone asked him. A smile flickered briefly over Harriett's face. Was it possible he had meant her?

Nervously Harriett fingered the reticule at her side and watched as the villagers sent their eggs down Meyer's Hill to the shouted encour-agement of their family and friends. Little Alicia Newpoke won the children's egg roll, her egg having gone not only down the hill, but into a gorse bush as well. And Mr. Findlay's egg, a spectacular red one which his wife had dyed with cochineal, was judged the winner of the egg roll for the men when it careened off an oak tree and Mrs. Smithburton's foot to land at the paws of Mr. Beauchamp's terrier, Betsy.

Reverend Haversham announced the winners, having a bit of difficulty being heard over Betsy, who was still barking vociferously, and then it was time for the ladies to assemble at the top of Meyer's Hill.

Harriett took a deep breath. She hadn't joined in the egg-rolling for years, though Augusta and Camilla were always there, laughing and giggling. Harriett stood among the village women, conspicuous for her solemn face among the carefree smiling ones.

"Do stop being such a Friday-face, Harry," Augusta urged her. "This is supposed to be fun, remember? And if we don't get near the front, our eggs will never have a chance of winning." Augusta took Harriett by the arm and dragged her off to one side and to the edge of the hill. "Now, stop looking so hangdoggish and don't dare lecture me on how this is supposed to remind us of the rolling away of the stone from Christ's tomb. Papa did that last year and it quite put a damper on things."

Harriett looked down, closed her eyes, and backed away a few steps. She had never been very good at heights.

"Did you see that Mr. Marsh is back?" Augusta asked, while they waited for Mr. Beauchamp to call the start. "He told me he was devastated to learn he had not been here when I was in need of him, but he had gone to see his nephew, who was ill. Where is your egg, Harry? Don't tell me you forgot to bring one for yourself?" Augusta gave her sister a look of disgust. "Well, I suppose you can have mine, if you wish, but—"

"No." Harriett shook her head and fumbled with the strings of her reticule. "I have an egg." She took it out and held it for a moment in her hand.

"Not very colorful," Augusta commented, looking from Harriett's golden brown egg to her own which had been colored a bright purple, using some of the scraps from Madame St. Germaine.

"I used onion skins," Harriett said, clutching her egg a bit nervously, and looking around at the people assembled below.

"Did you sketch a design on it?" Augusta asked, peering at Harriett's egg. "Why, it looks quite pretty, actually. Look, there is Mr. Marsh, over by the trees." She pointed down the hill. "Such a funny little man. He was quite cast down when I told him I was going to London next year. But then I told him I had missed him and gave him one of those green eggs you made with the leaf design. You don't mind, do you, Harry?" She waited a few moments and when Harriett remained silent, said, "Are you

311

feeling quite the thing, Harriett? I mean, aren't you going to scold me for teasing Mr. Marsh and tell me what an incorrigible flirt I am?"

"No. I—Gusta, do you see Lord Weston anywhere?"

"Lord Stiff Rump? I hardly think this the sort of thing he would attend. Besides, didn't he say he was leaving this afternoon for London?"

"Yes, but George Reading promised me he would be here."

"Oh, Mr. Reading." Augusta sighed. "Doesn't he have the most incredible blue eyes?"

Harriett turned to her sister with a look of alarm. "Gusta, you are not serious about Mr. Reading, are you?"

"Of course not," Augusta replied, a bit nettled. "I would not tie my horse to the post just as the carriage was about to depart. I am not such an addlepate. Though Mr. Reading did mention that he looked forward to seeing me in town next year. And I must say, I intend to save my first real waltz for him. But still, I mean to flirt quite outrageously and—oh, look. Mr. Beauchamp is about to call the start. Don't hold your egg like that, Harry. You're supposed to roll it, not throw it. If it's broken, it can't win."

Harriett nodded automatically, her eyes on the crowd of people below. Some were milling about the tables set with refreshments provided by the Upper Mourouby Ladies' Guild Society, others were lining the sides of the hill to watch the ladies' egg roll. But nowhere did she see Lord Weston.

"There! Look, Harry! Look how far my egg is rolling. If only Millie Furbank's red one does not go further . . . oh, drat! Why must my egg always come up against a rock or bit of grass or something? Really, it is almost as if—Harry, you have not rolled your egg. You can't just stand there and hold it, you know."

"Yes." Harriett said, "but there is no—" She stopped, her face breaking into a smile. Below was Lord Weston, being propelled along by an insistent George Reading. She gave a little wave, saw George Reading nod, and with a silent prayer, used all her might to fling her egg down the hill in his direction.

"Harry, I told you—you're not supposed to throw it, you're supposed to roll it."

Harriett barely heard her sister's words, her whole concentration centered on the golden brown egg as it bounced and rolled down the hill. George Reading pulled his friend first in one direction and then in the other, as the egg careened down Meyer's Hill. Biting her lip, Harriett thought for a moment that the egg would be stopped by a rock or clump of dirt, as Augusta's had, but it kept rolling, landing almost at the toes of Lord Weston's shining Hessians.

Watching with her heart in her throat, Harriett saw George Reading point it out, and Lord Weston bend to pick it up. Then, without looking at the egg, Lord Weston turned to a nearby child and handed her the egg, while Harriett watched horrified from the top of the hill.

Harriett had said she would shout it from the pulpit or the belltower, and she did not hesitate now to shout it from the top of Meyer's Hill. Pushing her way to the very edge, Harriett cupped her hands around her mouth and shouted as loudly as she could, "Dash it all, Phillip Sinclair. That egg was meant for you!"

Lord Weston looked up, saw Harriett standing tall upon the hill, and grinned. Extracting a coin from his pocket, he exchanged it for the egg, and then, while everyone watched, slowly turned it over and read the words scratched on the shell.

"Did you write something on the egg?" Augusta asked, pushing her way to Harriett's side. "What did you mean by telling Lord Weston the egg was meant for him? What does it say?"

On the ground below, someone echoed this question. "What does it say, milord? Read it out to us, then."

Harriett took a step forward. Surely he would not do so. Surely Phillip would realize the words she had taken such effort to scratch upon the egg were meant for him alone? In the silence, Harriett could hear a bird sing, and far to the left the croak of a frog. Lord Weston finished reading and smiled up at her. Then he pocketed the egg and turned to the villagers who waited expectantly to see if Mrs. Micklewaithe had been right.

"It says that she'll have me," he told them. "Harriett Haversham has accepted my proposal to become the new Lady Weston." And with the villagers cheering, he held out his arms to Harriett, who suddenly found she had quite lost her fear of heights as she went running down Meyer's Hill and into his arms.

"Disgraceful," Augusta murmured, watching as her sister heedlessly ran down the hill. "Quite disgraceful. Who would have thought my staid, prosy sister could be such a brazen minx?" And with a grin and a whoop that quite belied her words, Augusta followed Harriett down the hill.

Later, as they walked together in the home woods, Lord Weston took the golden brown egg from his pocket. Slowly he read the words out loud,

> *When we're apart I ache inside*
> *I hardly feel that I'm alive.*
> *A foolish heart I do possess*
> *Forgive me, for my answer's yes.*

"Bad verse, I'm afraid," Harriett excused herself shyly. "And I'm rather surprised you can read it! I had a difficult time fitting it all on the egg, some of the letters are terribly ill formed."

Lord Weston said nothing, but stood turning the egg over in his hand for a few moments.

"And you do forgive me for thinking such terrible things of you?" Harriett asked diffidently. "It was just that I couldn't believe you could really love me. And I was hurt and confused."

"Forgiven," Lord Weston said, punctuating the word with a quick kiss. "George told me what happened, and I do not blame you." He bent to kiss her quickly once more. "And I think I shall have a small glass case made to make sure your bad verse does not get broken."

"Yes." Harriett nodded. "I am very sorry about the egg you gave me, but I did go back, you know. And I found just a small piece of the shell that Bessie and the hens had missed. See?" She held out a small golden fragment on which a heart had been carefully scratched. "I meant to keep it. Even when I thought you had written the words for Miss Dade, I meant to keep the heart for myself. But I wish now that I still had your bad verse as you have mine."

Lord Weston looked down at her. "Your sister is right. Beneath that quiet exterior beats the heart of a brazen minx. And do not doubt that I still have a copy of my proposal. I must have rewritten it ten times at least. And do you have any idea how many eggs I spoiled before I had it right?"

"I ruined six," Harriett confessed. "And it

would have been seven, but I had no more time."

"Ah, then I am much the better, for I spoiled only four. Harriett?"

"Yes, Phillip?"

Lord Weston put the egg back in his pocket and brought out a long gold chain with a small golden Easter egg at the end. "I had this sent down from London. I was afraid for a few days that I would be returning with it still in my pocket, but now . . . it is really a locket, you see, and the egg opens up."

Harriett was delighted. "I shall keep my egg-shell heart inside," she said, and turned so he could fasten it about her neck. "You know, Phillip, eggs are supposed to be a sign of renewal."

"Yes," Lord Weston agreed. "Renewal and beginning, my love."

On a branch of the tree above, Rusty Brown peered down. He tilted his head to one side and then the other, not sure what his two bene-factors were about, so entwined as they were to appear not two but one. All he knew for certain was that if they did not start throwing some crumbs down yes, and raisins and some nuts, too, he would have to start cawing to remind them.